To d

w

Faith

Mary Doyle.

A DYING BREED

Mary Doyle

MINERVA PRESS
LONDON LEICESTER DELHI

A DYING BREED
Copyright © Mary Doyle 2000

All Rights Reserved

No part of this book may be reproduced in any form,
by photocopying or by any electronic or mechanical means,
including information storage or retrieval systems,
without permission in writing from both the copyright
owner and the publisher of this book.

ISBN 0 75411 302 7

First Published 2000 by
MINERVA PRESS
315–317 Regent Street
London W1R 7YB

Second impression 2002

Printed in Great Britain for Minerva Press

A DYING BREED

All characters in this book are fictional
and any resemblance to actual places, events or persons,
living or dead, is purely coincidental.

*With love to Anna, Terry and all the family.
Goodnight, God bless.*

Prologue

'Bastard! Bastard, your baby is a bast-a-a-ard!' The r's trilled on the frosty night air and a bitter wind carried the shrill echo out towards the harbour. A dumpy little woman clad in black swayed on the doorstep of a villa in Hove, bawling through the letter box and kicking the door with the toe of a kid boot.

Curious eyes peered through twitching lace curtains; it was past midnight and there was a curfew in the town. The voice rose to a banshee wail. 'Let me in William, I'm tired and I want to go to bed.' Fumbling in her handbag for the missing latchkey, she sent a shower of coppers across the garden path. 'Merde!' A handful of earth and pebbles hit the balcony window, and William rolled out of bed.

'That old woman is as drunk as a fiddler's bitch.'

Anna heard the clip-clop of heavy feet padding down the staircase then the door was flung open to reveal the dark shadow of a man looming against the orange electric light in the hall. He was clasping a toilet jug painted with blowsy red roses, and with one swift movement raised it high in the air and poured a flood of ice-cold water over the woman's head. A piercing scream rent the air as he dumped the empty pitcher on the mat, grasped her by the waist and lifted the sodden body over the threshold.

'I will carry you upstairs to bed Anna, but you leave this house tomorrow! I never want to set eyes on you again as long as I live, you bloody old tarantula.'

Part One

Chapter One

'Mopsy is doing a wee-wee, Louise. Ring the bell for François.'

Anna was sitting on a Persian rug in front of the nursery stove stroking her puppy's ears when there was a thunderclap and one of her china cats fell off the mantelpiece shattering on the hearth.

'The Prussians are camped on the hills around Paris, it might be the sound of their guns.'

A small brown puddle spread from Mopsy's bottom towards the child's petticoats as the old woman waddled to the bell-pull, summoned the kitchen boy and thrust the leaking puppy in to his arms.

'Take the little beast into the courtyard to do his business, then feed him before the journey.'

The nursery was a shambles with a pile of toys from le Singe Violet in one corner of the room and garments hanging from every piece of furniture. Louise mumbled as she packed yet another valise. 'The citizens of Paris are starving, filling their bellies with cats and dogs and sewer rats. Butchers slaughtered Castor and Pollux, the elephants in *Les Jardins Botaniques* but only the very rich could afford to buy the meat. Your Mopsy would make a fine stew with a few herbs, he's as fat as butter.'

'You are horrible Louise – Zaza! A crazy woman!'

Anna ran to the window. It was a misty November day, but she could see the burnt out candles on the chestnut trees and a hot air balloon floating high above the roof tops of Paris. Jumping up and down with excitement she called out to her nurse.

'Look, Louise, look. Maman says they can sail all the way across the Channel and take our letters to Uncle André in England.'

'Stuff and nonsense. They are only paper balls stuck together with glue. Little better than a child's kite.'

Anna had known Louise all her life and loved her dearly, in spite of a wart with whiskers on one side of her chin that tickled when she kissed goodnight, but she could be as obstinate as a pig.

At that moment maman glided into the room, lovely Marguerite Van Maaskens, tall, cool and elegant with a long neck like a swan and enormous dark grey eyes. She gazed around her in amazement at the utter chaos.

'You are doing well Louise, but remember everything must be stowed in the carriage tonight.'

'I understand, Madame.' She turned to the child: 'Will you take Trudi with the blonde plaits or your old favourite Didi?'

'Didi, Didi, you know I love her best of all. Don't forget to pack her trousseau and the blue sailor suit.'

The doll sat in her own high chair, blue glass eyes gazing into space, rosebud lips pouting to show two pearly-white teeth.

'We shall leave at twilight and travel under cover of darkness; the barricade at the Porte Maillot should be our first stop.'

Anna shivered. 'A goose walked over my grave.' Maman took the little girl in her arms.

'I think we are all a little scared – it is only natural. I am as nervous as a kitten. Be ready to leave about six o'clock after your croissants and hot milk. Wear the blue cloak with the hood and carry your little white ermine muff to keep your hands warm on the journey.'

'I want to stay in Paris, maman and eat tartes aux fraises on the pavement outside the café on the Champs Elysees. Papa promised to take me on a bâteau mouche one Sunday after Mass. Uncle André used to say that England is grey and foggy and the people are not very friendly. *Please* ask papa to stay.'

'This is the only way, Anna.'

There was a frou-frou from maman's grey silken gown as she swept out of the room.

Anna caught sight of her best straw hat with the velvet ribbons adorning the head of the old rocking horse and gazed at her china dogs and cats and frogs, pantalons trimmed with lace dangling from a commode and the fairytale paintings on the nursery walls. She would say au revoir to Cendrillon and Puss and the Babes asleep under a giant oak tree in the forest, but she knew in her heart that she would never see them again as long as she lived.

It was almost time to leave. Feeling sick and wanting to cry she stuck her chin in the air and walked down the broad marble staircase hand in hand with Louise.

Pale saffron light from the iron gas lanterns flowed over the scene in the courtyard. Servants were scurrying to and fro loading the luggage and a large picnic basket. A brace of pistols lay on the carriage table in front of papa's corner seat.

Anna kissed the twelve-year-old kitchen maid goodbye and her father frowned at such unseemly behaviour. A man of the people could be a terrible snob.

The carriage steps were high for her short little legs but Pierre took her elbow and helped her aboard. Mops curled into a ball on her lap and fell asleep; Albert climbed on to the box and they were away. Her eyes were blind with tears.

The pair of greys veered left into the Boulevard Haussmann where two soldiers were guzzling wine on a street corner, their weapons stacked against a lamp post.

'Vive La République,' murmured papa.

A handcart loaded with goods and chattels loomed out of the shadows and an old peasant was followed by his wife carrying a tiny babe wrapped in a coarse shawl while another slept in an upturned table. The girl huddled beside the carriage window stroking the smooth rolls of fat round the puppy's neck, comforting them both – she loved pug dogs all her life.

Albert called from the box: 'I take a short cut, Monsieur.' He drove through narrow alleyways beneath low crouching hovels. Mopsy growled and Anna screamed at the top of her voice – the high piercing shriek of a terrified child. A toothless old hag clung to the carriage door beside her, baring pink gums and mouthing foul words. 'A bas les riches. On meurt de faim. Foutez-moi-le—'

'Whip up, Albert... faster, faster – we shall end up with our throats cut. Return to the boulevards.'

The starving crone fell backwards into the gutter her hands clawing the air, cursing them to hell and damnation. Looking back Anna could only see a heap of rags and bones lying in the mud and sewage.

Moonlight glittered on the Seine and Napoleon's orangerie lying silent under the stars; they drove past the Arc de Triomphe towards the barricade at the Porte Maillot.

Anna broke the silence. 'Why are we running away, maman?'

'It would be far too dangerous to stay. The citizens are crazy for blood and food, they wrecked the Tuileries Palace looting and rioting. The Empress Eugénie is a brave woman but her ministers persuaded her to leave for England.' Maman dabbed her nose with a cambric handkerchief. 'Thank God grandmaman is safe in Provence basking among her mimosas and olive trees.'

Mopsy lay in blissful ignorance once more dreaming of the chase – twitching and snorting.

'The gate might be unguarded if we are very lucky. We should be out of danger if we reach the Bois de Boulogne, although Prussian soldiers are abroad between Paris and the coast. Cuddle Mopsy and pretend to be asleep.'

Papa sat fingering the pistol lying on the table in front of him. The tension was mounting. Louise had said the family might spend months in gaol as enemies of the people, trying to escape from a city under siege.

Albert reined in the pair of greys at the barricade and a young officer of the guard came forward.

'Your papers, Monsieur, if you please. Perhaps you would be kind enough to step down from the carriage.'

Papa drew out a black crocodile wallet and showed his Belgian passport.

'It appears to be in order but the signature is a little faded and might be a forgery. I see that Madame was born in Paris.' He came nearer and poked his head through the carriage window beside her. Anna opened one eye to peep at him; he was tall, young and handsome. 'Good evening, Madame, Mademoiselle. Why are you going to England at a time like this, Monsieur?'

'Business and pleasure, Officer. My brother has bought a furnished house on our behalf in Chislehurst. I am a wine merchant and hope to fare better in England.'

'How the rich live! Chislehurst in the County of Kent? I understand the soi-distant Empress Eugénie lives there with her son and entourage since her escape from the Tuileries Palace.'

Papa realised he had committed a grave faux pas.

'I must ask you all to remain here overnight and my superior officer will examine your papers in the morning. He may find them to be in order. I fear the accommodation may not be to your liking; it is primitive to say the least.'

There was a long pause and father knew it might be their last chance to leave the country for years. 'Officer, I think I dropped my wallet near the rear wheel of the carriage. It contains a few francs but pray do not bother to ask one of your men to retrieve it now – the light is very poor.'

It was a wild gamble; he might be accused of trying to bribe and corrupt an officer of the Republic. There was a long pause while the man eyed him from head to foot – his expression was inscrutable then he laughed.

'I think we understand one another Monsieur. I have the authority to sign your papers if they are in order. Voila!' He scribbled on the passport with a flourish. 'We wish the citizens God speed. Bonne chance, your luck may not hold if you encounter the Prussians en route.'

The horses trotted through the Bois past Malmaison. Distant hoof beats clattered on the frosty ground but it was only a riderless animal careening through the trees.

Papa took the child's hand to comfort her. 'Courage mon ami, le diable est mort. The danger is almost past.'

Albert pulled up in a clearing beyond the outskirts of the city; owls hooted and the orange eyes of wild creatures peered from the bushes.

'I am frightened of the dark, Pierre, please take the puppy for a walk.'

'Thank heavens the young man was corruptible, Marguerite.'

'Machiavelli! Shall we picnic here and rest the horses for a while?'

Albert unpacked their tall silver candlesticks engraved with the fleur-de-lys (a wedding present to the parents from grandmaman), cold chicken, champagne and lemonade.

'Leave the napkins at the bottom of the basket, I have hidden all my jewellery in the baguettes.'

Now the suspense was nearly over maman was as gay as a lark. She began to sing in a low soft voice:

> Au clair de la lune mon ami pierrot,
> Prête-moi ta plume pour écrire un mot.
> Ma chandelle est morte, je n'ai plus de feu—

She burst into tears laying her head on papa's shoulder. 'You are overtired, my love. Albert remembers a wayside inn on the way to Mantes-la-Jolie, we might rest there till morning.'

The inn loomed out of the shadows dark and silent as the grave. The child was wide awake but Louise and Mopsy were snoring.

Albert climbed down from the box and knocked on the oaken door. A chicken squawked in the farmyard and a rusty hinge creaked overhead. Albert looked up into the silver barrel of a shotgun balanced on a window ledge, glittering in the moonlight and Anna screamed out to warn him as a voice growled: 'Who goes there?'

'My master, Monsieur Jacques Van Maaskens, and his family seek shelter for the night. We travel to Mantes, and sir will pay well for a little comfort.'

'Stay where you are... I am coming down... with the gun.' A few minutes later the door opened to reveal the middle-aged landlord with tousled hair and bare feet, an old grey blanket draped round his shoulders to keep out the cold.

Papa approached the door of the Inn. 'Good evening, my good man. We need two rooms: my wife, my young daughter and her nurse are waiting in the carriage.

'Your pardon for the delay, Monsieur, but we fear the Prussians. News travels fast hereabouts and they say Paris will fall in a week or two. Even the Republican soldiers steal our food and animals. Come in, fine sir, come in.'

He led the way up a narrow carved oak staircase and opened the door to show a four-poster bed hung with old tapestry. There were two pallets and a chest in another room under the eaves. 'Simple but clean, Monsieur. My wife is a good housekeeper.'

'They will suit us very well. We thank you for this hospitality so late at night.'

'A glass of wine before you retire to bed, Monsieur? Your servants are welcome to sleep in front of the fire downstairs or there is clean straw in the barn.'

Anna woke at the cockcrow and looked out of the window to see Pierre and Albert dowsing their heads under a pump in the yard. The landlady brought a copper jug full of hot water and papa was already eating when she came downstairs wrinkling her nose at the smell of coffee and hot bread.

'Coffee made with acorns is fit for pigs,' he muttered. 'But the rolls are good. There will be a pot of chocolate for maman and you.

Jean Baptiste and his wife Mathilde were scouring the pewter pots with sand, curious to learn more about the travellers. 'You are going far, Monsieur?'

'To Mantes, then Deauville and England.' It was pointless to be secretive with the man.

'Do not worry, we are not informers. My father served under Napoleon at Waterloo and we remain loyal to the Bonapartes. You follow the Empress Eugénie? I know she escaped with her American dentist, le beau Evans, after a mob broke into the Tuileries. He pretended she was a mad woman on her way to the asylum with her companion Madame Lebreton as the attendant.

My brother Michel Besançon has a boat at Trouville and smuggles brandy, tobacco and a few passengers in distress across the channel. He saw the empress sail with Sir William Burgoyne on his private yacht *The Gazelle*. You see we hear all the latest news in this neck of the woods.' He paused for breath. 'My brother might be of use to you. Cross the bridge into Trouville and you should find *The Hirondelle*. Tell Michel I shall expect some fresh fish and a bottle of his best cognac for the introduction.'

The carriage drove into Limay, a suburb of Mantes la Jolie, and Albert said they had covered about sixty kilometres since leaving Paris. Pierre bought croissants, fruit and cheese while Albert stowed luggage on to the train.

'We will sell the equipage for the best price, Monsieur, and follow you to England.'

They perched on high wooden seats and the locomotive rattled through flat open countryside towards the coast leaving the tall spires of the poplars behind. Anna pressed her nose against the windowpane and Mopsy yapped at the noise from the steam engine. Coarse grasses slashed the sand dunes, daylight was fading as the train puffed into the station.

'Bagages… Deauville… Deauville-sur-mer… Bagages, Mesdames, Messieurs.' A little old porter in a faded blue kepi unloaded the valises from the guard's van and piled them on the platform. 'The Hotel du Casino is the finest, only a stone's throw away. I will call a fiacre, Monsieur?'

The building was like a giant wedding cake covered with white icing.

'I will go to Trouville first thing in the morning, Marguerite.'

Papa told them the story word for word. He had found the skipper sitting on a coil of rope smoking an old clay pipe and gazing out to sea. They had struck a hard bargain over a glass of absinthe. The captain said his cargo was loaded and they could sail with the tide the following day.

Mopsy rolled up the gangplank like a drunken sailor and Louise stumbled aboard to collapse in a crumpled heap on her bunk, curled up in a rigid ball like a dead hedgehog.

'Look out of the porthole, Louise, the sea is as calm as a millpond.'

The old woman shuddered. 'Leave me alone, I can be sick in a bâteau mouche on the Seine.'

Anna ran up to join the captain on deck. Maman and papa were standing at the rail holding hands. On the crossing, Besançon told her stories about his three children, wicked pirates and wild adventures on the high seas. She kissed his bearded cheek and he swung her high up in the air on to his broad shoulders, her drawers and white petticoats billowing in the sea wind.

'Now you can see the coast of England for the first time, little one, but I fear the town of Newhaven is not a pretty sight.'

The port was grey, bleak and bitterly cold. 'One of the coachmen at the Victoria Inn should carry you to Chislehurst, Monsieur. It is not far off the beaten track.'

The two men shook hands and Anna blew him another kiss on her way down the gangplank. Pale winter sunshine filtered through the dying leaves. 'Look, papa, pheasants.' She was a town child so everything was fresh and exciting.

A light mist veiled the silver birches on the common as the coach rumbled to a halt outside The Tiger's Head.

The inn sign creaked as it swung on rusty iron hinges, the wild animal painted in red, yellow and orange against a stark black background.

'Hawkswood Lane, your honour. This is where I drop off passengers for Chislehurst. The Lindens I think you said? Your house lies a few hundred yards down the road, sir. I s'pose I could always oblige a gentleman such as yourself, seeing as you have a rare pile of luggage, and deliver you to the door. We might go out of our way for a small consideration... it wouldn't take above five minutes with wheels.'

Papa pressed a guinea into his hand.

'You're a gent, guvnor and no mistake.'

The Lindens was set back from the road behind a long row of lime trees.

'A gentleman's house, guv, if ever I saw one.' The coachman deposited the luggage, pulled the bell and retreated.

The new house was large, square and double-fronted, built of mellow red brick with a flight of stone steps flanked by decorative urns. A scarlet Virginia creeper scaled the walls and two monkey-puzzle trees stretched their distorted branches to the sky; the Emperor Hadrian gazed from a squat column in the middle of a flower bed. The doors swung open. 'Good evening Monsieur, Madame, Mademoiselle, I am your new butler Williams, engaged by Monsieur André.' He gestured towards shadowy figures gathered in the background. 'A skeleton staff, Madame, pending the arrival of your other servants from France.'

A small voice piped up loud and clear: 'I want to see the stables, papa, and the coach house.'

'It is long past your bedtime, Anna.'

'No, no, no papa. I am wide awake.'

'Louise, Mademoiselle Anna will wait until tomorrow.' She stamped her foot and burst into floods of tears, but Louise tucked the bawling child under one arm and carried her kicking and screaming up the stairs to bed.

'I am nearly ten years old!'

'Stop behaving like a spoiled little brat and I will make you a cup of hot chocolate… otherwise I'll smack your bottom, *hard*.'

Chapter Two

Anna sat up in a narrow black iron bed and rubbed the sleep from her eyes. The hands on the clock stood at half past six. Shadows from a guttering night light on her bedside table and a dying coal fire flickered across the patchwork bedspread. Louise was still snoring.

'Mops, Mopsy' she whispered, waiting in vain for his little black tongue to lick her hands and face. She crept into the bathroom trying not to waken Louise.

A giant thunderbox stood on a dais, the water closet was decorated with blue and white dairymaids milking spotted cows and a geyser to heat the bath water loomed overhead.

After a quick lick and a promise she dressed herself and wandered out on to the landing to look for the puppy. The banister rail swept in a long shining curve to the hall far below. Mounting it she rode astride at breakneck speed and landed with a dull thud on the tile floor. Still rubbing her bottom she opened the nearest door and peeped inside. The drawing room was gold and white with brocade curtains and a gilded chaise longue in front of a marble fireplace. Uncle André had been very busy putting the finishing touches to the house. A pastel portrait of maman hung on the far wall beside a black medallion of the Empress Eugénie.

She found an enormous box of Belgian chocolates tied with a violet satin bow. 'To little Anna with all my love. Dé-Dé.'

It was a great temptation but a sudden noise startled her and a young lad emerged from the shadows. 'Sorry if I frightened you, Miss. I was hiding because I thought you was a ghost. Me name's Charlie.'

Anna gazed at the boy in silence, her English was still very poor. 'Mister André, the foreign gentleman, give me the job... he put an advert in the paper – "Young man wanted as underfootman. Must be RC and good with lamps." That's me. Ma read it, and here I am.'

'Have you seen my little black pug dog, Mopsy?'

'He's a game 'un. Spent a night in the stables and caught a rat.'

'I go find him now.'

'It's dark outside, Miss. I'll show you the way, it's past the coach house. There's an old shawl hanging near the garden door, it's bitter cold outside, you might catch your death.'

They walked together down the garden path and met a freckle-faced lad mucking out the stables who knuckled his forehead. 'I'm Fred, Mamselle. If you're looking for the black pup he's fast asleep in the first horsebox. He's had a busy night.'

Mopsy ran out barking and jumped into her arms reeking of horses and wet straw. 'Mops, you stink!' She ran into the house calling Louise, surely she must be on her feet by now. 'Tell the maids to bring a hip bath and jugs of hot water, we'll bathe him in front of the nursery fire to make sure he doesn't catch cold.'

Poor Mopsy was scrubbed with green soft soap till bubbles foamed from his nose and ears, then christened with maman's most expensive eau-de-cologne filched from her boudoir as she slept.

'You look beautiful now, Mops, as black as night. I promise to buy you a scarlet jacket with a fur lining for Christmas if you keep away from the stables. That horrible rat might have bitten you on the nose and given you rabies.'

Chapter Three

1870

It was the coldest Christmas Day on record for many, many years. The cook at the Lindens poured a large nip of gin into her early morning cup of tea, kitchen maids blew on their chilblains to ease the pain, and Father Goddard asked his housekeeper to knit him a thick pair of woolly bedsocks. The orphanage children peeled a mountain of spuds for their dinner and Anna found a humming top, a musical box and a copy of *The Adventures of Sophie* in a scarlet stocking at the foot of her bed. A blanket of snow covered the land and there were skaters on the frozen Thames.

The Empress shivered, pulled the eiderdown up to her chin and peered through the bedroom window at this godforsaken country. She loathed England; years ago she had tried to escape from her boarding school in Bristol to stow away on a ship bound for India. Now she was condemned to live here with the remnants of her court in exile while her husband was imprisoned by the Prussians.

Memories came flooding back. Riding bareback under a blazing sun through the streets of Andalusia dressed as a man with a scarlet rose, a cigarello or a dagger clenched between her teeth; trying to commit suicide with crushed matchsticks soaked in milk after an unhappy love affair, (the man preferred her sister.). Life was never dull in those days – even her mother Manuela's many amours were entertaining. They left her beloved father alone in Spain and toured Europe with Prosper Merimée: perhaps Mamma had inspired Carmen.

It was amusing to hunt with the Emperor at Compiègne and keep him at arm's length till after their marriage in Notre Dame. Napoleon's endless affaires with les Grandes Horizontales – the Countess Castiglione, self-styled the most beautiful woman of the century, had bored the emperor to tears after a while. Sophie Metternich described the creature as a myth cut out of pink marble. One night the Countess appeared at a masquerade dressed as the Queen of Hearts in a diaphanous gown with delicate patterns on a few strategic parts of her anatomy.

Eugénie remarked, 'I see you wear your heart very low down, The Empress no longer feared 'the influences of the night' although her husband was irresistible to women a combination of power and charisma: even dear little Victoria had flirted with him in the old days. Eugénie was never passionate enough to satisfy her husband in bed but her beauty enchanted men and women, brilliant blue almond eyes, sloping milk-white shoulders and a mass of auburn hair. His last letter was under her pillow:

'I would like to settle in England when I am free, with you and Louis in a little cottage with bow windows and climbing plants.'

French spies were living in a cottage near the railway station watching Camden Place through a telescope and reporting to Paris. Many republicans were determined that her beloved son Louis should never reign as Emperor Napoleon IV.

The Duc de Bassano, Head of the Household, warned her of a possible assassination plot but she refused to stay indoors. No one had ever accused the Spanish woman of cowardice. She knew that every extravagance was kept on record, a ball or birthday party, together with details of her personal jewellery sold through her dear friend Sophie, The Princess Metternich.

Eugénie shivered, where on earth was her Spanish maid?

She flung a tortoiseshell hairbrush across the room narrowly missing the mirror on her duchesse dressing table, (seven years bad luck!) and tugged at the bell pull till Pepa appeared carrying a tray laden with coffee, croissants and honey.

'Today I will attend Mass in the village church of St Mary not my own Chapelle Ardente. Pray inform Madame Lebreton.' She wore a dark gown embroidered with jet beads and a mantle of black Russian sables against the cruel weather.

'Tell Monsieur Gamble to lay out his master's mauve silken pyjama suit with the golden bees embroidered on the collar, I know His Imperial Majesty is coming home.'

Two boys, muffled to the eyeballs with caps and scarves, were skating on the pond as the Imperial carriage passed by. The church was crowded so Eugénie led the way, incognito, towards the back of the congregation and sat on a hard wooden bench among the schoolchildren and the orphans. Harry the butcher's son kicked Madame Lebreton on the shins with his hobnail boots and she moaned, 'Clodhoppers!'

Only one man noticed the Empress as she knelt in prayer; Uncle André was spending Christmas with his only relatives and he remembered Eugénie from her early days escorted by her mother and Prosper Merimee.

The Van Maaskens were talking with Father Goddard after the service and looking at the finely carved and painted figures in the crib. Two women came towards them.

'Bonjour, Pere Goddard, I am very 'appy to be 'ere with you today.' The lady inclined her head scattering her h's like flower petals at a wedding. 'Madame, Messieurs.'

Anna's eyes matched the velvet ribbons on her new Christmas bonnet. 'Your daughter is a lovely child, her eyes are the colour of spring violets. I have an excellent memory, Monsieur Van Maaskens; you were presented to me at the last masked ball in the Tuileries – a purveyor of fine wines and a connoisseur of the arts?'

'Your Imperial Highness is too kind.'

The Empress turned to the priest. 'The Emperor hopes to be released before Easter, so we may be living en famille at Camden Place. It is almost time for my luncheon with my son, Lou Lou, I wish you all a very merry Christmas.'

She touched Anna gently on the head, her many rings gleaming in the candlelight. The orphanage children clustered around the fine lady as she left St Mary's waving to the bystanders while her companion scattered halfpennies and farthings among the small fry.

Chapter Four

Every day Williams handed an ironed copy of *The Times* to his master at the breakfast table and papa read long boring excerpts aloud. 'A Peace Treaty has been signed in the Hall of Mirrors in Versailles. The Franco-Prussian War is over January 1871.' 'The Third Republic is now in power. The Prussians have released Napoleon III and crowds thronged the streets of Dover when he was met by the Empress and their young son, pelting them with flowers. Following a royal reception in many parts of England, the imperial family are now living quietly at Camden Place.'

Jacques had established his business as a wine merchant in premises off the Strand; every day he took the train from Chislehurst to Charing Cross, while Marguerite visited the local milliner and haberdasher and called on the ladies of the neighbourhood with Anna. Sometimes they met Eugénie at tea in the doctor's drawing room and gossiped about Paris, Queen Victoria's vast family and fashion. The Empress was rumoured to possess three hundred gowns and fifty parasols in her wardrobe and was delighted to discuss la mode, from the outdated crinoline to the bustle.

On Sundays Anna rode side-saddle on her new pony Toby, accompanying papa across the common past the Rambler's Rest and Camden Place.

During the week she walked with Louise and Mopsy and visited Miss Brier's in her little sweet shop – established by my dear mamma in 1825.' The spinster displayed her homemade sweetmeats in tall glass jars ranged in the window of Well Cottage and along her polished mahogany counter; an assortment of striped humbugs, aniseed balls, violet and strawberry fondants. She was in her element bustling around serving a few select customers, pepper-and-salt hair pinned in a neat bun and a small pair of steel-rimmed spectacles perched on the end of her nose. 'Mother was a chocolatier, trained in Bond Street, but of course our dear grandmama was a distressed gentlewoman living in reduced circumstances when she met our grandfather. He created animals to decorate the King's table: swans and rabbits of spun sugar, like coloured glass – exquisite. She paused for breath.

'Dear me, I am a rattle. You want pear drops, my dear? I always think they are rather strong on the breath for a young lady of quality. You would not prefer my sugared almonds? A little more expensive of course but they are a great favourite with Her Imperial Majesty. I supply them to the Household together with my truffles and violet creams (a recipe from my dear mother, long dead, God rest her soul). Ah well, perhaps I shall be by appointment one day.' She raised her hands in mock amazement.

'Queen Victoria visits Camden Place from time to time, you know. Think of it... Miss Briers with a Royal Coat of Arms outside her little shop! What an honour. The Empress herself comes to see me nearly every week with Madame Lebreton or the Spanish maid.'

They escaped from the shop and walked on towards the orphanage where a very small girl was swinging on the tall white gate. The child had thick, tousled black curls and round eyes like boot buttons. She dragged the toes of her boots in the dust of the road as the gate creaked backwards and forwards.

'Allo, Frenchie. Me name's Kate. Wot's yours?'

'Allo.' Anna stopped and held out a small white hand which was clasped by a grubby brown one. 'My name is Anna Marie Rose.'

'Blimey, wot a mouthful. Pleased to meet you Miss Anna, if you ain't too toffee-nosed to talk to the likes of me.' She stuck one finger up her nose and assumed a hoity-toity expression. 'Wot yer got in that paper bag?'

'Pear drops. You like one?'

'If I stick humbugs in me gob I get lockjaw and can't talk proper but pear drops is all right.' She thrust a paw into the paper cone and helped herself to a couple: one dark purple, the other bright orange. She licked one and the colour came off on her tongue.

'See yer on the common tomorrow afternoon.' She slid down from her perch on the wooden five-barred gate and turned to

Anna with a parting shot. 'You can't turn cartwheels for little toffee apples. I bin watching.'

Louise hustled her charge away from the orphanage towards the safe haven of the Lindens for hot chocolate and four o'clocks.

'You should not talk to strange children even when you are out walking with me. They are very peculiar, these English.'

The following afternoon Louise and Anna were sitting on an old tree trunk when Kate popped out from behind a thick bush. 'You're like a Jack-in-the-box.'

Kate ignored the remark. 'Don't you never go out alone? Who's the old girl,' with a jab of her thumb towards Louise. 'Yer Gran?'

'No, she looks after me.'

Kate chuckled, a deep throaty gurgle for such a small girl. 'Not three sheets in the wind, are yer?'

'Three sheets?'

'Tuppence short of a shilling.'

They were getting nowhere.

'Oh Gawd.' She shrugged her shoulders and gave up the struggle to teach the Queen's English to the frogs.

Little by little, Kate told them the story of her young life. 'They send us to the board school in the village till we go out to work at about ten or twelve. I help in the laundry – suds up to yer elbows. We was all born in Stepney, there was eight of us kids. Me dad was a sailor. 'E took 'is belt to us when 'e was on shore leave. Ma died when the littlest was born dead, and Rose tried to bring us up on 'er own but the Poor Law sent the little uns to the orphanage. Mr Osborne tells everybody my sisters went into service, but I know our Rose isn't on her hands and knees scrubbing floors for the gentry. Not on yer Nellie. She's on the game up West, drops me a tanner when she comes down for the day.'

The child was a year younger than Anna. 'I'm off. See yer round, Frenchie. Sorry Anna... Mamselle Anna. I've heard 'em call yer that. Bloomin' grand! See yer at the fair next week.' She took to her heels and was gone in a flash.

★

Her Imperial Highness planned a reception in March 1874 to celebrate the eighteenth birthday of her beloved Lou Lou, and tickets were on sale to the public at Willis's Rooms in the King's Road.

A week before the coming-of-age, a Punch and Judy man set up his booth on the common and a glass vendor was blowing friggers, ships and birds of spun glass, even a hunt in full cry with a pack of hounds in pursuit of an orange fox.

Anna and Louise met Kate near the pond where a man from the potteries was selling china dogs and other chimney ornaments. 'Buy a pair of comforters, Miss, only threepence each.'

'One please, I only have three pennies.'

Anna handed over her week's pocket money, thinking the spaniels were like Kate, alert with long hanging hair and beady, black eyes. 'Here, Kate, I've bought you a present.'

The child gawped. 'Nobody ever done that before, 'cept Rose, once, and that was a rag book with pictures.'

Anna was strictly forbidden by Louise to buy cheap ice cream from the hokey-pokey man. Pedlars sold from trays hanging round their necks or makeshift wooden stalls: bright ribbons, cheap bead necklaces and trinkets.

Kate was clutching her dog in one hand and a lump of hokey-pokey in the other. 'Fancy a lick?' She began jigging up and down like a puppet on a string.

'Hokey pokey penny a lump

The more you eat the more you jump.'

Sister Rose came down at the weekend. She's got a new bloke she's daffy about and they're getting hitched, all lovey-dovey, so bang goes me job as a maid in a knocking shop. This new chap's big and burly but 'es only a fishmonger from Billingsgate Market.'

She turned to the nurse. 'You want to look out for the dips, Louise.'

'The Dips?'

'Pickpockets, you daft 'aporth. They nick your purse before you can say knife.'

The small village children were riding painted wooden rocking horses on a little carousel set up in a clearing among the silver birches and the two girls found Fred and Charlie nearby at a coconut shy.

'Three balls a penny,' cried the gypsy.

Charlie was brandishing a small goldfish in a glass bowl. 'I won it for me Ma, Miss Anna, she loves pets.' He grinned at Katie. 'You're pretty, shall I take you home to mother as well?'

'Bloomin' cheek.'

Louise went to the Romany fortune teller's tent and gazed spellbound at the crystal ball.

'You are not a happy woman, you should go back to France.' The gipsy clasped her gnarled hand staring at the maze of lines on the palm. 'I see two or three small children sitting round a kitchen table and you feed them with onion soup. There was a man many years ago, tall with broad shoulders, but he died young.

'That will be threepence please, Madame, unless you want me to read the tarot cards.' But Anna tugged impatiently at her elbow. 'Come on, let's go and hear the music.'

The girls ran off together with the old woman panting along behind them hitching up her bloomers.

The organ grinder and his monkey had found a pitch in the yard of The Ramblers' Rest where a few yokels loafed around with pots of ale watching the show. A couple of tankards were lined up on top of the hurdy-gurdy and the little animal dipped a gnarled finger into each one, sucked it, then grinned at the bystanders with the wrinkled face of a little old man. The Italian turned the handle and began to play a tarantella.

Kate picked up her skirts and danced faster and faster in between the tipplers around the yard, her skinny black legs flashing in and out in time to the music. She ended with a flying leap, the monkey jumped on her shoulder and waved his little red cap. Half pennies and farthings rained down. Kate picked up the scattered coins and gave them to the old man.

'I buy you a lemonade, bambina? We must do this again while I am here. You are far better than my little friend Umberto.' He gave her a silver sixpence. You come again tomorrow, ple-e-ase.' Anna watched from the fringe of the crowd till Kate came back clutching her bit of snow. 'I might dance on the halls one day. It's money for old rope. Our Rose told me all about The Oxford and

The Hackney Empire. I could get off with a stage door johnny and marry a lord!' She twirled an imaginary moustache and warbled, off-key:

'I'm the man who broke the bank at Monte Carlo.'

Chapter Five

Uncle André came over on a steamer from Ostend to Folkestone for the celebrations. He was curious about Louis Napoleon – the young man had a reputation as a reckless daredevil.

Marguerite dressed in the height of fashion with the help of a Parisian dressmaker in the High Street and a milliner at Marshall & Snelgrove. Today she wore a blue gown, pearl choker, and carried a parasol of coffee lace, her blonde hair dressed in a chignon at the nape of her neck. She bought Anna a little mauve jacket and a pillbox hat.

According to *The Times* more than six thousand Frenchmen crossed the channel in yachts, steamers and fishing vessels for the occasion; men and women cycled miles from the surrounding villages and The Bull Inn was crammed to bursting point with the gentry. Revellers with tickets from Willis's Rooms trudged up the hill from the station to Camden Place, hot and breathless. Trains from Charing Cross ran every ten minutes and the hoi polloi who could not gain entry to the grounds stood for hours with their noses pressed against the railings. The noise from the crowd was deafening as the Van Maaskens' carriage turned from Hawkswood Lane into the main road. Paper garlands of flowers and coloured lanterns decorated the trees and houses en route.

The orphanage children stood in a long row waving flags and Anna caught a glimpse of Kate clasping a homemade Union Jack and a small crudely painted tricolour. She did not hear the small girl call out, 'Allo, Frenchie.'

Albert drove through the tall wrought iron gates and up the avenue towards the house for the first time. A few hardy old dowagers were sipping wine or cassis at tables outside one of the marquees, and sheep grazed in a nearby field.

The Empress and her son received their guests to celebrate his eighteenth birthday and to further the cause of establishing a Third Empire under Louis Napoleon now that his father was dead following a seven-hour operation for gallstones. Dr Conneau thought the cause of death was a clot of blood. Father Goddard had administered the last rites, Eugénie was hysterical for weeks, sedated with chloral; Louis was shattered by the tragedy but life goes on.

'I am so happy to receive my fellow countrymen and loyal friends.' Louis bowed to the wine merchant and his family as they were presented. 'Monsieur Madame, Mademoiselle, enchanté.'

Anna bobbed a curtsey.

'Monsieur André Van Maaskens... a brother I presume. There is a great family resemblance.'

They moved away from the reception line towards the buffet.

'Look at the Princess Metternich. She is so ugly they call her the Singe du Monde but she is very elegant,' Marguerite whispered.

The Duke of Padua made an impassioned speech about the young prince. 'As you know he is training at the Woolwich Academy and may receive a commission in Her Majesty's Regiment of Artillery.'

This was received with wild applause from the English contingent in his audience. 'In spite of the many responsibilities resting on his young shoulders he has never lost his boyish love of practical jokes which many of you will remember with chagrin from the old days in Arenenberg. Now, at eighteen years of age, he is waiting to answer any call from his beloved country.' Rapturous applause. The Prince rose to reply, speaking in glowing terms of his dear mother and his late father and a glittering future for the Bonapartistes on their native soil. His charm, eloquence and patriotism received a standing ovation amid loud cries of 'Vive l'Empereur' and 'Vive Napoleon.'

A string quartet played the poignant national anthem of the Second Empire, 'Partant pour la Syrie', composed by his grandmother, Hortense, as the guests were leaving.

Chapter Six

It was a quiet Sunday afternoon, a drowsy time for snoozing after a heavy luncheon, working a tapestry or reading a romantic novel from Mudie's library. The blissful silence was broken by a wasp buzzing on a window pane and a comment from Anna. 'Louise says there is an artiste at the Moulin Rouge who farts and plays a tune with his bottom, then blows out a candle to wild applause!'

Papa tried to pour oil on troubled waters. 'It is quite true Marguerite, I read about this man in *The Morning Post* and *Le Figaro*.'

Marguerite glared at her husband and decided it was high time to change the subject. 'Chislehurst is dull after Paris and I am bored, Jean Jacques.'

'You can always dabble on the stock exchange if it amuses you to be une femme d'affaires or gossip with the local ladies in the doctor's drawing room about *The Gentlewoman's Magazine* and Mrs Beeton's latest recipes. André will take you to the theatre whenever he is in England.'

Once a year his brother stayed in the Empress Eugénie's old suite at Claridge's Hotel and brought gifts of lace and long white evening gloves for Marguerite and handmade Belgian chocolates and toys for Anna.

'Jean Jacques' (his wife was the only one to use his pet name), 'I know you have a warehouse in Bermondsey storing hides, skins and foreign feathers – that is how they are described in the census. I am good with figures and I understand furs. Please let me run that side of your business. It would keep me out of mischief.'

'I suppose we could try the experiment for six months and judge by the results.'

Marguerite had got her own way as usual. 'I love you, dearest. I shall go to the East End tomorrow.' She turned to her small daughter who was reading by the fireside and listening to the conversation at the same time. 'Uncle André thinks you are beginning to speak English with a Cockney accent although I can't imagine where you have acquired it. You are becoming a young lady, lessons with a governess and visits from the music master at Camden Place are not enough. I think it is time you went to the convent school near Bromley. I shall discuss your education with Reverend Mother, I am sure papa will agree with me.' Maman was the eminence grise. 'The years are racing past and you are almost fourteen years of age.

'Did I tell you how Uncle André started life as a rag-and-bone man and made his fortune? Now he is a connoisseur of the arts buying fine paintings at Christie's and Sotheby's for his gallery in the heart of Brussels.' She laughed. 'You have heard the story of André and the Swiss bear?' It happened in Brussels many years ago when we were all very young. André had been walking the streets for hours lugging an old sack and all he had collected was a few twisted pipes and some odds and ends of copper. He was on his way home when an old peasant woman flung open her front door, hair scragged back in a bun, sabots on her feet. She pattered towards him.

"'Young man I have something for you if you will take it off my hands, but I am not paying you a sou for carting it away."

"'Rags or metal, Madame?"

"'Neither, it is made of wood and I fall over it every day of my life so you may take it and good riddance. Come into the house."

'He left his half-empty sack on the cobblestones and followed her into a dark room and out into the backyard to see an enormous carved brown bear. It was taller than André with a dusty rail to hold walking sticks and umbrellas.

"'He stood in the hall of the château where I was in service as a girl and the son of the house gave him to me when the old lady died. What on earth am I to do with such a thing now? It is always in the way when I come out into the yard at night and he frightens me to death."

'Her stern old face softened. "My late husband was fond of the animal, called him Bruno and polished the rail every week. Take him away if you can find a good home. "

'André gazed at the animal and decided there must be a market for such a fine-looking beast. "I will take him, lady. May I leave the sack here till tomorrow?"

'He went to pick up the animal but it weighed a ton so he waltzed with him, from side to side, down the steps and across the road as the old woman watched, roaring with laughter. Panting and breathless he propped Bruno against a lamp post and counted the few sous in his pocket. There was just enough to buy a drink at the café nearby. A passing cabbie waved his whip and called out. "Where's the circus, sonnie?"

'The waiter left him alone with the bear to enjoy his cordial but as André braced himself to leave, the man began to flick the table with his serviette. A middle-aged man passing the Café Rose saw the boy and his strange partner. "Where did you come by such a fine animal, young man?" The stranger stroked the bear's paws and the original patina glowed through the dust and grime. "I am sure the rail is brass and the carving is superb." Taking a clean linen handkerchief from his pocket he began to rub away the green verdigris. "He was made in Switzerland many years ago and I think he would grace my gallery. Are you prepared to sell the beast or is he a constant companion?"

'The boy stuttered with excitement. "He is for sale, Monsieur. I think he came from a good family."

'"I am sure his pedigree is impeccable. I will give you so much," proffering a handful of money that was beyond André's wildest dreams.

'"Is it a bargain?"

'"Volontiers, Monsieur." He thrust the money into the pocket of his ragged breeches.

'"I am an antiquary with a gallery near the Grand Place and if you collect anything interesting I should be glad to offer you a fair price. I think you may have flair and a good eye. Now will you try to find me a cab while I stand guard over our mutual friend?"

'André and the driver helped Bruno into the fiacre. The antique dealer turned to the boy. "I know it is none of my business but what shall you do with the money?"

"Father and I will celebrate tonight with meat from la chevallerie and a carafe of wine... then tomorrow I buy a handcart."

"'I am sure that we shall meet again, young man. Here is my card.'"

Marguerite sighed. 'Your uncle has told me that story so often I know it by heart. I can almost see the old woman and the bear now and André with the seat out of his trousers.'

'Maman tells wonderful stories papa, I shall always remember 'The Frog's Wedding' when I was very small... all the animals came and a big fat toad was the clergyman.'

'We must be serious now and talk about your education as a boarder in the convent.'

Chapter Seven

On the first day of the autumn term, Albert loaded shiny black metal trunks and a tuck box on to the carriage and drove them to meet Reverend Mother. She had skin like old parchment, a high nose and knuckles that cracked when she rubbed her dry tapering fingers together. 'You will share a dormitory with Maureen, Hannah and Mimi.' She rang a silver handbell on her writing desk.

'Send Maureen to me, Sister Agatha.'

A tall girl with flaming-red hair tied in a black velvet bow came in to the room to find Anna on the verge of tears, longing to go back with her mother to The Lindens.

'Take good care of Mopsy, maman, and dear papa... he didn't want me to leave home. If I am desperately unhappy I shall run away,' she whispered in her mother's ear as they kissed goodbye.

'Try to be good, Anna. God bless you, darling.'

The girls mounted a steep flight of stone steps to the dormitory on the third floor. 'You will sleep in the bed next to me with Hannah underneath the window. Borrow my handkerchief and stop sniffing, it's not the end of the world, you know. Mimi is in the far corner and she can be a pain because she always gets a crush on one of the girls.'

The room had bare whitewashed walls, high barred windows throwing a beam of light onto a large silver crucifix and black iron beds. Homemade rag rugs lay on the bare scrubbed floorboards.

'The nuns make us wear a brown hair shift in the bath and wash underneath it – to look at our own bodies would be an occasion of sin. I had a governess once who made me wear a blindfold.' She rattled on to set the new girl at ease. 'I'm Irish, the youngest of four brothers and sisters. The father came over from Waterford and was a wharfinger till we lost nearly everything in a fire on the docks at Rotherhithe. The poor old boy is a bit ga-ga these days since the mother died but Aunt Bridget looks after everyone. You are so very tiny.'

'I am nearly five feet tall and I can take care of myself.'

'Come and scrounge some hot chocolate from one of the nuns.'

Lights out. Anna was cold and miserable after a supper of soup and dry bread, stodgy pudding and watery coffee. She began to weep into her pillow. Hannah was fast asleep and snoring and Maureen was quiet after a last 'Good night, God bless.' A sibilant whisper came from the far side of the dormitory. 'Stop snivelling, new girl.' Then a few moments later:

'Anna, I dare you to take off that frilly cotton nightgown and stand naked in the moonlight. Pretend to be an artist's model then we can all look at your torso.'

'No, it would be an occasion of sin.'

'Cowardy, cowardy custard. I dare you… I dare you.'

A tornado swept across the bare room then Maureen grabbed Mimi by her long blonde hair and banged her head against the wall.

'You are an evil little creature, Mimi Leclerc. Leave the new girl alone or I will report you to Reverend Mother for indecent behaviour. Go to sleep Anna. We'll keep you safe and sound but for God's sake stop crying.'

The next morning Mimi had a splitting headache and refused to get out of bed in time for breakfast.

'Why did she want to see me without my clothes on?'

'She's a bit weird, but she dreams of being a great artist like Rosa Bonheur and studying in Paris one day; Sister Theresa says she lacks talent and is self-obsessed.' She hesitated. 'I have seen my brothers in the bath and of course there is a difference. John said they measured their willies on the windowsill.'

'C'est quoi, le guillaume?'

Maureen blushed to the roots of her hair and bent over her plate of porridge. The little one's innocence was incredible, still she was an only child.

'Forget it, Anna, you will soon learn English slang in the convent, but remember that men are not born wearing fig leaves.'

Sickly-green linoleum covered the floor. The baths were crouching animals on giant iron paws with orange rust slavering from their jaws. Anna waited in a line of girls holding a new sponge bag and a bottle of bright pink dentifrice. It was her first bath at the convent.

'Your turn, Anna.' Sister Josepha held out a brown hairy shirt. 'Put this over your head, undress, get into the bath and wash beneath the garment without looking at your body.'

'These rags will scratch me and it stinks!'

'Anna, do as you are told. It is the healthy smell of carbolic disinfectant.' The wizened face of the nun peered at her through a cloud of steam and she thrust the offending garment into the girl's hands. Creatures giggled in the corridor listening to the fracas through the half-open door, peeping into the bathroom. 'Cover yourself child.'

Anna was already half-naked and seeing her small breasts, pale pink nipples and belly button, blushed crimson. She flung the brown rag on to the bathroom floor.

'Put on the shift at once Anna.'

'No, Sister. I don't care if you expel me, I want to go home.'

Maureen pushed open the door. 'Make believe, Anna. Hold your nose and float like Ophelia on the water.'

Anna pulled a horrible grimace at the nun's back and climbed into the bath.

The coarse sackcloth was clinging to her arms and legs. She lay inert then rose shivering and dried herself on a prickly towel.

After lights out the girls huddled under the bedclothes and whispered.

'Have you any eligible Frenchmen in your family, Anna?'

'They are all old men like Uncle André.'

'My brother John was at St Edmund's College near Ware. The fathers thought he might have a vocation, but he is going to work at Somerset House.' Maureen sighed.

'The Donellys came over to Liverpool in the fifties when thousands of our countrymen were evicted. In the long days of the hunger, many Irish men and women were dying with the green stain of the nettles on their mouths.'

★

They spent several weeks in the South of France with Grandmaman de Savonnet – a lady with a will of iron. She lived alone with her cats and a scattering of servants in a lovely old house on the outskirts of Nimes by courtesy of a distant cousin. Being related to the Bourbons and Madame Roland, the family fortunes had never recovered since the Revolution.

Rolande de Savonnet survived without male issue. Now she was too old and tired to travel far but when her husband was alive they spent months abroad in Brussels, Evian and Lausanne. Anna adored her grandmother, a frail exquisite miniature always dressed in black from head to toe. When she was a young child living on the Boulevard Haussmann, they often rode together in the Bois.

The old lady died peacefully in her sleep when Anna was nineteen years old.

Chapter Eight

One sultry afternoon during the Easter holidays, Anna was dozing in a hammock slung between two apple trees in the orchard with a romantic novel by Jane Austen lying open on the grass beside her. She was lonely. Maureen lived somewhere near Orpington, Kate was her secret friend and Louise was too old for any rapport, with brown liver spots on her hands and a hairy mole under her chin.

Papa emerged from the house and sank into a low wicker chair that groaned under his weight; the good life was apparent in his added girth, the waistcoat buttons straining across his paunch, heavy dewlaps and dark complexion. 'Anna, your mother works too hard as a femme d'affaires. Now she has cornered mercury.' He laughed, a deep throaty chuckle.

'Cinnabar, she wants to use it in the manufacture of felt hats from rabbit skins.'

He puffed on his meerschaum pipe, a mermaid with scaly tail and bare bosom, and the warm sweet smell of tobacco wafted towards Anna. 'Let us take a holiday by the seaside. They say Brighton is the queen of watering places and the sea air might act as a tonic (and an aphrodisiac),' he murmured under his breath.

'How soon can we leave, papa?'

'Some time during the school holiday, I will book a suite at one of the hotels on the promenade.'

A few days later they left The Lindens for Tunbridge Wells where papa retired to his room for an afternoon nap leaving the ladies to their own devices.

★

The Royal Assembly Rooms dominated the Pantiles, a large sign proclaimed, Chalybeate springs. There was a tracery of black and white railings and balconies, decorative iron columns supported finely wrought canopies of the Trafalgar period. Madame Stephanie's bow window displayed a lilac gown embroidered with pale mauve violets.

'It is lovely, I want to buy it, Maman.'

'My dear Anna, you will wear white at your first ball. Monsieur Worth's ingenue gowns of tulle are all the rage this season, or you might prefer la Maison Dieulafait.' She looked at her daughter with narrowed eyes. 'I think your waist is eighteen inches but we will ask Louise to measure you.'

'I have my own dress allowance, Maman.'

'I forbid the lavender. You have been besotted with the colour ever since the Empress said your eyes were violet.'

'I was about nine years old at the time.'

In the haberdashery Marguerite bought a Berlin woolwork pattern of a cocker spaniel with an arrogant parrot and a tortoiseshell etui case for Anna.

A plain young woman looking in the saddler's window turned and ran to greet Anna. 'Forgive me, Madame Van Maaskens, I am a pupil at the convent. I believe my mother is an old friend, Alexandra Lansdowne?'

'I remember her well. Will you join us in a citron pressé? I see there is a free table on the pavement at the little café across the way.'

'I should be delighted, Madame. We leave for Paris in the autumn, I shall go to finishing school and mamma will spend a few months with the Crown Prince Feodor at his château near St Cloud.'

Maman's verdict on the young woman was brief and to the point. 'A pleasant girl with a great deal of vitality.'

'Moya, Hannah and I are dear friends but Mimi dreams of la vie de boheme in a garret, living on a diet of champagne and caviar.'

*

Sweat poured down the horses' flanks as they dragged the carriage up the School Hill in Lewes and into the yard of The White Hart Hotel. A fine figure of a woman clad in black bombazine with a white starched apron tied round her ample girth stood at the mahogany serving table carving wafer-thin slices of roast sirloin of beef to be served with feather-light Yorkshire pudding and horseradish sauce that burned the throat, followed by apple pie and clotted cream, and black coffee laced with brandy.

'On Guy Fawkes night they roll burning tar barrels down the streets. In olden days, pugilists fought with bare fists on the Downs, cock fighting was all the rage and bull terriers baited black Russian bears.'

Anna shuddered.

'That was in the time of the Prince Regent, long before you were born. The widow of Windsor casts a shadow over the Prince of Wales and his sister Beatrice.'

The equipage moved at a leisurely pace along the Old Steyne towards the promenade, past the gilded minarets and dome of the Royal Pavilion and stables glistering in the spring sunlight.

The fish market lay at one end of the Marine Parade and although the catch had landed hours before, there was still a stench of herring lingering on the air. Girls with raw-red hands were gutting fish on the stones.

A little boy in a sailor suit bowling his metal hoop along the sea front drove it straight between the legs of a portly old gentleman who roared with anger and discomfort. Nanny slapped the bare legs of her small charge and he squealed like a piglet.

They passed young couples spending a day or two at the seaside to escape from the sweltering heat of London's streets to a boarding house with a sea view. Errand boys and servant girls, scions of the aristocracy with their mistresses, bourgeois families – Brighton welcomed them all. Brighton, a lady of uncertain age with a few wrinkles but great charm – a happy bawd.

Flower beds were a blaze of colour. The Palace Pier stretched far out to sea above the glittering water, at the entrance were two kiosks of painted iron offering penny dreadfuls, sweets and copies of *John Bull* and *Titbits*.

The Queen's Hotel where Eugénie had stayed on her arrival in England lay on a corner past the ornate aquarium. Brown's Eating House displayed deep tin trays full of sizzling sausages, bangers and mash with fried onions for the hoi polloi.

Albert pulled up the horses before the stone steps of their hotel, a vast red brick edifice surmounted by copper domes slowly turning acid green in the ozone. Papa turned towards the water waving an all-embracing arm and announced, 'La Manche.' The main entrance was decorated in gold and white with columns of rouge marble and led to a wide staircase edged with pots of azaleas. The whole scene was illuminated by crystal chandeliers. The Winter Gardens lay at the far end of the foyer.

The hall porter, an old man in maroon livery with epaulettes of gold braid, carried their valises to the suite followed by a pageboy struggling with Gladstone bags, a Louis Vuitton dressing case and Marguerite's red leather hatbox.

A large drawing room furnished in the style of Louis XV led to a double bedroom, a pale green and silver room for Anna and a small adjoining dressing room for Louise. The old woman ran bath water, scented it with eau de toilette by Guerlain and tested the temperature with her elbow. 'Comme un bébé!'

A sprigged gown and a pair of black kid-slippers with French-paste buckles lay beside the chaise longue.

Papa was a proud man as he walked down the staircase between his two elegant ladies. He had been a Belgian street urchin, becoming a Paris boulevardier and a successful wine merchant. (He had chosen the only trade acceptable in polite society and was now purveyor of fine wines and spirits to the household in Camden Place.)

The windows of the restaurant were wide open but there was not a breath of fresh air – the flames of the pink candles on the tables were still. Anna looked round the dining room. All the guests seemed to be d'un certain age – what Kate would have called 'old codgers with one foot in the grave'. 'Tout passe, tout casse, tout lasse.' One could afford to be cynical at seventeen years of age.

The food was a delicious consolation: hors d'oeuvres, sole béchamel with a glass of chablis and meringue glacé. Papa sprawled in a fauteuil in the lounge after sipping his cognac, while Anna pretended to be engrossed in a small leather-bound volume of poems by Ronsard. Marguerite glanced at her daughter: Louise had dressed the pale gold hair in a wreath of lilies of the valley with ringlets framing the girl's lovely oval face.

'Mignonne, allons voir si la rose qui ce matin éclose. Sa robe pourpre au soleil.'

Tears pricked her eyelids, the romantic days of the troubadours were dead and gone.

'I should like to take a breath of fresh air in the Winter Gardens, if you will excuse me?' Silence, suffocating torpor.

'I am tired after the journey and papa is having a little nap already. We shall retire soon. Do not be longer than half an hour.'

Life was a fabulous adventure with Anna as the Sleeping Beauty waiting for a prince galloping on a snow-white charger. She walked in the conservatory between scaly palm trees and a giant cactus that caught her gown, the heavy smell of damp earth in the tropical undergrowth was overpowering. Glittering stars pierced the glass roof and the dense foliage overhead. Iridescent water shimmered like the wings of a dragonfly. A waterfall cascaded from a flint grotto while gold and silver fish flashed in and out of the light cast by gas lanterns beside the pool. A black carp swam by and the ripples cleared. For a moment in time Anna gazed at her own reflection then saw 'in a glass darkly' the image of a man with a long thin face and a pointed beard. Caught in a dream world she turned to see if this apparition were a figment of her imagination. Trembling on the brink of the shallow pool she swayed towards him and he caught her by the hand. She saw dark brown eyes and a flashing smile. 'Pardon, Monsieur, you startled me. I thought I was alone in the Winter Garden.'

The young man was flesh and blood, wearing a loud check suit like a yellow and brown horse blanket and a cinnamon waistcoat. She was fascinated by the rainbow colours and the large golden horseshoe tiepin in his flowing cravat.

'Mademoiselle's accent is enchanting. Pray forgive my garish attire. I have not had time to change for dinner after a hard day at the races. I beg your pardon.'

She gave him one of her sweetest smiles and he was fascinated. 'It is a little unexpected, Monsieur.'

'My name is Feldmann, Robert Feldmann. May I ask your own name?'

'Marie Anna Rose.'

The stranger bowed, gently took her hand and brushed it with his lips. 'I must leave you now, otherwise I shall be in disgrace with my good friends the bookmakers. Au revoir, Mademoiselle. I am sure we shall meet again.' The rainbow man turned away and passed out of sight among the overhanging branches of the trees. While Anna stayed behind in an enchanted world of make-believe, listening to the buzz of tiny insects in the warm scented air.

Anna kept a journal with little drawings beside the script. That night she wrote:

> *I have met an amazing young man dressed like a mountebank in all the colours of the rainbow. He has enormous dark brown eyes and I think I have fallen in love.*

She drew a picture of Robert in the margin showing the beard, the cravat and a horseshoe tiepin, with a big kiss and 'Roberto, Roberto.'

Meanwhile the object of her affections had done a runner and was sitting in a third class carriage on his way back to London mulling over his losses on the turf and the hole in his belly.

Chapter Nine

Anna scanned the hotel and the promenade in search of her romantic beau but he was nowhere to be seen for the rest of their holiday in Brighton.

Jacques and his daughter bathed from a wooden hut on the beach while Marguerite sat under a pink parasol and announced she was far too exhausted for such tomfoolery. Papa wore a long bathing suit with horizontal stripes to enhance his figure, Anna dressed in a navy and white costume with a collar, bloomers and a mob cap.

'André and I spent hours in the river when we were boys, washing off the grime of the city and the scrapyard.'

He taught Anna to swim.

'The English are antediluvian. They want me to use a beach for men only.'

They tried to perform a balancing trick on the sand at low tide but papa became puce in the face and his wife called out to him: 'This is not a circus, my dear. Put Anna down at once, I do not wish to be a widow like the queen of England.'

He sank into a deckchair beside her, puffing and blowing like a grampus. 'I think I am getting old.' He looked up at his daughter, narrowing his eyes against the strong sunlight. 'This young lady will be a belle one day.'

Anna blushed and ran back into the cabin to change into her afternoon dress.

'She is not a cocotte, Jean Jacques. Take off those ridiculous garments and I will meet you both on the terrace of the hotel for a thé citron.'

Louise was worried. Her old face looked wrinkled and careworn as she tried to discuss her future life with Anna before the family left Brighton. 'I am an old woman, little one, I want to live with my sister in Provence and care for the grandchildren.

You know my own baby died when you were born and I nursed you with all my love, but it is now time to go home.'

'You can't leave me alone, Louise.'

She tapped the side of her nose with a stubby forefinger. 'We shall see what we shall see. Madame will insist on a lady's maid when I leave. Shall I suggest one from the orphanage, Katie the horreur? I could say we met a few times in the village which is true.' She mumbled under her breath, 'A little subterfuge. The child would be good company although she is only fifteen; I can see she thinks the world of you. I cannot leave you alone in a foreign country. Your parents are too absorbed in one another.'

Anna kissed the old wet nurse on both cheeks. 'If you must go it is a wonderful idea, Louise. I will mention it to maman as well.'

She touched on the subject several days later after Louise had sown the seeds. 'Why not engage a maid through the orphanage, maman. You would be doing a great kindness.'

The supervisor, Mr Osborne known as Old Misery guts, arrived at the house with a small baggage in tow: Kate, unruly black curls scragged back with hairpins, woolly stockings darned at the knees with fine stitches like a young lady's sampler, and a pair of high buttoned boots.

She was still very small at fifteen and three-quarters. Anna's kitten Mitzi began weaving round the skinny black legs purring like a steam engine. Kate bent down and picked up the little creature. 'Cor, 'er whiskers don't arf tickle.'

Misery guts frowned. Young servant girls should be seen and not heard.

She dumped the animal on the hearth rug and went back to playing statues, dying to cock a snook at the pompous old man as he droned on and on recounting the story of her life.

'Mother and father are both dead. She is the youngest of eight brothers and sisters, all the others have joined the forces or gone into service.' He ignored her presence as if she were a lump of horseflesh on the butcher's counter. 'A bright young woman, but she needs a firm hand, Madame.' The urchin raised her eyes from the carpet and winked at Anna.

Marguerite agreed to engage her for a trial period to be trained as Anna's personal maid at a wage of ten pounds a year and all found, sharing an attic bedroom with one of the other servants.

*

Marguerite felt a wave of nostalgia for the old way of life. 'The grapes were pale green like spring water and I shall always remember the sun-baked earth of Provence and the blazing sunflowers.' The village curé wrote letters for Louise enclosing small gifts of herbs and a necklace of wooden beads for Anna, then she passed away leaving her a carved jet locket on a chain – her dearest possession.

*

'Maureen, he is the handsomest man on Earth, with black hair and dark brown eyes like one of Jane Austen's heroes and I found him lurking among the tropical palms in the Winter Garden of the hotel. He kissed my hand and I fell head over heels in love with him, then he disappeared!'

'Tell me all about this Brighton holiday and your Prince Charming.'

'We bathed in the sea every day and papa taught me to swim, and we watched the giant octopus stretching its tentacles against the sides of the glass tank in the Aquarium.'

'Enchanting! I am sure any young blade was better looking than a dirty old squid. One day this knight in shining armour may ride up Hawkswood Lane on a milk-white steed.'

The girls were sitting on their beds in the dormitory and Mimi broke into the conversation. 'I go to finishing school in Paris in the autumn and I shall wear trousers like Georges Sand and smoke black cheroots.'

'And fall in love with Frederic Chopin and live on the isle of Majorca.'

'You know I hate men and never want to be a wife and mother, not even a mistress.'

'Poor Mimi, forever worshipping Sappho on the shores of Lesbos.'

'At least I shall not be gross with child, waddling around like a fat Christmas goose in the bogs of Ireland.'

'Her Majesty told maman she might ask me to be one of her ladies-in-waiting after the ball at Camden Place.'

'Queen Victoria?'

'No, the Empress Eugénie, of course.'

'A great honour, with the court in exile.'

Hannah, the fourth girl sharing the dormitory, was large and plain, although her mother, Lady Lansdowne, was a famous beauty. 'I shall live in the country and ride to hounds and follow the shoot with my brother. Daddy owns a thousand acres, so we shall have room to breathe. I expect to meet a middle-aged landowner looking for a dull faithful wife with childbearing hips and a kind, understanding nature.'

'Like the Duke of Fife? They call him le petit écossais roux qui a toujours la queue en l'air. The little red-headed Scotsman with his tail always in the air!' Maureen had a bawdy sense of humour at seventeen years of age. Hannah could laugh at her own shortcomings. 'I came to terms with my appearance years ago; Mummy is the belle of the ball in our family and we are never allowed to forget it. She has a new amour, Prince Feodor, equerry to Nicholas, Tsar of all the Russias.'

Mimi flounced off in a huff. 'I think you are all disgusting, especially Maureen who has no reticence whatsoever.'

*

Kate was at a loose end after cook chased her out of the kitchen where she was nibbling the left-overs from luncheon.

'You must have got worms girl. You never stop eating. Get out from under my feet, you're neither flesh, fowl nor good red herring. Training to be Miss Anna's lady's maid at your age. I never heard the like of it!'

Kate made a face at the old girl behind her back and slipped out of the back door and down the flagged path towards the stables where she came upon one of the lads polishing a lady's saddle on a rough hewn table under one of the trees. 'Ullo.' A pause. 'How d'you like working for the nobs?'

'Mam'selle Anna's lovely but her ma's a bit stuck-up, don't even say kiss my arse. I think the old man's a one for the ladies.'

'Want to have a look at the horses?'

'I'm scared stiff of the ugly brutes.'

Fred stopped work on the saddle. 'Don't be daft. Come on, I'll show you round. This is Miss Anna's Toby – fourteen hands. You can feed him some grass if you like.'

Toby kicked his stall and Kate backed away.

'You're a townie, right enough. Here you are.' The boy wrenched up a handful of coarse grass and gave it to her. 'Keep your hand flat or he'll eat your fingers. Now stroke him on the nose, silly.'

They toured the loose boxes. 'You're doing fine, Blackie.'

Kate grinned. 'Thanks, Freckles.'

His nose was spattered with ginger dots.

'My Mum says they're sun kisses.'

'Your Mum's a silly old bitch.'

He flung himself on her, temper blazing, and they rolled over and over down the grassy bank. He landed on top of her, grabbed the black curls and tugged.

'Say you're sorry.'

'Shan't.'

He tugged again and she let out a piercing yell just as Albert and Pierre were coming round the corner. The youngsters leapt to their feet and bolted behind the potting shed. Fred looked at the small, bedraggled figure in front of him then stuck out his hand. 'Friends, Blackie?'

'Me name's Kate. Wot's yours?'

'Fred Harris. I'll walk you to church next Sunday if you like. All the froggies go to St Mary's but we'll go across the road to the other one, St Nicholas.'

'Alright, Freddie. Don't mind if I do.'

Chapter Ten

Mr George Leybourne pranced around the stage of Wilton's Music Hall in Whitechapel and the whole audience joined in the chorus.

> Champagne Charlie is my name,
> Champagne drinking is my game,
> I don't care what becomes of me—

Jean Jacques swung his short swagger cane backwards and forwards and eyed the ladies of the night; music and pretty girls amused him but he was not looking for an affaire de coeur, merely killing half an hour or so before his train left Charing Cross. Tonight he was alone as his usual drinking companions had deserted him in favour of a business meeting near London Bridge.

A handsome young man leaned against the bar counter resting one foot on the brass rail and drumming his fingers in time to the catchy tune. Applauding the entertainer he knocked the tankard of beer at his elbow splashing a few drops of liquid into the air. 'I beg your pardon, sir.'

'Pas de problème, Monsieur.'

The ice was broken. The barmaid wiped the gleaming mahogany counter. Jacques thought he recognised his companion's face – he was most probably a 'regular' at Wilton's on Friday nights.

Noise erupted during the interval. The company of merchants and working men were enjoying their night out on the town.

The two men stood idly watching the cocottes promenade in pairs at the back of the hall, casting a roving eye in their direction from time to time. 'The tall blonde is a fine figure of a woman but a little mature. Perhaps your fancy is for ladies with red hair or a raven-haired beauty like la contessa behind the bar?'

'They say all cats are grey at night. In any case I cannot afford such luxuries at the moment – I am not in gainful employment.'

'Shall we share a table for supper? It is included in the ticket price.'

They sat together eating in silence and watched the next act, a long-boot dancer called Little Tich – a droll eccentric. 'What is your profession, young man, if I do not intrude on your privacy by asking such a question.'

'Horse flesh and the turf at the moment, but I worked in the office of a textile firm in Aldgate. My greatest assets are fluent French and German, and I write a good hand.'

'I wonder if you would consider a future in the wine trade? My firm is called Van Maaskens and we have premises off the Strand. I am looking for a young male secretary who is bilingual, there is a great deal of correspondence between my office and the vineyards in France.'

'I should be greatly honoured if you would consider me Monsieur. My name is Feldmann, Robert Feldmann, at your service. I presume you would require references from an employer?' It was a wild gamble as he left under a cloud after a slight difference of opinion, and giving one of the staff a black eye. 'I always prefer to trust my own judgement. Another man s opinion of you might be quite worthless.' They cracked open a bottle and Van Maaskens came to an intuitive decision. 'I suggest you stay at my house in the country, and we can work from there for a trial period of say three months.'

The suggestion was beyond Robert's wildest dreams.

His future employer caught a quizzical expression on the young for the post your my last man's face and misunderstood the reaction. He was certainly not looking for a sweet boy 'I can assure you that my wife and daughter will make you very welcome. Remuneration to be agreed later. 'Salut.'

They clinked glasses and shook hands. The bargain was sealed and it was agreed they should meet for a luncheon at Simpson's in the Strand the following day to discuss the details.

Papa was drinking a glass of wine with his family and holding forth as was his wont. 'His name is Feldmann, Robert Feldmann.'

Anna's heart missed a beat. 'I have engaged him as my secretary and he will stay here for a few months to enable me to catch up on the arrears of work. I thought he could sleep in one of the small rooms at the back of the house then he will not be under your feet all the time, Marguerite. Do you agree?'

'He will take his meals with us?'

'Of course, my dear. I took him to Simpson's for luncheon and his table manners are impeccable. You really are an incredible snob sometimes, Marguerite. His father is a German refugé and the young man speaks excellent French. He appears to be ambitious and is most anxious to learn.'

Marguerite and Anna were waiting in the drawing room to greet papa's new protégé. A clatter of hoof beats announced their arrival as the station cab turned into the drive followed by the sound of voices in the hall. Sally the parlour maid opened the door and papa entered followed by the rainbow man clad in a dark suit of charcoal grey and a delicately flowered waistcoat. The transformation was complete: the peacock feathers had moulted, even the rakish beard had been trimmed to a neat Napoleon.

'May I introduce my new secretary, Mr Robert Feldmann... my wife Madame Van Maaskens and my daughter Mademoiselle Anna.'

Marguerite inclined her head. 'Monsieur Feldmann.'

'A pleasure to meet you, Monsieur.'

Anna was radiant as she held out a slim white hand to the newcomer. This was a gift from heaven.

Feldmann bowed to each of the ladies in turn. Marguerite noticed that his manners were excellent – he rose to his feet in deference every time she entered or left a room.

During the evening Anna played the piano, Mendelssohn's 'Songs Without Words' followed by a gay waltz, while Robert stood beside her turning the pages of the music. Papa stifled a yawn, his own taste was more rumbustious. 'The Carnival of the Animals' or bawdy music hall songs. One of his greatest pleasures was a night out in the West End with supper at Romano's although he resisted the private rooms.

'Time for bed, my dears. Robert and I must work early in the morning and I think we should retire.'

'May I show Mr Feldmann the conservatory, papa? The camellias are lovely now.' Mademoiselle was a picture of wide-eyed innocence.

Her father nodded. 'If you wish, but remember it is almost ten o'clock.' He turned to Robert, 'These things interest you?'

'I am dedicated to the study of nature, sir.' The young couple passed through the double doors out of sight. He took her hand and kissed it for the second time. 'You are enchanting, Mademoiselle.'

'You also, Monsieur.' She blushed like a damask rose.

'This is no mere coincidence. I bribed the clerk at the reception desk and copied your address from the register then I was forced to do a 'moonlight flit' from the hotel due to lack of funds. Your father's office boy was most obliging with further details of Friday nights at Wilton's in Grace Alley.

Come, Mademoiselle Anna,' he caressed the name. 'I am sure it is long past your bedtime. We do not wish to annoy your father... for the time being,' and he ushered her back into the drawing room.

Robert was shown to his room in a small turret at the rear of the house by a skinny little maid with boot-button eyes. Simple comfort – a spotless white marcella quilt covered the bed and he found a brown stone hot water bottle at the foot.

'Will that be all, sir?'

'What is your name, my dear?'

'Kate.'

'Short and sweet.' He chucked her under the chin and she glared at him. The child was as plain as a pikestaff, darting here and there like a ferret, turning down the bed, placing a copper jug full of hot water on the washstand, then scuttling off as fast as her legs would carry her to the attic room she shared with Sally.

'That one's a bit lively. Thinks he's God's gift to the ladies.'

Robert leaned on the window sill and gazed out over the lawns and orchard. The Weald stretched beyond the grounds as far as the eye could see by moonlight. The cold air hit him like a blow between the eyes so he began to prepare for bed. A small iron grate held a few glowing coals. He filled it from the painted metal scuttle, climbed into bed and pulled the blankets up to his chin. The Lindens was quite a spread. He knew from gossip in the Strand that his employer was a warm man, well-breeched, and it was a stroke of good fortune that he had been able to ingratiate himself at the music hall.

Anna was the loveliest girl he had ever met apart from a young Italian, la contessa, the barmaid at The Oxford who was generous with her favours. Anna with her violet eyes and hair like spun gold, all youth and innocence, was like the princess in a fairy tale.

Maybe, if he played his cards right... he dreamed of l'amour, a life of luxury, a touch of class for the first time in his life. Robert was not a fortune hunter, but no one's motives were entirely pure.

Meanwhile Anna lay in bed gazing at the crescent moon; falling in love was the most wonderful sensation in the world.

Chapter Eleven

'Feldmann is years older than Anna but they seem to enjoy spending time together and he may have a steadying influence on the child.'

'She rides like a mad creature, la Diablerette.'
'The stable lads call her a pocket Venus.'

Anna and Robert were strolling in the garden. She wore a bonnet trimmed with wild roses and carried an ivory prayer book – a gift from Uncle André on the day of her confirmation.

Robert stooped to pick a small flower growing wild in the herbaceous border. 'Love-lies-bleeding, for you Mademoiselle Anna.'

She blushed. The sleeve of his jacket brushed against her breast as they walked side by side along the garden path, her heart beat faster and faster and a small pulse was throbbing at the side of her neck. 'Robert, why don't you attend Mass with the family? I am sure my parents would be happy for you to accompany us.'

'Young Anna, there are many things about me you will never understand as long as you live.' He gestured with a long lazy hand.

'Your family lacks the spirit of adventure to discover the New World. Sometimes one must take a chance in life and gamble against long odds.' He laughed at his own grandiloquence. 'Come and sit beside me and I will tell you the story of my life as a gentleman of fortune. I have never lied to you, Anna.' He hesitated for a moment then began. 'My father is a German Jew who came to this country many years ago and now works as a tailor's cutter in Bethnal Green. He made all our shirts and knickerbockers when we were kids and even cut those garish tweeds for the races. I fancied myself as quite a card till I saw those swells in the ring. My old lady is a goy, half East End, half bog Irish. She runs an eel and pie shop in the Mile End Road and you could never imagine the steam and sweat, water streaming down the windows and ma dishing out grey, slimy jellied eels. It makes me sick.'

'You love her very much.'

'Yes, and I'm proud of them both for dragging themselves out of the gutter. I got a job as a bookie's runner when I was ten, taking tanner bets from punters and scarpering when I saw a bobbie. Then I worked as an office boy, made a few bob on the horses and learned the three r's and French and German from my old man. Now I am falling in love with a little rich girl, a convent child living in a world of make-believe.'

His manner changed. 'Beware, my motives are not always as pure as the driven snow. I might carry you away to a château in Stepney.'

Anna laughed. 'Do the eels swim around in an aquarium like goldfish?' In spite of his blinding honesty she could never understand his old way of life in a thousand years.

'I met your father for a glass of wine in The Bull and bought a copy of *The Times* to create a good impression. It carried a long leader article about life in the United States of America and emigrants who made their fortune on the East Side in the rag trade, on the railroad or in shipping. You must be strong to survive. Mavericks are gamblers who spend their lives playing cards on river boats up and down the Mississippi.'

He sighed. 'I am tired of England, even this little corner of France, but I have not saved enough money to pay the steerage fare to America.'

'There is always my dress allowance.'

'I do not ponce on children. Besides I could not take your money and abandon you... everything is in the lap of the gods.'

Her face fell. 'Anything is possible when you grow up.'

He kissed her lightly on both cheeks, she clasped his hand and they sped away between the trees. 'Dance with me, Roberto. It is a grand waltz by Johann Strauss, and we are in the ballroom of the Tuileries Palace.' She danced alone between the trees then drifted towards him but he was not in the mood for childish games.

'Anna, your father is sending me to Brussels to supervise the dispatch of some merchandise and meet your uncle André. I shall be away for weeks, little one. Do not forget me and marry a lecherous old prince from Camden Place in my absence.'

She tripped on the gnarled root of an apple tree, he saved her from falling and she flung her arms around his neck. He kissed her for the first time: her eyes, her neck, her throat, and she was floating on air. He thrust his body against hers, the tip of his tongue flickering against her lips like a snake.

Mopsy was grunting and growling under the garden seat with pale wild roses and straw sticking out of his mouth. One pink ribbon lay along his smooth black flank. 'It was a present from maman. She will be furious with me.' Her cheeks were burning.

'Robert, I love you best of all the world. Will you marry me?' She caught her breath and waited. His answer was flippant.

'I want you very, very much, little one, and we could live happily ever after, but I am sure your father would reject a mongrel from the East End as a suitor for his daughter's hand. He might consent to Louis Napoleon, the Prince Imperial.' His low drawling voice was bitter. Robert took her gently in his arms. 'Sweet seventeen, never been kissed. My love.'

A pink blossom from one of the apple trees fell on to her hair. He cupped it in his hands for a moment then put the delicate flower in the breast pocket of his jacket. 'I shall keep it close to my heart, Anna, in remembrance of you. I will marry you anywhere in the world, but only with your father's blessing. Remember you are under legal age and I do not intend to serve a gaol sentence for abducting a minor. Dare you ask for his consent? He dotes oh his only daughter. I will stay at The Tiger's Head tonight and wait for you to send me the answer.'

He kissed her gently on the mouth then turned away leaving Anna alone in the garden. A brimstone-yellow butterfly brushed against her hand and a thrush was singing its heart out in a lilac bush. She ran indoors and up the stairs to her bedroom. Papa came home every evening at six o'clock, put on a smoking jacket and retired to his study for an hour's peace and quiet before the evening meal. She would beard him in his den.

Anna bathed, splashed lavender water on her handkerchief, Kate brushed her hair and tied it back with a velvet ribbon. 'Kate,

I have a secret but if I tell you it may never come true.' The little maid gave her a sideways glance.

'Maybe I can guess. Tell me tomorrow morning. It's my evening off, so I'm going for a walk on the common with Fred and taking a birthday cake to Miss Briers; the poor old girl's knocking on a bit.'

Anna sat on the edge of the chaise longue at the foot of her bed and waited... and waited and waited. She was terrified of her father when he flew into a black rage with one of the servants and she detested scenes of any kind. She shut her eyes and prayed.

Maman was spending the night in London and could not intercede. She left the bedroom at five minutes past six with Mopsy waddling down the staircase at her heels, panting and breathless – a mature fellow now eight years of age.

Voices rose from the back of the house. She could hear cook chunnering on about a lumpy white sauce and blaming the kitchen maid. Another world lay behind the green baize door.

Anna crossed the hall. 'Stay, Mops.' He lay outside the study his dark bulging eyes watching every movement. A few white hairs sprouted from his velvety black ears and his muzzle was greying. She took a deep breath and knocked. Papa was warming his coat tails at the fire, holding a glass of whisky in one hand and a cigar in the other.

'Anna, how good to see you so early in the evening.' The top of her head reached his middle waistcoat button as he bent forward to kiss her on the cheek. A heavy gold Albert stretched across his paunch with a hunter in one pocket and two, large seals dangling in the middle.

'I have brought you a present to celebrate your debut in society.' He turned towards the marqueterie escritoire and took out a blue jewel box to show her a coral pendant, eardrops and brooch, fashioned as stars set with tiny seed pearls. 'I thought you might wear them to the ball with the white gown your mother has ordered from Worth.'

He eyed his daughter from head to foot. 'You are a lovely young lady now and maman says you speak English far better than your poor old father. I shall never lose this execrable accent.

'The English sisters say I roll my r's and it sounds like an affectation; it is always worse if I become excited or angry.' Butterflies were fluttering in the pit of her stomach as she tried to be calm.

'I have received the invitations from Camden Place and decorations will be worn, I still have some from my younger days and an order from the King of the Belgians.' His deep voice droned on reverberating in her ears like faint thunder. She braced herself gazing straight into his full brown eyes.

'*Courage mon ami, le diable est mort*: courage my friend, the devil is dead. You taught me to believe that when I was a little girl, I must always be brave, comme les garçons.' She took a deep breath and blurted out her secret. 'Papa, I am in love.'

There was a deadly silence. A pulse ticked in the man's throat and his large brown hands knitted together behind his back. 'Who is the man?'

'Papa, I love Robert and we are asking your permission to marry. Please give us your blessing.'

She was aware of a clock ticking on the mantelpiece and her father s heavy breathing. 'Feldmann.'

'He loves me too papa, we can be married when he returns from Brussels.'

'The scum of the earth, a whipper-snapper. The man's a bloody fortune hunter.' His voice was hoarse with emotion.

'Papa, if you refuse I shall marry him on my twenty-first birthday. We met last Easter when he was in Brighton for the races and he came here to find me. I love him more than anyone in the whole world.' She stood before him with her chin up and eyes shining.

His face was magenta. A thick blue vein at one side of his forehead throbbed against the dark skin and his hands were shaking. 'Anna, come to me.' She was still. He seized her by the arm. 'This man has violated my hospitality. If he has harmed you in any way I will kill him. I want you to swear before God that you will never see him again as long as you live. Go down on your knees.'

'No, papa, No.'

He thrust her body towards the floor. She writhed to escape from his grasp, but he caught her by the shoulder, nails biting her flesh through the thin gown. Snatching his horse whip from a rack on the wall, he raised it above his head and slashed his daughter. Hissing like a snake, the leather thongs curled in the air lacerating her skin till she screamed in agony. Blood was seeping through the white silk bodice as Anna gazed into the distorted face of a madman. His gold signet ring glittered like the evil eye, a crimson mist veiling her eyes darkened to purple and pitch-black as she fell senseless to the ground. Jean Jacques loosed the horse whip and bent over the girl lying in a crumpled heap at his feet. There was a flickering pulse... Anna was still alive.

The finely wrought coral necklace lay beside her on the carpet. He ground it to fragments with the heel of his shoe, then stooped to pick up his daughter and cradled her in his arms.

'Anna, my little Anna – it was all a bad dream, a nightmare.' He caressed her face, then sobbing, carried her out of the study and across the hail towards the staircase.

*

Mopsy saw this man with his mistress, hurled himself across the tiles and embedded his razor-sharp teeth into a fleshy calf. Cursing, Jacques shook his leg free and kicked the little pug dog across the floor. Mops shuddered and lay still, curled in a small black ball against the newel post at the foot of the stairs.

*

Anna was clawing at the bars of a cage, crawling on a glass ceiling, trying to escape. Now she was awake and screaming, clutching a piece of white linen she had ripped from her father's shirt as she fell. Strips of cloth from her gown were embedded in the wounds on her back and shoulders where the flail scored the pale flesh. She bit her lower lip in pain till blood flowed between her small white teeth and trickled down her chin.

She could remember papa shouting, 'No Anna... No Anna... No!' and lashing her time and time again. Sliding across the sheets she lowered herself gently on to the carpet and crawled towards the bathroom retching from the pit of her stomach.

Yellow bile splashed the blue and white milkmaids and the spotted cows in the bowl of the lavatory.

Anna turned on the bath taps, climbed over the rim and lowered herself into the tepid water that darkened from a pale shade of pink to crimson. She lay inert for a long while then took a wrapper and draped it around her naked body. Kate was out of reach so she was alone with the other servants and papa. Anna could imagine him saying: 'Mademoiselle Anna has a slight headache and will not come down for dinner this evening.'

If only she could reach the presbytery for help. She tried the bedroom door. It was locked. In a fit of white-hot rage she crashed on the door with her fists. 'Let me out of here... out out out. I shall run mad.'

No one came.

Robert had promised to wait at The Tiger's Head till he knew about her father's consent to their wedding. There would be a terrible scene if he should come back to The Lindens and confront papa. She must escape from this house. They could elope to France on the night coach. Grandmaman de Savonnet would give them food and shelter in the old château if they travelled south to Nimes, and Robert could find work in the vineyards. Her head was spinning round and round like a top.

There was money for the journey in her dressing-table drawer – the dregs of her monthly dress allowance and the contents of her jewel box. Everything was falling into place.

'Kate, Kate, why aren't you here tonight when I need your help? You would know how to escape from this room.' It was nine o'clock and her little maid was due back at ten but sometimes she climbed in through the kitchen window at midnight to be met by cook with a rolling pin.

There was only one way out of this prison cell: through the long window and over the balcony, and there was no time to lose. Anna pulled the smallest wicker valise out of the cupboard and began to pack, underwear, a dress, the small pink and blue holy water font that hung over her bed – a present from uncle André. It was agony to raise her arms and slip a dress over her shoulders.

She tugged at the bell pull again and again but there was no answer, the house was silent as the grave. Still there might be a way out. Marguerite was terrified of fire and had taught Anna to knot sheets together, lower them from a window and drop to safety. Anna stripped the linen from her bed to form a rope, tied one end round a stone baluster on the balcony and let it fall to earth, throwing her valise on to the flower bed. Anna followed, hand over hand like a monkey at the zoo, blood seeping down her spine and between her buttocks.

She crept down the side of the carriage sweep in the shadow of the laurels, crouching in the shrubbery for a few moments watching the flickering light in the study window. 'Adieu, papa.'

Anna was feeling very weak as she dragged the valise through the gates and out of sight of the house.

Noise burst from the small leaded windows of The Tiger's Head Inn. The church clock struck ten. The clanging of pewter pots and the raucous laughter of men echoed down Hawkswood Lane. Anna moved into the back courtyard and knocked on the door. It was raining now, a light fine drizzle.

Once papa knew she was missing he would raise the alarm, call the Police and take her home by force, if need be.

'Dear God, please let Robert come quickly, then we can run away together.' She knocked again. This time the door opened and a sluttish servant girl stood on the threshold in the half-light, a greasy lock of hair hanging over her dank forehead.

'Well?' The upward inflexion was insolent.

'I want to see Mr Robert Feldmann at once. He has taken a room at the inn and we have arranged to meet here.'

The girl eyed her from head to toe. 'Oo are yer, gel, one of 'is tarts? Charlie from the big 'ouse up the road brought 'im a big envelope. 'E bought Charlie a pint of ale for 'is trouble and said, "I'm off to the smoke on the last train tonight". Sorry, but you're backin' a loser.'

She flung a bowl of scummy slops across the yard past Anna's feet and went back into the public house slamming the door behind her. Anna was sick on the cobblestones. She stood in the shadows leaning against an old outhouse, hiding her face. Two men were leaving by the back door.

She turned towards the open common, tears streaming down her cheeks. It was dark now. Scudding clouds obscured the moon as she stumbled over the rough grass in the blinding rain. She hated Robert and loathed papa, she would never go home again. Anna fell in a dead faint among the reeds at the edge of the pond where Fred and Charlie found her an hour later after leaving the inn.

'God, it's Mamselle Anna, I thought it was a ruddy corpse.' Charlie bent down to feel her heartbeat. 'C'mon, we can lift her between us. She's only a little 'un. Got a flask? She's still alive.'

Fred poured a few drops of spirits between her clenched teeth then they carried her back to The Lindens through the tradesmen's entrance and up the maids' staircase. Kate had already seen the makeshift rope hanging from the balcony. 'Go and tell the master you found Mamselle Anna lying on the common. She looks near death.'

'I fail to understand why your daughter was wandering alone on the common at midnight. The young lady has been mercilessly flogged.'

Dr Enright was called out in the middle of the night and demanded a second opinion on the case to no avail.

Jacques had been drinking heavily for hours. 'She was punished for disobeying her parents.'

'Flagellation?'

'She refused to conform to our code of honour, Monsieur le Docteur.'

Marguerite was distraught to learn that her husband had demanded a medical examination of the girl while she was till unconscious. 'Who knows, she might be with child.'

'Your daughter is *virgo intacta*, Madame. She has not been deflowered. I am far more concerned about the punishment inflicted which was a gross abuse of power.' Dr Enright knew this might well have been a case of manslaughter. 'The young lady could still die of bronchia pneumonia, brought on by shock and exposure. I refuse to fudge the medical evidence.' He was beginning to lose his temper. 'Good God, man, do you realise that your daughter may never regain consciousness? She is in a deep coma and her back and shoulders are slashed to ribbons. Thank Heaven you did not touch her face.'

Marguerite took him by the arm. 'Let us discuss the matter in the privacy of my room, Doctor.' He followed her along the corridor while Jacques remained hunched in a chair, his head clasped between his hands.

'I understand that our daughter became enamoured of my husband's secretary, Feldmann. She was...' she hesitated for a moment groping for words, 'punished for refusing to obey her father. She is a headstrong girl and tried to run away. You must realise, Doctor, it would have been a most unsuitable liaison.'

This woman was trying to protect her husband from the law. When she looked up her eyes were bright with tears. 'I shall never be able to forgive him.'

'Your daughter is a virgin. Why does he seek to punish her?'

'The sins of the flesh are a danger to us all.'

Anna lay in a twilight world of moving shadows. She opened her eyes to find water trickling down her neck and into her ears as Kate sponged her face and body. She was lying naked in her own bed on a cool linen sheet.

'The doctors have been buzzing around like blue-arsed flies. Fred and Charlie found you by the pond and thought you was dead. You have been asleep for days, Mamselle Anna. I am going to draw back the curtains and blow away the cobwebs.'

Anna's pale face was pathetic with deep hollows gouged out beneath her violet eyes. The sharp bones of her brittle wrists were breaking through the lace cuffs of her nightgown.

Kate had been sleeping on a rug at the foot of Anna's bed like a small animal guarding her mistress: the doctors prescribed absolute peace and quiet and forbade all visitors including her parents. 'That man Feldmann wasn't fit to lick your boots.' Kate propped Anna against a pile of down pillows and began to feed her with broth as if she were a baby. The silence was broken by a knock at the door. 'Sir.' The maid stepped back to allow her master to enter the room. Jacques sat on the bed beside his daughter and a scent of eau-de-cologne wafted towards him. Instinctively she shrank away into the nest of pillows.

'My little Anna I love you so much.' He began to cry crocodile tears, mopping his face with a silken handkerchief before making his confession. 'I have some bad news: poor Mopsy died in his sleep. I have bought a puppy to keep you company – a little griffon bruxellois. His name is Felix and he is only two months old.' He fumbled under his smoking jacket and thrust a small furry bundle into her arms, tears streaming down his face.

'Poor little Mops, I adored him.'

'He was an old dog; we buried him in the orchard under an apple tree with a small wooden cross to mark his grave. Frederick carved his name and "born Paris 1870".'

Felix was burrowing under the bedclothes. Anna kissed her father's cheek. 'I forgive you everything, papa, you were trying to protect me, but I shall never forget that night as long as I live.'

She spent hours on a chaise longue in her bedroom pretending to read or sew, dreaming of another life far away from Chislehurst, in the Australian bush or living in a brownstone house in Manhattan. Mimi wrote long disjointed letters about living with 'the disenchanted' in Venice, Café Florian, the Piazza San Marco and the gondoliers. She was sharing an apartment with peeling shutters and scarlet geraniums on the windowsill in an old courtyard near the Grand Canal. Encore la vie de bohème.

Anna told Maureen the bare bones of the affaire, enough to salvage her wounded pride, how papa had refused his consent to the wedding and thrashed her with a horsewhip.

'The man is a maniac, although I know that Cardinal Newman's friend flagellated himself for eating too many slices of buttered toast. It's the truth! The sins of the flesh.

We are all going to the ball at Camden Place except the father who is very frail and away with the fairies most of the time.'

★

A letter was delivered to The Lindens some months later. It was addressed to Mademoiselle Anna Van Maaskens, bearing an American stamp and marked 'personal'. The notepaper was headed: 'Broadway'.

My dearest Anna,

When your father refused his consent to our marriage I went back to my roots in the East End, bought an overcoat with an astrakhan collar, and sailed for New York.

My heart turned over when I saw the Statue of Liberty for the first time. America is big, brash and beautiful, not miniature and adorable like you Anna, but I love her.

I gambled, worked as a roustabout for Barnum's Circus and a barker at the Chicago Fair. Now I am helping a friend run a burlesque show off East 14th Street. They all say that I am looking for the crock of gold at the end of the rainbow.

I think you would hate the life in New York, but I was born 'on the wrong side of the tracks' as they say in the States and I enjoy the pulsating vitality of this great city.

Please give this draft for one hundred pounds to Monsieur votre père with my compliments – I told you that I do not ponce on little girls. I am betrothed to a young Italian girl called Lucia and we hope to marry in the new year.

I shall never forget you, Anna, as long as I live.
Bonne chance, bonne nuit, Adieu.
Robert

Robert would always remember her as a poor little rich girl – his spoiled brat. He would never know about papa thrashing her with a horse whip, the insolent slut at The Tiger's Head and the time she lay unconscious in the reeds. 'Tout passe, tout lasse, tout casse.' One could not reply to Robert Feldmann, Broadway unless he made a name for himself on the 'great white way'. She flung his letter on the open fire.

Kate was watching her mistress in the mirror; over the years she had picked up a crude smattering of French with an atrocious accent. 'Ça va, Mademoiselle?'

'Oui, ça va très bien, Katie. Now I am free to marry anyone I please when I am twenty-one and if papa tries to interfere again, he can jump from the top of the Tower of London.'

Chapter Twelve

André Van Maaskens received an invitation to the birthday ball at Camden Place because of his past dealings with Sophie Metternich and sailed from Ostend a few days ahead of time. Marguerite had written him a most disturbing letter.

My dear André,
 Help me, help me. I am distraught. Anna fell in love with her father's secretary and Jean Jacques thrashed her with a horse whip to within an inch of her life. Little Mopsy has died of old age, so they say. Please spare a few days to comfort us.
 Your devoted sister-in-law,
 Marguerite

He arrived at The Lindens, kissed all the family on both cheeks, played with Felix the griffon bruxellois and waited for his brother to tell him the whole story. Jean Jacques was silent, ignoring the affair.

One evening Anna came to his bedroom. 'May I talk to you, Uncle André, in confidence?' She told him all about Robert and his desertion. 'I think you will understand. I loved him with all my heart but I suppose there would have been other girls in his life even after our marriage. I could never endure that.'

'Try to be patient, little one. I know from experience how difficult that can be at seventeen years of age.'

Charlie was acting as André's valet and told him that Mopsy had been kicked to death.

'Sally found him all bruised and bloody at the foot of the stairs, Monsieur André, and the master told me to wrap the body in a blanket and hide it in the stable.'

André decided to broach the subject the following evening while drinking an apéritif with his brother in the study. 'Marguerite has told me about your problems with Anna.'

There was a long pause.

'If you hurt either of them again, I will recount the story of your affair with the little midinette in Paris and how you killed Mopsy. Remember, my dear brother, I am not playing the fool or making idle threats.'

'You are trying to blackmail me.'

'Bien sur. I think we understand one another very well.'

The whole episode was closed, swiftly and without argument.

★

The night of the ball Marguerite wore a gown of eau-de-nil, Anna 'the white tulle' with her pale golden hair dressed in ringlets with lappets and a fall while Jacques was resplendent in tails, a brocade waistcoat and a row of Belgian medals 'for valour' across his chest. In his youth he had saved a man from a burning building and a soldier in full pack from the river.

The yellow equipage of the Princess Metternich drawn by a fine pair of café au lait horses led the slow procession of carriages across the common.

'They say the doctors operated on the emperor for seven hours then Father Goddard was called to administer the last rites. Poor tragic empress.'

'Ssh, Marguerite, that was a long time ago. Now we are going to a ball not a funeral.'

They alighted at the open doors of Camden Place. The wooden panelling in the small vestibule, carved with strange creatures, dog's heads and gargoyles, gleamed from the light of hundreds of candles blazing in the chandeliers.

Louis and Eugénie stood side b side in the hall to receive their guests. A footman announced the Van Maaskens family.

'A pleasure to receive you both, and Mademoiselle Anna.' The girl was enchanting.

The exiled dowager empress of France was radiant in a gown of peacock blue with her auburn hair piled high on the crown of her head. 'Anna, my Christmas child, the gown is charming.' She had heard rumours in the village of an unhappy love affair, both

Miss Briers and the doctor's wife were incorrigible gossips. 'An amethyst necklace to match the spring violets!'

She turned away to greet le Singe du Monde while they moved on into the ballroom. An elderly gentleman approached. 'You may not remember me although we were neighbours on the Boulevard Haussmann.'

'Baron de Hahn. Allow me to present you to my wife Marguerite and my daughter Anna.'

'Enchanté.'

The old man bowed and kissed the ladies hands. 'May I have the honour of adding my name to your dance programme, Mademoiselle? Not a galop, I think, or the lancers at my time of life; the knees are a little crotchety these days. Perhaps the first waltz?'

The dance programme was suspended by a silver ring from the little finger of her left hand, and the baron was the first to inscribe his name on the blank surface.

The ballroom was like a hothouse with the scent of carnations, madonna lilies and poudre de riz. Carved painted caryatides of women and children rose from floor to ceiling in the oval drawing room, painted with pastoral scenes in the manner of Watteau. An army of maidservants had rubbed the wooden parquetry blocks with French chalk till they glowed. Huge gilded mirrors reflected the rainbow gowns, the military uniforms of scarlet, royal blue and gold, and the magpie civilians in their tailcoats.

Many young sprogs from the shop, the Woolwich Military Academy, asked Anna to dance. After supper Anna found Maureen sipping a glass of champagne and deep in conversation with a very handsome escort.

'Anna... may I present my brother John Louis Eugene Donelly... this is my dearest friend at the convent... Mademoiselle Anna Marie Rose Van Maaskens.'

He rose and gave her a smile that would fetch the ducks off the water. 'I have heard a great deal about you already, Mademoiselle Anna. I know that you are four feet eleven inches tall, wear children's shoes, ride like the wind and win all the pillow fights in the dormitory. Maureen says the stable lads call you the Pocket Venus or the French Devil!'

'I am no longer a child, Monsieur.'

He was like a portrait of the Prince Consort as a young man by Winterhalter – tall with dark brown hair, large grey eyes and a monocle on a broad moire ribbon.

John looked down at the tiny exquisite creature and smiled. 'No, you are the loveliest girl I have ever seen. Let us walk across the lawns, the night air will be refreshing after this heat and the powerful scent of the flowers. It is all a little overwhelming.'

The three young people passed through the French windows on to the terrace.

Maureen whispered to Anna 'The monocle is not an affectation. He is as blind as a bat without it.'

'This well is a very romantic place. The servant girls fetch water every night and the footmen and kitchen boys leap out of the bushes to steal a kiss.'

'You thought of that on the spur of the moment, John.'

'It is true, I know an old gardener who met his wife down by the well fifty years ago.

'And they lived happily ever after. You live in a dream world little brother.'

'No, on my word of honour.'

The owner had tried to Frenchify the building with fancy balustrades around the roof and a porcelain fireplace encrusted with flowers and cherubs imported from a continental hunting lodge. 'Will you dance with me, Mademoiselle? I am sure my sister will not lack a partner – her red hair is like a flame to the moths, irresistible.'

Anna learned that John was twenty-four, madly in love from afar with Adelina Patti, and working as a civil servant in Somerset House for the princely sum of five hundred pounds a year.

'It helps Aunt Bridget make ends meet. The father came over from Ireland in the early fifties and I was baptised in Southwark Cathedral when I was four days old. Now you have a potted history of my life.'

Maureen announced that she was going to marry the young farmer she met in Limerick during the school holidays. 'We shall live in a long white farm house with a thatched roof in Adare; it's like a picture book village.'

Anna kissed her on both cheeks. 'I wish you every happiness but we shall miss you. Remember me.'

Kate knelt on the top landing and watched her young mistress leave the house then nipped down the back stairs to find Fred in the stable yard. 'Mamselle Anna looks a picture. All the young men will fall in love with her. If that wicked old devil ever touches her again I'll do for him myself.'

Fred looked at his ragamuffin girl and thought she knocked snots off all the others. She had tried to put up her black curls with a few of Anna's tortoiseshell hairpins but stray hairs were already beginning to fall round her ears and over her forehead.

'C'mon, Cinderella, let's have a dance of our own out here on the grass.' He put an arm round her waist and they twirled in the moonlight while Fred hummed a gay little tune… one two three… one two three. 'You know I'm going to marry you, Kate, when my ship comes in.'

'Chance 'ud be a fine thing. You haven't even asked me yet.' He knelt on one knee in the muddy grass, the damp seeping through his corduroy trousers. 'Miss Kate, will you do me the honour to become my wife?'

'Charmed, I'm sure, I thought you'd never pop the question. I'll spend the rest of me days cooking and washing and scrubbing for you, love. Oooer To think I might have been a chorus girl at the *Gaiety* and married a lord! But I love you, Fred Harris… I must be off me rocker.' She kissed him lightly on the tip of his freckled nose and ran away into the house as happy as a lark.

*

Aunt Bridget, Maureen and John became frequent visitors to The Lindens and the parents were aware of a budding relationship between the young people.

'He is a gentleman in every sense of the word, and Father Goddard assures me that he is a good Catholic.'

However, the pater familias had already made up his own mind. 'They have only known each other a for just a few months, and you are matchmaking.'

'Five hundred pounds a year is a respectable income, and I would give Anna a handsome dowry and a dress allowance if the relationship matured.'

'You try to encourage the romance by inviting John to a traditional Sunday luncheon. He is Irish so perhaps we should serve potatoes in their jackets wrapped in a fine linen table napkin and lying in a ring of antique silver instead of the rosbif.'

'Pooh, woman, you are always making fun of me.'

The Donellys lived with their frail old father in St Mary Cray. Brother Declan had returned to Ireland as a school teacher in Roscarbery while Violet had married a doctor and lived near Waterford.

Papa issued invitations to the opera, a pug dog show and the display of fireworks at the Crystal Palace. 'Sydenham is not far away and they tell me Brooks put on a fine show of pyrotechnics.'

Anna was enchanted by the brilliant fountains of light, rockets, golden rain and cascades of silver stars splattering the sky.

'I want to explore Chislehurst Caves, sir. May I take your daughter with me? Accompanied, of course. We could stop outside The Rambler's Rest for some refreshment on the way.

'Certainly, my boy. I will tell Pierre to saddle Toby, and you may ride one of the greys if you wish.'

Pierre brought their mounts into the stable yard early in the morning. Anna loathed riding side-saddle although it was de rigeur. The folds of a habit skirt clung to her legs and she wanted to be free and ride astride like a boy.

It was a clear day, and they set out in fine fettle with the groom in attendance, cut across the rough grass of the common and turned aside in to a hollow to visit the old clapboard inn where Kate danced the tarantella to the tune of an Italian organ-grinder years ago. Pierre fetched two glasses of strong ale and a cool lemonade for Anna then they set off down the hill leading towards Bromley. The caves lay hidden near the railway station and the entrance was very dark – a giant hale almost obscured by a few large boulders.

The groom was uneasy for his young mistress. 'Shall I go first, Mademoiselle Anna, to make sure it is safe? There are strange stories of cliff falls and people buried alive under the rocks.'

John brushed him aside before Anna had time to reply. 'Tether the horses. Pierre, and wait for us at the mouth of the caves. I have brought a lamp and a ball of twine in case we lose ourselves. I leave one end with Pierre and play out a little at a time. If we are gone longer than an hour he must be on the qui vive and follow us, otherwise we might be interred in the bowels of the earth or suffocated by nauseous gases.'

He might be teasing but Anna shivered.

'I am not frightened. A goose walked over my grave.'

'Early Romans camped here on their way to Londinium and the history of these caves goes back to the Stone Age.'

They walked into the darkness and she dared not admit that she was terrified. The air was dank and evil-smelling, with water dripping in the depths of the caves.

'John, can we get out at the other end? I want to turn back, papa will worry about me if I am late for luncheon.'

He ignored her, lifting the light high up in the air and a frightened creature swept past her hair. 'Look at those bats hanging from the rocks overhead.' Grey shadows like thick cobwebs brushed her face.

'The ghosts of children… I want to get out of here.'

He laughed at her. 'You are such a baby, Anna.'

She was scared of the dark and frightened by thunder and lightening, although John told her it was only the angels playing marbles up in heaven. She was even nervous of John Louis Eugene. She tried to put a hand in his but he was busy tying the string to an old tree stump in the first cave. Something moved in the cave, a rat or some strange creature, and she screamed, 'John.!'

'You squeal like a stuck pig.'

They passed deeper and deeper into the caves. Anna was too scared to go back alone and he was determined to explore. At last there was a faint glimmer of light at the far end of a tunnel and one could see uneven steps hewn out of the rock. They emerged into the daylight at the top of the hill. A thick film of grey dust lay on their clothes and a small spider ran across the skirt of her riding habit.

'A money spinner to bring you luck, my little Anna.'

'I'm terrified of spiders.'

'I might have guessed.' He brushed away the small insect without hurting it. 'Look at the wonderful view, it stretches for miles around like the Wicklow hills.'

'I would not go into those caves again for a king's ransom. I will race you down the hill.'

Anna gazed across the Weald of Kent, at the Railway Station far below them and the distant common. 'I cannot see our house.'

'Home-sick already, little one, after a couple of hours?' He took her in his arms and kissed her very gently on the mouth. 'Will you marry me, my dearest Anna? I cannot offer you a grand life but I promise to love you for ever and a day.'

She kissed him on the forehead. 'Yes, John, please and thank you.'

They scrambled down the hillside like two ragamuffins on a day out in the country to find Pierre fast asleep in the sunshine with the cord tied to his thumb. They nudged him awake and rode back to The Lindens in time for the midday meal. John washed the grime from his hands and face while Anna changed out of her habit into a new gown in an effort to charm papa into consent.

The young couple sat at either side of the enormous mahogany dining table. The père de famille was in a good mood but it could all change. 'Le rosbif, comme d'habitude.'

'May I speak with you, sir, after we have finished eating.'

'Any time, my dear boy. You know that I try to avoid work at the weekend.'

'It concerns your daughter, Sir.'

Papa bristled. 'In that case, young man, perhaps we should discuss the matter in the presence of my wife.'

He motioned the servants to leave the room after they had served the main course. 'En bien?' There was a brief silence.

Anna gazed around the table, at the ruby-glass finger bowls and maman's favourite silver epergne filled with mignonette and tiny scarlet and white rosebuds. She dared not look at her father's face.

'I wish to ask for your daughter's hand in marriage. It would be a great honour, sir. I am not a rich man, but our family is descended from the kings of Ireland and...'

'Anna?' The young girl was holding her breath waiting for an outburst of rage. She cast down her eyes.

'With your permission, papa and maman, it is my dearest wish.'

There was a long pause, then Jean Jacques thumped the table with his fist, plates jumped in the air and the flowers trembled. 'Volontiers. I have been waiting for you to make up your minds. I know your circumstances, John, and your background. I consent... we consent... heh, Marguerite?'

The eminence grise was smiling. 'Nothing could give me greater pleasure. You have our blessing. Let us drink a toast to the happy couple – John and Anna!'

Chapter Thirteen

Louis Napoleon left Southampton for the Zulu Wars amid wildly cheering crowds. His mother fell in a dead faint on the quayside and was carried back to her hotel.

Letters came over the following weeks telling her of his prowess: commanding officers were determined the young prince should not become embroiled in any serious fighting, but he was a soldier and an adventurer.

Now the Prince Imperial was dead, killed on a scouting expedition and Eugénie was heartbroken by the loss of her only son at twenty three years of age.

'They say she will neither eat nor sleep and exists on black coffee and chloral, spending hours alone in the Chapelle Ardente at Camden Place. His colonel had refused to send the prince with his regiment but his mother and Queen Victoria overruled him.'

There were many conflicting tales abroad in the village. He was killed by seventeen assegai wounds after a small party of men was taken unawares by the natives. Soldiers found him stark naked save for a gold medal of the Virgin and a seal of the first Napoleon around his neck. Dr Evans identified the corpse by the presence of a gold tooth. The Zulu warriors said later that he fought like a lion.

In spite of some government opposition a day of national mourning was declared.

Victoria and Beatrice travelled to Chislehurst bringing a laurel wreath with two white paeonies. The coffin lay in the main hall of the house and everything was draped in white to signify the purity of Louis' life.

Victoria and Eugénie clung together at an upstairs window as the cortège passed down the avenue between the trees winding its way out of sight along the road towards St Mary's Church.

The empress covered her ears to shut out the deafening salute of the guns, the sound of pipes and the muffled beat of drums.

Two hundred soldiers marched in the procession, while thousands of men and women stood with their heads bowed in respect and homage as the hearse passed by – its glass windows revealing the coffin covered with flowers and a pall of purple velvet embroidered with bees.

The Prince of Wales and Prince Leopold were among the pallbearers, glossy black horses bent their plumed heads and the Prince Imperial's horse, Stag, led by Monsieur Gamble, followed the coffin. Other Princes of the English Royal family, Arthur and Clarence, the Dukes of Cambridge and Padua and officers of the household formed part of the long procession stretching several miles.

The Nation honoured the Prince and his youthful gallantry. The Imperial dream is at an end, reported the Paris newspapers.

Jacques and Marguerite knelt in prayer in St Mary's Church where Alexandra, Princess of Wales, waited with many others for the Requiem Mass to begin. Together they mourned the last hope of a French Empire.

Anna and John stood behind the lattice windows of Miss Brier's cottage which gave a clear view across the common.

'He was such a lovely young man. I remember when they first escaped to Chislehurst. His mother often bought my sweetmeats for the boy.'

She burst into tears and Anna began to cry too.

'One of the gardeners from the house told me the Princess Beatrice was almost out of her mind with grief as she stood weeping beside the coffin; they were mere children. Oh dear, I do feel poorly, I can feel one of my turns coming on. Look at our Prince of Wales! My that's a fine uniform – the epaulettes. All that gold braid must have cost a fortune. It seems strange that Tum-Tum and the Princess Beatrice are brother and sister, but of course there are many years between them... the oldest child of our dear queen and the youngest.'

John and Anna were in tears praying for the soul of the departed as the old woman rattled on.

'Hail Mary, full of grace...'

Miss Briers broke the tension by collapsing into an armchair like a deflated balloon. She always enjoyed a good wedding or a funeral, but they often brought on a touch of the vapours.

The cortège had passed. Anna offered to fetch smelling salts and sal volatile from the medicine cupboard, but the lady demanded a burnt feather and a tot of brandy instead then declared they must stay for tea and muffins as she was far too overwrought to be left alone, and after all, it was a social occasion.

★

The empress wanted to buy a field next to the church and build a mausoleum in memory of her dear husband and Louis but the farmer was adamant: he would never sell to a Catholic.

Eugénie was offered an estate in Farnborough with many acres of land and decided to leave Camden Place and try to rebuild her life. All her dreams and ambitions for a brilliant Imperial Court in Paris died with Lou Lou.

The local people missed her many gifts to charity and the poor when she departed with her entourage. Anna was in floods of tears. 'I think she might have come to our wedding, Katie. Maman wants a marquee on the lawn with caterers from Bromley and crates of papa's vintage champagne. I want to give a party for the orphanage children with cakes and buns, jelly and custard, washed down with gallons of ginger pop and fizzy lemonade. Let's organise it together.'

Katie was over the moon. 'Perhaps you could hire an organ-grinder with a monkey and a hokey-pokey man? Do you remember that day on the common and my china dog? He's sitting on the windowsill upstairs in the attic.'

John and Anna visited Father Goddard in his presbytery to discuss their forthcoming wedding and listen to a homily on the joys of a married life blessed with many children.

Anna was confused about the facts of life. She understood the habits of dogs and cats and horses, the birds and the bees, but surely human beings were different?

Maureen tried to explain in simple terms. 'Babies simply pop out of your belly button.'

But Kate said 'They use the same door to come in and out.'

Marguerite and Anna pored over the ladies' fashion magazines and finally ordered a white lace gown embroidered with pearls, and Uncle André sent an exquisite bridal veil from Brussels. The local court dressmaker was busy with a white satin confection for Maureen, the only bridesmaid.

Anna bought a present for Kate out of her dress allowance; a pale yellow dress and a row of amber beads. Fred was given a cravat decorated with horseshoes and riding crops.

'Something borrowed, something blue. Something old and something new.'

'Wear those split-arse mechanics you made at the convent – they're second-hand.'

Anna had won the needlework prize with a pair of long drawers decorated with French knots.

'I think I prefer my blue satin garters.'

*

John and Anna were sitting in the library at The Lindens waiting for dinner; her parents were late home after a long day in London.

'There's nothing half so sweet in life as love's young dream.' John was reading aloud in his soft Irish brogue from a book of Tom Moore's poems, a fine first edition bound in red Moroccan leather and inscribed on the fly leaf: 'To my beloved Anna with all my love, now and always. Sean.'

'We shall be married in seven weeks, my dearest dear.'

'It is all too good to be true.'

Anna looked at her fiery engagement ring, an opal circled with brilliant diamonds. 'Mimi tells me opals are unlucky unless one is born in October. She pretends to be a white witch.'

'I think your friend is a very odd creature with her spiritualism and her artistic pretensions.' John was not enamoured of her school friend.

'The cottage next to Miss Briers sweet shop is for sale. It has red tiles, a bow window and lilacs in the garden. Will you come and look at it with me tomorrow morning after Mass? Katie and I crept through a hole in the back fence and peered in the windows.

We could see oak beams in the living room. The house must be hundreds of years old.

Papa might buy it for us as a wedding present. We could borrow furniture from The Lindens and take things from my old day nursery. There's a linen press and a chest of drawers with brass handles. Please come with me, John. Pretty please.'

There was a deadly silence.

'I prefer to be independent and choose my own house. We might rent for a while.'

'You must not be too proud to accept a gift. It would be part of my dowry.'

There was a sudden clatter of hoof beats on the gravelled drive. Anna ran to the window.

'They are home at last. The train must have been almost an hour late.'

She drew back the heavy brocade curtains and saw a young boy in ragged breeches hesitate for a moment at the foot of the flight of stone steps, then run swiftly to the top and tug at the iron bell pull. The noise jangled through the hall and kitchens and set Anna's nerves on edge. A few moments later the parlour maid came through the heavy baize door leading to the servants' quarter, her feet pattering on the black and white tiles and Anna could hear the boy's breathless voice through the library door which was slightly ajar.

'Is the young lady at home, Miss? I think the name is Van Maaskens.' He stumbled over the foreign words.

'What on earth do you want, lad, coming to the front door at this time of night? Miss Anna is waiting for the master and mistress to come back from the station so they can start dinner. They're late already. She won't want to see the likes of you now.'
'They ain't never coming back, Miss.' He took a deep breath. 'A fox ran across the road, the horses took fright and bolted, and the carriage turned upside down in the ditch. The lady died straight away – broke her neck in the fall when the door burst open. They called a doctor to the old gent but it was too late. The coachman bid me come at once and tell the young lady, break it to her gently like. He's crushed an arm and is too sick to ride here so they've

83

taken him to the hospital. He was thrown clear of the box. I'm riding one of the horses.'

Anna stood in the doorway of the library clinging to John's arm, her face as white as a shroud. 'Papa, maman, I must go to them at once.'

John crossed himself. 'It is too late now, Anna. Come and sit down. Kate will fetch you a brandy.' He turned to the maid. 'Here, give the boy some money for his pains and thank him. You must stay here for the time being, Anna, I will go alone.' He knew she must be kept away from the morgue and the sight of her dead parents. 'Call the doctor and tell him what has happened. Ask him to come at once. Your mistress must not be left alone for a moment. Try to rest, my love, I should be back within the hour.'

Anna was wild with grief, sobbing hysterically and beating her fists on the window panes. 'I can't wait here alone. I am going to find them. Are they lying by the roadside?'

The doctor came swiftly and administered a strong dose of laudanum to the patient. 'I am confident your mistress will sleep through the night.'

Anna woke early the following day and her mind was crystal clear. 'I am going to the chapel of rest to say goodbye. No one can stop me. I want to be alone with maman and papa for the last time.'

A sickly sweet smell filled the air, and sent Anna reeling against the wall. But she dare not faint in this bare candle-lit cell. The first sight of death in a young woman's life, the horror of the mutilated bodies she could imagine beneath the shroud.

Jacques and Marguerite lay together in death as in life, wrapped in fine linen covered by a Belgian tapestry.

Anna whispered 'I love you, I love you,' and kissed each one gently on the forehead. A fine network of tiny lines etched the cold stone. 'Hail Mary, full of grace…'

She left the chapel in a mist of tears to find a concerned uncle André and John waiting for her in the carriage. 'The ceremony of marriage seems to be a farce now, a childish charade. We must postpone the wedding.'

Her parents were buried in a vault at Honor Oak Cemetery in Bromley with a white marble angel weeping over them, and candles burning day and night.

Part Two

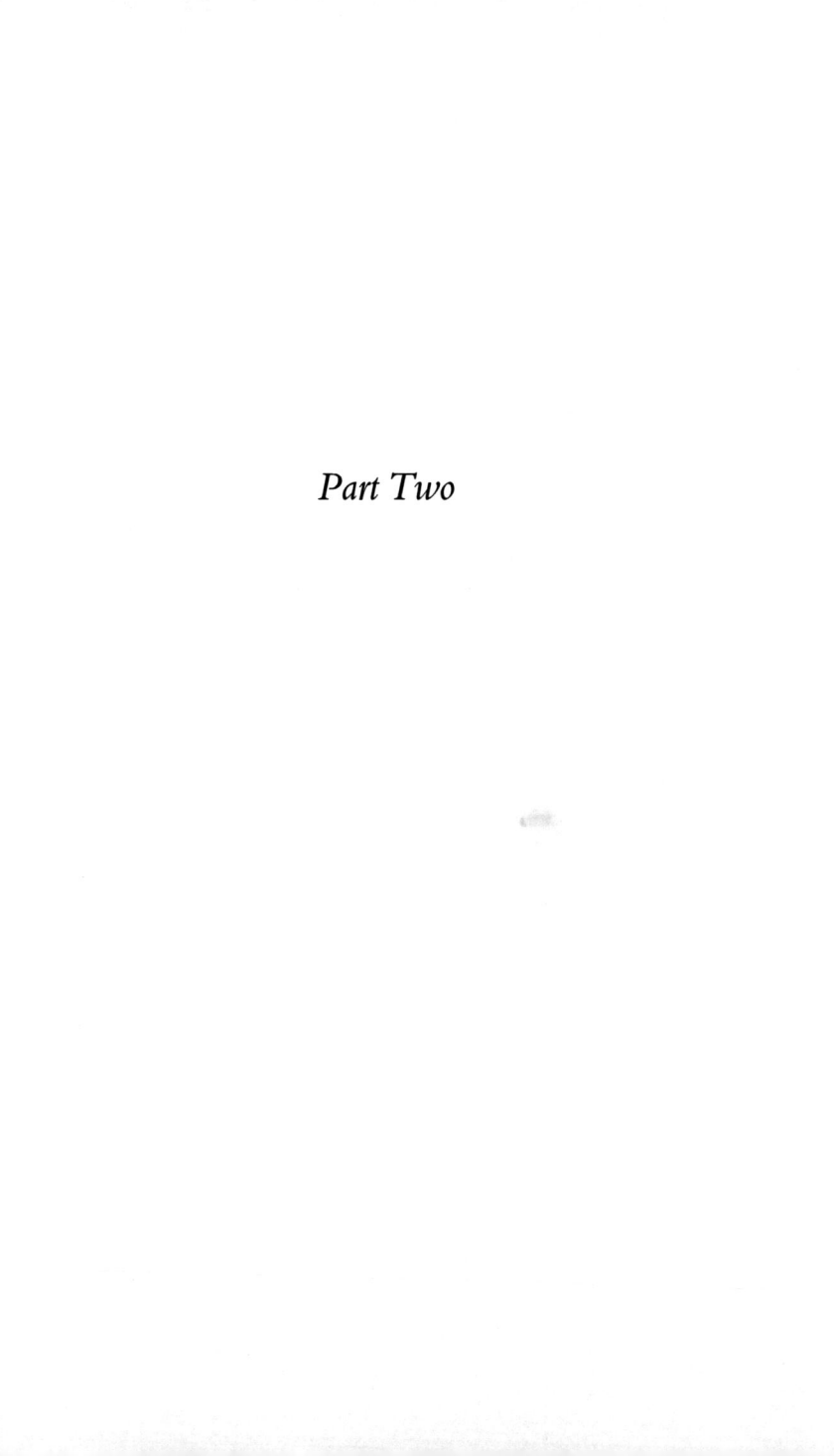

Chapter Fourteen

André, John and Anna were sitting in the library drinking an aperitif when her uncle decided to broach the delicate subject of the wedding for the first time since the funeral.

'You could marry in John's church at St Mary Cray and I should be honoured to give you away.'

Anna whispered, 'I might become a nun.'

'Over my dead body.' John was adamant his dearest love would never become a bride of Christ.

'You are not alone in the world, Anna, John is always beside you and I can be there within hours if you need me. We all respect your feelings, I know you could not bear to live in this house.'

Everything was strangely quiet without papa to bellow at the servants or discuss the latest news in a loud voice. The old horse whip was still hanging on the wall near the escritoire. Anna shivered and Felix, the griffon bruxellois, licked her hand. Maman's white terrier, Fritz, lay in front of the log fire. Her parents might walk into the room at any moment.

There was a long silence.

'We were happy together. Papa was a naughty old man with a foul temper but we loved him.'

'We must talk about the future, Anna. I am my brother's executor and he left a considerable fortune. According to the coroner's verdict my dear Marguerite was the first to die so you inherit the entire estate worth in the region of sixty thousand pounds.' André's voice was husky with emotion but he was in control.

'I do not want blood money.' He ignored her and continued. 'The will lists everything in detail, The Lindens, statuary, furniture, jewellery, objets d'art, horses, carriages, even harnesses. There are commercial properties in Bermondsey and Southwark and considerable liquid assets together with his second interest as an importer of skins, hides and foreign feathers. Jacques was a shrewd business man and he wanted you to inherit everything of real value. If you waste the fruits of his labour it would be, as they say in England, "Clogs to clogs in three generations". "L´ Chaim" is the Jewish toast, "To Life!" Everything will not grind to a halt because of our great tragedy.'

He turned to John. 'What do you intend to do on your wedding night?' and was met with a look of blank amazement.

'No, No, No, I am not being indiscreet.' André chuckled. 'I was about to suggest a night in London to break the journey to Ireland. I could book two stalls at the Savoy Theatre. The Savoyards are presenting a new Gilbert and Sullivan operetta and their music seems to be all the rage.'

'You are very kind, Sir, I am sure Oscar Wilde or Pinero would bore Anna to distraction at the moment.' André blew a smoke ring in the air and watched it dissolve.

'I know you were happy in Brighton with your parents, Anna, and the town might be ideal for you both. A reputable firm of estate agents has recommended several properties that might be suitable as a gentleman's residence.' He smiled at John. I could view them on your behalf, if you wish.'

'We give you carte blanche, Uncle André.'

'Then I will make arrangements for a quiet wedding.'

You might sell The Lindens to a family man, the orchard and rose gardens could be a wonderful playground for children.'

She burst into tears.

'I shall never be une femme d'affaires like maman, so perhaps you could sell the warehouses to the managers. I am putty in your hands, mon oncle.'

He caught a glimpse of the naive, vulnerable Anna.

'Leave all the decisions to me, little one, and I will take great care on your behalf.'

The following morning Anna tugged the bell pull for her maid. 'Kate, I want you and Sally to pack all the clothes in the dressing room and maman's boudoir and send them to the mission in Southwark. I cannot help you. Tell all the servants to gather in the library in half an hour. We need to talk about the future.'

The buzz of chatter ceased as the tiny blonde young lady walked into the room and stood behind her father's mahogany pedestal desk facing the staff of The Lindens.

'I am to marry Mr John Donelly three months after the tragic death of my parents. Father left a small bequest to each of you in his will.' She took a deep breath and carried on after a moment's pause. 'My uncle Monsieur André Van Maaskens will supervise all my affairs including the upheaval in this house when all the goods and chattels are removed, probably to a house in Sussex. You have been loyal to our family for many years, ever since my childhood, and I should hate to lose you now.' Anna was on the verge of tears.

'I know that Mr Williams and cook wanted to retire in the spring and we wish them well with a special gift from me in recompense for their long years of service.'

Her voice was husky as she came to the carriages and horses. 'Albert wishes to leave for France following the accident, so Pierre will be the new coachman with Fred as head groom, while Charlie and his wife Sally will act as footman and parlour maid. You know I will care for you all, please do not desert me now. I wish you all a happy life in my new household.' She turned to her adopted orphan. 'Kate will always be my lady's maid and dear companion.'

Papa would have been proud of her. The weeks drifted by in a haze.

Albert came to say goodbye, although he was driving her to the wedding, and tried to explain the cause of the accident in his own bumbling way. 'It was the fox, Mamselle, a great orange fox with a black bushy tail ran across the road in front of the carriage and terrified the horses. They reared out of control and I was thrown off the box; there was nothing I could do. I shall never forget that night as long as I live. Dear God, I am so sorry.' He buried his face in his hands.

Kate tried to create a small diversion with some gossip. 'I think Miss Briers may have a beau. He's a retired Major with a passion for sugared almonds and Elsie Briers! Mr Osborne has been given the sack. They say the Empress is building an enormous tomb for her husband and Louis.'

Confession with Monsignor Goddard, a last fitting for the bridal gown and a visit from aunt Bridget and Maureen trying to console Anna.

The days were flying past and there was no way back. Tomorrow Anna would be a married woman and she might never return to The Lindens.

★

Bridget drew the curtains in Domenic's bedroom when she took her brother an early morning cup of tea in bed. The leprechaun was sitting bolt upright, a paisley dressing gown draped round his skinny shoulders, plucking at the sheets with long bony fingers and gazing into space.

His bright blue eyes darted round the room before coming to rest on his sister. 'You are still a fine-looking woman. It's yourself should be getting wed this spring morning. I am bracing myself to get out of bed on my son's wedding day.'

'Enough of your Blarney, Domenic. It is only six o'clock so you can rest there a while longer.'

'Then I will have a lightly boiled egg with two thin slices of bread and butter cut into soldiers.'

'Dear God, the man is away with the fairies! I am far too busy to cope with such nonsense. There will be sausages and bacon in the kitchen for everyone at eight o'clock.'

Domenic came downstairs when Bridget banged the small copper gong in the hall, nibbled his sausage like an aging field mouse with a grain of corn, then banged on the table with his fist. 'Where's the tea, woman? Hot and sweet as love. You and Bridget will see me to the church, Jim boy, when I totter off down the road. The poor old legs are like matchsticks and I do not wish to collapse in the aisle and make an exhibition of myself. Where's my ebony cane, Alice?'

The little maid of all work scuttled off to the umbrella stand in the hall. The master was the most charming man in the world at one moment, an absent-minded ill-tempered old devil the next.

Never the same for two minutes since the death of his wife Helena.

'The hip flask, I shall need my silver hip flask in case I feel queer. Fill it to the brim and I can take a swig during the ceremony.'

'You will do no such thing.' Bridget heaved a sigh of relief, even these constant demands were better than one of his black moods when he sat for hours without a word to throw at a dog.

'Remember you are the one who refused to ride in a carriage, Domenic. It will soon be time to leave the house, but even you cannot go in your shirtsleeves and dressing gown brandishing a silver-topped ebony cane.'

'Dear Bridget, I always did like a woman with an edge to her.' He scuttled up the stairs 'for a pussycat wash' and to dress for the occasion.

*

Anna rode in the new brougham that smelt of leather and polish. André sat beside her, drumming his fingers on the grey topper balanced on his knees. The handsome mature face and dark brooding eyes were framed by silver cat's whisker moustachios and sideboards. A small bald patch on the crown of his head gleamed in the pale sunlight. He was waiting for trouble.

'I feel sick uncle. I want to go home. I'm frightened to death.'

'Nonsense, child. This was never a marriage of convenience arranged by your father?' Anything was possible with Jacques.

She shook her head. 'John and I love one another.' Her heart was fluttering like a caged bird.

'Then nothing has changed and you have waited long enough. Albert, take us to St Joseph's with all speed, or we shall be late for the wedding.'

He helped her to alight from the carriage and could feel her trembling. The damn girl might faint at any minute.

A small crowd of villagers gathered round the gates of the church to stare as André ushered the bride along the brick path towards the porch.

Maureen was waiting to spread out the folds of the short bridal train. Her auburn hair was crowned with a wreath of gardenias. Anna carried a posy of mauve and white violets and mignonette. The organ began to play Mendelssohn's *Wedding March* as they walked slowly up the aisle.

Kate and Fred sat in a pew at the back of the church wearing their Sunday best with black armbands as a sign of respect for the dead master and mistress. She grabbed Fred by the elbow and whispered in his ear, 'I shan't understand a word of their foreign lingo, but the music's lovely. Ooooer!' She caught sight of Mademoiselle Anna coming through the doorway on her uncle's arm, an exquisite miniature, pale as the lilies on the church altar.

Domenic knelt on a hassock saying his prayers, and Bridget nudged him with her handbag in case he had fallen asleep. Jim fumbled for the ring in the inner pocket of his waistcoat while John screwed the monocle into his eye and glanced at his watch for the umpteenth time. At last Anna promised to love, honour and obey, and John swore to cherish her for the rest of his days. The high sweet notes of the 'Ave Maria' pierced the air.

Domenic raised his eyes to gaze at the stained glass windows above the altar then whispered to Bridget. 'The service is almost over and I want to go home. I need to pass water.'

'Sign the register in the vestry, then we can leave by the side door. I am sure the father will turn a blind eye.'

The Donellys lived in a terrace house a few hundred yards away, so the guests walked to the reception while John and Anna, strewn with rice and rose petals, travelled in the brougham. Domenic was fumbling with his fly buttons as he walked along the pavement.

'You must wait to relieve yourself till we reach the house. Hurry!'

'You omadhaun!'

He set off with a hop, skip and a jump, with Bridget racing him down the road, calling, 'Domenic, come back here, Domenic!'

Laburnum Villa was carved on a stone slab above the door. Aunt Bridget, Maureen and Alice had prepared all the food themselves: raised pork pies, boiled ham, soda bread, caraway cake and a great concoction from a recipe in Mrs Beeton's *Book of Household Management* – sponge cake, light as air, layered with whipped cream and covered with snowy-white icing, the whole surmounted by a silver vase and two porcelain figures representing the bride and groom.

The oldest son Jim was doing the honours for his father. 'Champagne or a glass of good Irish whisky from Kilbeggan?'

Fred took a swig of the hard stuff and it scorched the back of his throat like a flame making him splutter. 'Give me a glass of strong ale any day.' 'It all looks good enough to eat. See that glass dome, isn't it beautiful?'

'I prefer the stuffed kingfisher and the snowy white owl.' Kate admired the embroidered antimacassars on the backs of chairs to protect them from the pomade on men's hair, and the swags of tasselled chenille draping the pianoforte legs and the mantelpiece. 'Dust traps. Their skivvy must work all hours of the day and night.'

Although it was a spring day, Domenic was ensconced beside the fire with his sister fussing over him like a mother hen. 'Anna is a lovely girl.' He gazed into the coals.

'The Wharf was ablaze, flames lit the sky for miles around. My Helena died soon after. They say it broke her heart. Thank God the Hunger is over at last.'

Maureen dropped a light kiss on top of his head. 'Poor Da.'

'It's a lovely wedding, ma'am.' Kate's eyes were like stars.

'I'm very happy, Katie,' Anna burst into tears.

'Ssh, everybody's looking at you. Here's my hanky. It's clean.'

Anna staunched the flow and gave a watery smile when André rose to his feet and proposed a toast to t he young couple.

'John and Anna, we wish you long life and happiness and the blessing of many children. Let us remember the living and the dead in our prayers. May God bless us all.'

★

Business men in their bowlers and dark city clothes were waiting on the platform at the end of their working day as John and Anna alighted from the Chislehurst train at Charing Cross Station.

'If we take a hansom cab to the Norfolk Hotel I can show you some of my old haunts. Do you remember passing Somerset House on your way to the pantomime? The Norfolk lies near the Embankment – it's a small private hotel close to Villiers Street.' He was as eager as a schoolboy playing truant.

As they drove down the Strand memories of papa and maman came flooding back to torment her. She could visualise the office in a side street, empty now and smothered in dust.

The family went to Drury Lane every Christmas, and papa's belly laugh echoed through the stage box. Anna remembered that her father had taken Robert Feldmann to luncheon at Simpson's in the Strand after their first meeting at the Wilton's Music Hall.

'You are quiet, little one, you must be very tired.' He screwed the monocle into his left eye. 'There is Somerset House. I worked in an office at the back of the building overlooking the Thames. It had a fantastic view.

I thought I could be independent on five hundred pounds a year, but now you have persuaded me to be a gentleman of leisure for a while. Brother Declan said I had sold out to the English. There are three hundred and sixty windows altogether – my friend Stephen Phillips gave me that useless piece of information. We worked together for a while after he left Oundle School, but he has other ambitions.' He told her bowdlerised stories about *Romano's*, *The Gaiety*, the actresses and their lordly suitors.

'We are here. Let me give you my hand.'

Anna's handwriting was a little shaky as she signed the hotel register as Anna Donelly for the first time.

A pageboy in buttons was hovering near the reception desk. 'Boy, please take the small green crocodile dressing case to the vestiaire... the cloakroom attendant.' She sounded exactly like her mother, cool and arrogant. She followed the small boy across the foyer to the toilette where an old woman came forward, clad in black from head to toe with her hair pinned back in a severe bun.

'I do not wish to go to my room till after the theatre. Will you be kind enough to help me?' She was trying to avoid being alone with John in the intimacy of a double bedroom.

Anna unhooked her lilac dolman, the attendant untied the tapes at the back of her waist and the young woman changed her bodice. The low cut top revealed her sloping shoulders and gently curving breasts. A dusting of poudre de riz on nose and forehead, a tortoiseshell comb through the wisps of hair curling around her ears, and she was ready to join her new husband in the vestibule.

The lad was waiting outside the door for further orders. He was probably no more than ten or eleven years of age. 'Take my case to room twenty-one, boy.' She took a sovereign out of her reticule and pressed it into his soft little hand.

'You can celebrate my honeymoon, child,' and she left the hotel clinging to John's arm as they strolled towards the theatre. They were still too early for the show.

'Yer pays yer money and yer takes yer choice, lady.'

Anna picked an apple from the costermonger's barrow and gave him a penny.

John looked down at his child bride, standing four feet eleven in her shoes, heiress to a fortune munching an apple in the Strand. She threw the core into the gutter and wiped her hands on a fine cambric handkerchief as they entered The Savoy to see *Princess Ida*.

The house lights dimmed and only the newfangled electric footlights separated them from the stage. 'They are the first ones in a London theatre,' John whispered. 'The light is brilliant.'

When they left the theatre after the show darkness had fallen. 'Are you hungry? I am ravenous. Shall we take a light supper in Maiden Lane?'

Anna nodded. The operetta had banished her memories for the time being and she was living in a world of make-believe. All thoughts of the hotel bedroom were frightening.

They sat in the romantic candlelight of Rules. Champagne bubbles tickled her nose.

'Stephen says that oysters are an aphrodisiac. He knows about these things. My friend's a man of the world not a simpleton from the bogs of Ireland. His father is precentor of Peterborough Cathedral but dear Stephen's a little on the wild side.'

He was talking a great deal to hide his own lack of confidence on their wedding night.

Aphrodisiacs! The word conjured up visions of Bacchanalian orgies. The grey slimy gob of fleshy oyster on the end of her fork made her feel sick. She nibbled a thin slice of brown bread and butter, then sipped her champagne gazing across the table at John. What in heaven's name was she doing alone with a stranger in a West End restaurant at midnight?

'I think it's time to leave. The place is almost empty and the waiters are becoming restless.' He paid the bill and remembered Stephen's maxim, useful when stony broke – too great a tip is a sign of insecurity.

They returned to The Norfolk hand in hand, he unlocked the bedroom door, caught her in his arms and carried her over the threshold. 'You're as light as a feather. Come on, I'll race you into bed, Anna.' John disappeared into the bathroom to undress, leaving Anna alone. Her white nightgown of fine, embroidered cotton was lying on the pillow case, unpacked by the hotel chambermaid. There was no time to waste. She was terrified by the idea of her first night in bed with John and knew she must win the race. Anna tore at the fastenings of her violet gown, dropped her drawers and petticoat in a heap on the floor and kicked her slippers into a corner of the room. Dragging the nightgown over her head, she scrambled into the high tester bed, frightened that John might come into the room and see her naked. Anna sat rigid, her knees drawn up to her chin, clutching the coverlet. She began to finger the beads of her blue rosary whispering, 'Hail Mary, Mother of God.'

John tapped on the door and called out, 'Are you in bed? May I come in now,'

He poked his head round the side of the door, wearing a striped red and white night shirt that reached as far down as his knobbly knees, a tasselled nightcap and the monocle.

Anna took one look at this appartition and collapsed into a fit of helpless laughter. 'You clown, John, you look like a barber's pole.'

He climbed into bed beside her and lay propped against a heap of pillows talking of all manner of things: their honeymoon in Ireland, the old high kings crowned on the Hill of Tara, and the wild thrift blowing on the brown rocks of Wicklow above the sea. He was lulling her to sleep. They lay still in each others arms then she felt his body moving against hers. 'Anna, darling, I have never made love to a girl before, so I am as nervous as yourself.' He stroked her hair and kissed her.

She looked at John's body rising above her in the moonlight and, in her fuddled imagination, saw papa's face distorted with rage and the flail lashing her bleeding flesh again and again and again. She was shaking like a leaf.

'My little Anna, you know I would never hurt you. I can wait, I have waited for you all my life. The nightmare will pass.' He rocked her to and fro like a baby, humming an old Irish lullaby, then wrapped her in the eiderdown and turned away. It was nearly dawn when he fell asleep at last waking early to find Anna lying quietly with her tear-stained face buried in the pillows.

The Norfolk served breakfast in bed – croissants and hot coffee. Anna was thankful John did not mention their wedding night. Perhaps she had been a little tipsy and it would never happen again. The rattle of the locomotive's wheels beat a ceaseless rhythm: *married woman, woman... married woman*, over and over again till she pressed her hands over her ears to shut out the deafening noise.

'They are serving luncheon in the restaurant car if you fancy it.'

It was a grand day for the crossing from Holyhead to Kingstown. Gulls swooped overhead screeching for scraps from the galley floating in the wake of the ship. Every Donelly in Ireland seemed to be waiting at the docks, and Anna braced herself to meet them for the first time.

Brother Declan rushed up the gangway and swept her off her feet in a great bear's hug. Violet kissed her new sister-in-law on both cheeks, while the children clung to her skirts and everyone else shook hands, wishing her a 'thousand welcomes' in Gaelic. Aunts and uncles, distant nephews and cousins had taken advantage of the occasion to travel up from the country for the celebrations. It was better than a horse fair, a good excuse for a bit of a party.

Declan was the driving force behind the reception committee. 'I booked a private room for the wedding breakfast. I know you will want to rush away soon afterwards, but this is our gift to you both – a feast! Kieron, take your sticky paws off the lady's gown or your new Aunt Anna might just clip you round the ear. The cabs are waiting, John. May I have the honour of riding with you in the bridal carriage?

Do you like the garlands of flowers on the horses, Anna?' His excitement was catching and Anna began to enjoy herself. 'Look at our fair city, Dublin, a whore with tattered petticoats and a heart of gold. Ireland is very dear to me, Anna, not the soldiers in Dublin Castle or her fat little Majesty, Queen Victoria. We live beyond the pale. God bless Parnell, although he is an Englishman.'

The cavalcade swept through narrow streets and fine Georgian squares till it reached a small private hotel in St Stephen's.

Like a swarm of locusts the family devoured poached salmon, roast sirloin of beef, 'pink as a baby's bum', according to Declan, followed by summer pudding and clotted cream.

The wedding cake rose like the Ice Palace of Catherine the Great; a special gift from Declan out of his meagre salary as a school teacher in Roscarbery. Waitresses with starched aprons and beribboned caps moved swiftly among the guests, and the wine waiter poured a sweet sticky liquor the colour of dark amber – mead, the ambrosia of the gods made from fermented honey by the friars. 'We brew poteen in illegal stills and it has the kick of a mule.' Declan bent over to whisper in Anna's ear. 'I think you should both disappear from the feast, my little sister Anna, before the relatives become maudlin and pass out under the table in sweet oblivion. There will be stories to make your hair curl, and Brendan is sure to recite *The Midnight Court*. He kissed her lightly on the cheek. 'Farewell, nymph. In thy orisons be all my sins remembered.' He clasped his brother's hand. 'You are a lucky devil, John, I envy you. I am madly in love with the bride.' He turned to the guests with a flourish. 'A toast to the bride and groom before they leave us. May your hens lay gold eggs and may your butter be sweet. Schlainte!'

John and Anna slipped away and a hackney carriage took them to the station. 'Waterford is only about ninety miles away, but the trains are often late. There is always time enough. A boneshaker picked them up on arrival. 'Green Gables, cabbie, a small hotel at Passage East, close by the Strand.'

He remembered fishing and paddling with his father at the water's edge when he was a boy.

The old horse dragged them higher and higher into the steep green hills rising above the harbour, between tall hedges of fuchsias and dog roses. Once upon a time sailing vessels ventured into Waterford bearing cargoes of silks and spices, now only small fishing boats with terracotta sails skimmed the water.

A broad stretch of pale golden sand lay far beneath them. Everything was quiet at the day's end, without a soul working in the fields. Then rounding a bend in the road they came upon a tinker family camped by the wayside near a broken-down shebeen. A skewbald horse was tethered to a stake nearby and two small urchins played tag round a campfire. The mother sat in the shade of a tree beside a painted wagon, a black woollen shawl draped around her shoulders, suckling her infant. The father squatted astride an old tree stump whittling a piece of wood with a clasp knife.

Anna called out to the cabbie asking him to stop, picked up her skirts and ran back along the white dusty road. John followed and spoke to the family in Gaelic.

The woman did not say a word but smiled and fed the baby at her breast.

Anna bent down to stroke a greyhound bitch sniffing at their ankles.

'My wife is French and does not speak our language. We were married yesterday.'

The swarthy Romany had dark brown eyes set in a long, narrow face – Spanish-looking. He came forward and offered Anna his carving of a small doll shaped from a piece of reddish-brown cherry wood polished by the man's fingers as he worked. Anna was about to offer money but John came between them.

'It is a talisman, a sign of friendship. He would be deeply offended if you offered money.' Anna sat in the carriage stroking the wooden doll. 'A fertility symbol. The tinker hopes we may be blessed with many children.'

That night they lay together in a cool white room overlooking the harbour with a wide empty space between them.

'Shall I place a bolster between us to act as your silent knight?'

Anna moved towards him and snuggled her head in the hollow of his shoulder. 'I am sure this is the safest place in the whole world.'

Soft blonde curls tickled his cheek and he turned away from her wrapping the sheets round his nether regions. 'Go away, Anna, or I shall make love to you.'

He rolled over towards the far side of the bed, but she ran her fingers up and down his spine following the stripes on the cotton nightshirt, and he could feel her nails, like the claws of a playful kitten, pricking his skin.

'This creation of yours is like a circus tent.'

'Stop teasing me, Anna, or I shall do something you will regret.'

'Eh bien, we are man and wife, I think.' Her slender arm was around his waist and he sprang to attention.

'If you scream tonight I shall divorce you.'

'Darling, John, perhaps I should apply for a dissolution by the Vatican on the grounds of non-consummation.'

'My dearest, Anna, I love you far too much to lose you now.'

The bedcovers fell to the floor where thy lay in a discarded heap till morning.

Anna fell asleep and dreamed of the holy family with the gipsy mother as the Madonna.

*

Donkeys grazed in the meadow at the back of Green Acres and the young lovers rode bareback with carrots dangling at the end of sticks to encourage their mounts to gallop while screeching peacocks strutted the lawns, their weird eerie cries piercing the still air.

After a few days seclusion at Passage East, they visited Violet, Brendan and the boys in their small farmhouse outside Dunmore. A wicket gate at the end of the garden led on to the Strand where they wandered hand in hand along the water's edge as beachcombers in search of treasure or a bottle with a message washed up by the rippling little waves, and finding only broken spars and rotting oranges. Every evening at dusk they walked Violet's red setters through the woods. He warned her about his sister's cooking. 'You may not care for boiled bacon and colcannon, a mixture of leeks, potatoes and butter, but the seafood is marvellous: enormous Dublin Bay prawns and lobsters that melt in the mouth.'

Violet had been a plain child with a shock of flaming red hair like her younger sister Maureen and a long nose. Soon after leaving school she fell in love with doctor Brendan Kehery, a middle-aged bachelor who became her devoted husband and they had been together for twelve years working in a small country practice and raising three sons.

The living room was crammed with photographs and daguerrotypes of all the family from John, or Sean as she always called him, the Benjamin of the litter, lying naked on a fur rug, to Brendan in his cap and gown.

'Anna is a lovely girl, but I think she will lead John one hell of a dance unless he keeps her on a tight rein. Remember, she holds the purse strings and your brother will be poor now that he has left Somerset House.' He paused for a moment puffing on his briar pipe. 'Do you know what hubris means?' Violet shook her head. 'Arrogance in defiance of the gods – from Aristotle and the ancient Greeks. It brings tragedy in its wake.'

'I think you are being melodramatic Brendan about a young couple deeply in love. They are both cradle Catholics and I am sure they will lead a good life and raise a fine family.'

'And live happily ever after in a romantic fairy tale? You are very naive, my dear. That young lady spells trouble.' Brendan changed the subject, his wife would never understand his premonition in a thousand years. 'There is a Home Rule meeting in Kilkenny next week. I suppose Declan will be there as usual. Your brother is a great rabble-rouser.'

*

On the first day of May, flowers were strewn on cottage doorstep as a gift to Our Lady. 'They say the sun dances on the water every Good Friday so, to be sure, villagers bring a hip bath out on to the street to catch the rays.' John and Anna spent hours in the old Apple Market of Waterford, browsing through books and bric-a-brac in Mary O' Grady's corner shop.

'I will buy you this pair of Cork decanters, John, with three rings round the neck to steady your hand.'

'My dear little wife, I am not an inebriate yet although you might drive me to the bottle after a year or so.'

A company of players was barnstorming in Dunmore, and Anna wept copiously at the travail of Dion Boucicault's Colleen Bawn.

At last Uncle André wrote to say that he had acquired a property on their behalf but he must return to Brussels forthwith otherwise his business would crumble about his ears.

> *Hollingbury Copse is a fine house with nine bedrooms including the servants' quarters on the top floor and ten acres of land. The property has lain empty for a while since the death of the previous owner, so the price is fair. As I had Anna's written authority to purchase, the Bromley solicitors proceeded and I have instructed a firm in Sidcup to remove all goods and chattels from The Lindens to Brighton before you return to England. The sale of the house in Chislehurst is near completion so you need not go back unless it is your wish.*

The young couple sailed by the night boat from Rosslare to Fishguard breaking their journey in town before travelling to Brighton. The train steamed into Preston Park Station and a cabbie picked them up on the rank outside. 'Did you say Hollingbury Copse, guvnor?' The man flicked his whip across the horse's back. 'It's been empty for years now. Seems the new owners are spending a fortune on the place. Old Paton the gardener is staying on. He's been there, man and boy, for nigh on forty years, I reckon. You friends of the newcomers, sir, if I may make so bold?'

'We are the family, cabbie.'

'Beggin' your pardon, guvnor, I'm sure. My missus always does say I've got a lot of chops; I will go rabbiting on when I ought to keep me trap shut.'

The chalk-white ribbon of road wound over the Downs, and when they rounded a sharp bend the cab turned right into a wide drive while the left fork meandered into the valley towards Ditchling village. A plantation of young silver birches and ash trees masked the house from view.

John raised his monocle and quizzed the rose-red brick of the lodge and the encircling walls. 'Crinkle-crankle, we have a few of these in Ireland built by the English planters. They flow in and out like the waves.'

The house stood on a gentle grassy rise with a coppice beyond and a bronze fountain fashioned as a boy with a dolphin splashed an arc of water into the pool below.

André had engaged one Walter Godden to act as butler and valet to the new master. Kate, Fred and Charlie were standing in line with the rest of the staff, Kate grinning like a Cheshire cat because her Fred had been promoted to head groom.

Pale gaslight shone softly on the old Aubusson carpets splashed with overblown pink roses and a Gobelins tapestry depicting Diana, goddess of the chase, and her lean hounds. The library shelves were already lined with her father's leather-bound books. Blue and white china, burnished copper pots and pans, jelly moulds and giant fish kettles gleamed on the vast Welsh dresser in the kitchen. Maman's collection of enamel boxes lay in a display table on the landing with a tiny china doll in a walnut shell belonging to Anna as a small child, her cold Charlotte.

That night John climbed into the tester bed and waited for Anna to join him, but she began to pluck the petals from a flower in a bowl of damask roses standing on a table in the window embrasure. 'He loves me, he loves me not...'

'I think you know the answer without playing games, Anna. Come to bed and stop being a silly goose.'

Chapter Fifteen

Hollingbury Copse was a wonderful new toy for Anna. She bought William Morris curtains for the study and a few pieces of scarlet Japanese lacquer at Liberty's emporium off Regent Street. She hunted with the Southdown, met the Gages of Firle Place and made a few new acquaintances but no real friends.

John planned a new herbaceous border with the old head gardener, and researched his book in the library surrounded by old dusty tomes and ancient manuscripts.

Didi had been unearthed from the attic at The Limes and sat, bathed and laundered, on a cushion in the boudoir watching Anna undress for a bath. Her mistress gazed down at her swelling stomach and stroked the bump. Even the sisters at the convent could not suggest this was an occasion of sin. 'Katie, Katie, come and look at my tummy... I'm going to have a baby.' The little maid came running into the room.

'I look a fright. I'm pregnant and I'm terrified.'

'I'm so happy for you Mam'selle Anna. Oooh, 'spose I mustn't call you that any more, now that you're a married lady *and* in the family way. (Rose calls it being in the pudden club.) What shall I say? Ma'am, mum or Madame Anna? That sounds real ooh la flash!'

'Madame Anna sounds like the directrice of a fashion house, but it will do very well.' She turned and hugged her little friend and they both began to cry, tears streaming down their faces, Anna clutching a pink towel round her midriff.

'Ere, we're both soft as a brush. This won't buy the baby a new bonnet.' Kate took a clean handkerchief from one of the drawers in a commode and handed it to her mistress.

'I'm tired of spending hours alone while my husband pores over old volumes in the library. He seems to think I should take a siesta every afternoon like the Spanish women. I think I will visit the habit maker tomorrow and order a new flared jacket and a flowing skirt, dark blue, perhaps, I detest green and they say it is unlucky. Black always reminds me of funerals.'

'Don't take any chances riding to hounds, missus. The master is going to think the world of that kid. You're in a delicate condition, now.' She giggled and sniffed. 'Carrying on like a pair of snivelly guttersnipes! Never heard the like. I'm your maid, Madame Anna, and don't you forget it. I must learn to keep my place.' There was a long pause then a gulp from Kate. She took a deep breath before asking: 'May I have the day off on Sunday, please M'm? Fred wants to take me home to meet his mum and dad, and I'm scared stiff. The old boy's a fisherman and they live in a back alley near Brighton Station. I think Fred's going to pop the question again. You know we've been walking out for years.'

Anna laughed. 'The lodge cottage is empty. You could live there as a married couple and still look after me. I never want to lose you, Katie.' Anna kissed the girl on both cheeks.

'I hope you will both be very happy.'

'That's the last time you get sloppy, Madame Anna. We ain't kids no more.'

'I shall claim the respect due to my status as a sober and godly matron.' And they both roared with laughter.

★

The fallow months dragged by and Anna was bored, craving possessions for the first time in her life: a wrap of dark Russian sables and extravagant presents for her husband, handmade shoes and a pair of ruby and diamond cufflinks and studs.

'You are becoming extravagant, Anna.'

'I am free to do as I please, and it is my only amusement now.'

John wanted to buy her a gift before the birth of the child and chose an amethyst ring circled with rose diamonds. The jeweller put it in a purple leather case and John slipped it into the pocket of his overcoat.

'I have brought you a present, my dearest, and I will buy an amethyst for every newborn child in our family.'

'Do you think I'm a mother hen sitting on a clutch of eggs just waiting for them to hatch out?'

He slipped the ring on to her finger and she held it up against the light from an oil lamp on the table beside her.

'Thank you, John, it is a lovely deep colour. There is a tiny flaw in the stone, but I believe that is usual.' She kissed him gently on the lips.

'I must show you what I found today on my shopping expedition.' She drew a magnificent pair of diamond ear drops from her reticule. 'They are the finest Mr Sturgeon had in stock, and you know he is by appointment to Her Majesty.'

*

Dr Nicholson advised great care while she was expecting the birth. 'You would be well advised to remain at home for the last few weeks. I suggest you recline on the chaise longue in your bedroom every afternoon come rain or shine, feet up, blinds down. A lady of your volatile temperament should rest.'

'I am not an invalid, doctor. Will you be satisfied if I agree to ride side saddle for the time being?'

He shook his head looking rather more lugubrious than usual. 'Not until you have been brought to bed of a normal, healthy infant. You are *very* tiny, Madame Donelly. There could be complications.'

A letter came from Declan.

Dear John,

You know the English have imprisoned Parnell. Someone asked him who would be the new leader and he replied 'Captain Moonlight'.

Boycotting, rick-burning and the evictions go on after the countless Coercion Acts of the British Government.

Come over and join us.
Declan

'Our Fred wants to bring a young lady to tea next Sunday, father.' Alfred Harris puffed on his old briar pipe and waited quietly for his wife's comments.

'It must be serious. Fred's knocking on a bit, it's time he settled down.'

'Let's have a look at the young woman before we jump to conclusions, mother.'

Kate and Fred caught the train from Preston Park to Brighton and walked downhill to Crown Gardens where ten flint cottages stood in a row, each with a long tidy front garden and a painted wooden gate.

'Walk round once more, Fred, before we go in.' She was shaking in her shoes when Fred's mother, Martha, opened the door and showed them into the front parlour.

'Come in my dears and sit you down.'

'This is Kate, mother.'

'Pleased to meet you I'm sure. Let me take your pretty bonnet my dear. My, my, all the flowers in May.'

Kate had been up half the night sewing artificial buttercups and daisies round the brim of her old straw hat to brighten it up for the occasion. The young couple sat side by side on the edge of a black horsehair sofa and Kate could feel the coarse bits sticking through the cover and prickling her bum and the backs of her legs.

Fred's dad came into the room wearing his best shirt and braces but left his jacket hanging on the hall stand.

'Meet my husband Alfred.'

Alfred Harris liked the look of this young woman – no airs and graces, straight as a die. He held out his hand and gave hers a firm squeeze.

'Glad to know you, Miss, I'm sure. So you're our Fred's intended.'

'Alfie! We've only just met the young lady and nothing's been said so far. You're a terrible one for jumping the gun. I'm so sorry.' Mrs Harris was flustered, she wiped her clean hands on a spotless white apron and bustled round the room straightening ornaments on the whatnot and twitching her lace curtains.

Fred was pleased that his father had broken the ice.

'Dad's right, mum. We want to get married as soon as possible.'

He caught his mother's eye. 'It's nothing like that, ma.'

'Ooooh, I'm not up the spout, Mrs 'Arris,' announced Kate, 'chance 'ud be a fine thing.' Then she blushed scarlet to the roots of her hair.

'There, there, my dear, don't you fret. Call a spade a spade, that's my motto, always was. Come into the kitchen for your tea, my loves. I hope you like winkles.'

'Not 'arf.'

She led them into the small back room where the table was laid for high tea. It was Kate's idea of a good blow-out: a blue and white willow pattern dish piled high with cockles and winkles and a paper of pins at the side of each plate to wheedle them out of their shells. A bowl of watercress was flanked by a batch of scones, a heap of golden bread and butter and a ginger cake.

They all tucked into Mother Harris's tea with relish.

'Now, my girl, what are your plans?'

'The mistress says we can move into the lodge of the big house as soon as we get married. She's giving us money as a wedding present and some furniture, but it's all old stuff and Fred and me want everything brand new if we can manage it.'

Alfred went to an old tin box on the mantelpiece, took out ten sovereigns and gave them to Fred.

'There you are, my boy. We had a good catch this summer so you may as well have it now as later.'

Kate jumped to her feet, flung her arms round his neck and kissed him. 'Thank you both ever so much. We'll go to the Co-op in the Lewes Road first thing tomorrow morning. We've been gawping in their windows for days. The Lodge has got one room and a kitchen downstairs and two bedrooms.'

'One for the nippers!' said Fred and they all laughed.

The next day Fred and Kate caught the penny tram down Elm Hill to the emporium where they bought a bamboo table to carry an aspidistra in a green pottery jardinière, an oak bedroom suite with stained glass panes in the wardrobe doors and a blue and white willow pattern toilet jug, basin and po. The shop assistant suggested a large iron bed with brass knobs and a glossy commode topped with red and blue carpet.

Kate chose a roll of pink casement marked 'slightly shopsoiled' to make into curtains for the bedroom windows and Nottingham lace with pictures of windmills for the front room. They both fancied a walnut table and four chairs with curly legs, but their money ran out, so Anna ordered them to be delivered to the lodge as a surprise.

The banns were read in St Nicholas, the fishermen's church, high on the hills overlooking the town and the sea.

'The Missus can t come to the wedding cos she's RC. They're not allowed.'

Sister Rose was to be matron of honour, with Ernie as best man. She dallied in the bedroom of the little house while the others were downstairs waiting for the hansom cab. Kate had chosen a dress of sprigged muslin and carried a bunch of primroses. Fred brushed his hair till the ginger curls sprang away from his head like small snakes, carried a brown derby of dad's, and polished his best pair of boots night and morning for days beforehand.

After the ceremony he gazed at his bride, kissed her, knuckled his forehead and murmured, 'I can't believe it. I can't believe it's ruddy true at last.'

After a bun fight in Crown Gardens, Alfred paid for a cab to carry the newly-weds back to Hollingbury Copse. They tumbled into bed tired but happy like two puppies rolling in the hay, but kitchen bells rang out across the Downs and the garden, tied by Rose to the underframe of the bed.

'I'll murder that sister of mine. Take them off, Fred, take them off.'

'Sod the ruddy things, it's too late now.'

*

Sometimes the carriage and pair took John into the heart of Brighton and he spent the day roaming the lanes looking at antiques and bric-a-brac, and enjoying a quiet drink in The Cricketers, a small public house near Prince Albert Street, frequented by strolling players from the Theatre Royal.

He was sitting at his favourite table in the window when mellifluous tones interrupted his reverie.

'John old boy, how good to see you again after all this time.' He looked up at the newcomer and stretched out a hand. 'Stephen, my dear Stephen, sit down and join me in a drink. What on earth are you doing in the back streets of Brighton? do you remember our last night out in the Strand?' He screwed the monocle into his left eye and gazed at his friend. 'You're looking flush.'

Stephen Phillips lifted two glasses of porter from the bar and returned to the table. 'Your faithful servant is appearing at the Theatre Royal with Frank Benson's Shakespearean Company, and today we perform *The Merchant of Venice*.'

'So that accounts for the cloak and dagger style, the wide-brimmed hat and the panache. You were never a shrinking violet, Stephen, but you seem to have made your mark with a vengeance.'

'It's the Theatre now, old boy, with a capital T. The civil service was never my metier nor yours, if I may say so. I did not fancy working all my life for a pittance – rather starve in a garret. What was your salary, around five hundred pounds a year? Not too bad for the poverty-stricken minions, I suppose, but I hear that you have married an heiress and live in the lap of luxury.'

'You are jumping to the wrong conclusions, my friend. Anna and I were engaged long before she inherited her father's fortune.'

'I never meant to offend your delicate Irish sensibilities, you know I am an incurable romantic at heart – obsessed with phantom lovers and Italian tragedy.'

'We await the birth of our first child.'

'That calls for another drink. I'm very happy for you both, and we must wet the baby's head in advance.'

There was a long companionable silence as they drained their glasses. Stephen Phillips cut a fine figure of a man in the bar: over six feet tall with large brown eyes and an aggressive aquiline nose; his whole persona larger than life.

'I am writing a play. You must bring Anna to my first night when it is produced in the West End. George Alexander will be the impresario, so we can look forward to a glittering occasion. I am working on a book of poems too with Laurence. You remember my cousin Laurence Binyon? We often met for a drink after a hard day in the office. Oh the dear, dead days of yore.'

'You are a nostalgic devil, Phillips. I want to research a book on Celtic mythology so I am studying the Gaelic again.'

'I know two words only – *pogue mahone* - it means arseholes, but I have never found it very useful in common parlance. Do you remember our evenings at the Café Royal with that dreary Frank Harris and Oscar? Talking, talking, talking about everything and nothing. I met Oscar once in Regent Street carrying an enormous sunflower like a banner. Who wrote that wonderful line about a flaunting, extravagant queen?' Stephen pulled a gold half hunter from his waistcoat pocket and glanced at the time. 'Oh God, I shall be late for the matinee unless I hurry, and Frank's good lady will create ructions. I am placing Bassanio in *The Merchant*. Come to the theatre with me, John, and we can talk in my dressing room. I have so many things to tell you about our friends in London, Elgar's latest work and the divine Patti. You can watch the show from the wings when I am on stage. Let us fly, my public awaits.' He flung the cloak over his shoulder with a grand gesture and they departed, taking a short cut through the Lanes and past the Chapel Royal to the stage door at the rear of the Theatre Royal.

'Good afternoon, Mr Phillips. Henry is waiting in your dressing room as usual.'

'Thanks, William. Be a good fellow and send one of the lads out for a couple of bottles of porter before the show. This is my old friend John Donnelly and we both have a prodigious thirst.' He pressed a coin into the man's hand and they set off down the corridor. 'Frank has the star dressing room, of course. We are second cousins but his good lady does not approve of yours truly and watches me like a hawk. She thinks I lack dedication to my art.'

The dresser Henry was like a black beetle, scurrying here and there with costumes for *The Merchant*, brushing a cloak, sponging a jacket, caressing the feather on a red velvet hat. 'We are running a little late Sir.'

Gas jets spluttered casting a yellowish light on the long mirror. Stephen stripped off his outer garments, donned a silk paisley dressing gown and sat down to make up his face with a few sticks of colour taken from a battered old tin box. 'What do they say? The smell of the greasepaint and the roar of the crowd... it sounds like Barnum's American circus. Where's the hotblack, Henry? You know some actors use drops of belladonna to enlarge the pupil, but I think it might ruin the eyesight.'

John was fascinated by the transformation. The looking glass was surrounded by cards and odd messages of goodwill on scraps of paper. Someone had scribbled a message in carmine on the glass signed May.

'May Lidyard.'

There was a knock at the door. 'Ten minutes to curtain up, Mr Phillips. I've brought your beer.' The curtain rose to a typical matinee audience of elderly matrons and their captive daughters rattling teacups on trays and rustling their programmes. The whispered conversation in the stalls died slowly.

John peered out from his vantage point in the wings.

The Theatre Royal was one of the oldest in England retaining its original chandeliers, red velvet curtains and gilded mirrors. The story of Shylock and his pound of flesh unfolded with Frank Benson playing the sinister Jew. 'If you prick us do we not bleed?'

They had reached the casket scene, and Stephen's mellifluous tones were echoing to the back of the gallery, when John heard the low clear voice of the call boy from the corridor behind the scenery.

'Mr Donelly... Mr John Donelly... wanted at the stage door. Urgent.'

Fred was talking to William, cap in hand. 'It's his wife. The doctor sent me. She's having a baby.' He caught sight of his master running towards him.

'The carriage is waiting. Come quick, sir. The missus is having the baby and Dr Nicholson says it's two months early.'

'I hate my body Kate. It looks like a pink balloon.' Anna was bored to tears. She spent days in her boudoir using a steel hook and the finest cotton thread to make a baby's bonnet of Irish crochet encrusted with tiny roses and shamrocks.

It was a very hot summer's day and John had gone off to explore the antiquarian bookshops in the Lanes. The expectant mother wandered into the nursery to look at the cradle draped in white muslin caught back with tiny pink rosebuds. The infant was sure to be a girl. They might call her Marguerite in remembrance of her mother.

The layette was ready and Kate had knitted a pink matinee coat.

Anna was feeling restless and uneasy as she left the house and wandered into the garden, taking a deep Sussex trug and scissors from the greenhouse to deadhead the roses. A green wooden wheelbarrow stood on the terrace at the head of a flight of stone steps leading down to the rose gardens. Anna grasped the handles and tried to push it out of the way, but it was far too heavy for her to move. A sharp pain like a knife pierced her body. Breathless, she sat on a low iron garden seat and waited for it to pass, but the contractions were regular now and she leaned forward with her head between her knees. The midwife had warned her about birth pangs, but this was agony and the baby was not due for weeks.

'Kate,' she screamed. The high thin wail peeled across the garden. 'Katie... John... John, where are you?'

Kate was tidying a closet in the room above, heard the shriek through an open window and pelted down the staircase.

'Come indoors with me, Madame Anna. One of the men will fetch the doctor and the master in no time at all.'

It was hell to move a few steps. She wanted to die.

'You should lie down at once. Don't you fret M'm. I know from our Rose that mum always had a terrible time with every one of us kids, but they say, it's soon forgotten. Lean on my arm and we'll get you into bed, quick.'

Anna's heart was pounding. She clung to the mahogany bed post, her teeth embedded in her lower lip, as Kate loosened her stays and helped her up the bed steps on to the four-poster where she lay twisting and turning and tearing a small lace handkerchief to shreds. 'I am trying to be good.'

She sounded like the nine-year-old in the Boulevard Haussmann. The doctor came at last and examined his patient, shook his head mournfully and applied a pad of ether to Anna's nose and mouth 'Hot water, girl, and be quick about it; your mistress's life is in danger and we may not be able to save the baby. Tell one of the other servants to fetch the priest, then we shall be prepared.'

Kate's eyes were like jet beads, her face white as chalk, but she fetched and carried running backwards and forwards with copper jugs of boiling water and piles of freshly laundered towels.

'Where is the layette for the infant? Bring me a nightgown and shawl.'

Anna's body was racked with pain, but after a while she lay still on cool linen sheets, her pale tapering fingers resting on the coverlet. When she recovered consciousness she passed one hand inside the bed and felt her flat stomach. 'The baby... where is John?'

She knew the sickly sweet smell of death hanging in the air. 'Your husband is not here, Mrs Donelly. I understand the coachman left him at The Cricketers public house, but he walked to the Theatre Royal with an actor from the Benson company. We sent for him post haste, but the birth was premature and totally unexpected.'

The man was talking too much.

'I want to see my baby.'

'There is bad news, Madame. We lost the infant, a perfect stillborn girl weighing three pounds.'

Anna covered her face and wept.

Godden's countenance was grave when he answered the door to his master. 'The mistress is in her room and the doctor is with her. He asks you to join him immediately when you return.'

Anna lay motionless, her eyes closed.

'I have given your wife a sleeping draught; she was nearly out of her mind. The baby was stillborn and there were certain complications.' The pompous old man droned on.

Kate came out of the dressing room carrying the dead baby wrapped in a pure white shawl. John took the child in his arms and kissed the cold little forehead, murmuring a prayer in Gaelic.

The infant was buried in a small coffin lined with satin and Father Rossigny celebrated the Mass of Angels.

117

Anna was bedridden for days, but the weeks dragged past. Sometimes she lay for hours in a wicker chair on the terrace gazing across the rosebeds, remembering. One cool, still day towards the end of summer, she rose with tears coursing down her cheeks and walked blindly towards the coppice. The babe lay buried at her feet under a small carved cross in earth blessed by the priest in the name of the Holy Catholic Church. Anna shivered and prayed for strength to accept the will of God, crossed herself and walked back towards the house to meet John at the end of the day.

*

Bridget and Domenic visited Hollingbury Copse from time to time, but it was a long journey for the father who was becoming more and more fragile as the years went by, living in the past.

He died in his sleep without seeing a grandchild born to his son John.

Bridget was philosophical. 'It's a blessing in a way for poor Domenic's mind was failing. Now he's in peace at last. God rest his soul.' She made the sign of the cross. 'I shall go back to Ireland, there's nothing to keep me here now. There is a cottage in Carrageen overlooking the castle ruin. It stands on the brow of a hill and I know it's been empty for years. They tell me it's going for a song. I shall be near my niece, Brendan and the boys, and I'm sure Declan will come to see his old aunt when he's not fighting for Home Rule. I shall look forward to a visit from you both very, very soon.'

Chapter Sixteen

'I suggest we invite your friend Stephen Phillips to dinner the next time he appears at the Theatre Royal. I should be happy to meet this flamboyant personality for the first time.

Stephen came to Hollingbury Copse several months later in his guise of 'actor laddie' and Anna disliked him on sight. Everything about the man from his frilled evening shirt to the wide silken lapels of the jacket was a little larger than life.

'Night's candles are burnt out. Thank you, dear lady, for a most entertaining evening.' He bowed to kiss her hand with a flourish then bade farewell to his friend in the hall. 'Your wife is far lovelier than I imagined, John, but I am sure she does not care for me.'

'You steal the limelight, my dear fellow. Anna is a born prima donna.'

'Let us meet in The Cricketers and talk to our heart's content – the milieu is sympathetic. Cissie the barmaid will minister to our needs with hunks of fresh bread and Stilton cheese laced with port wine and we can crack a bottle. What more could a man ask? My own good lady does not understand my temperament and I fear we will become estranged. The exquisite Anna is fragile, but methinks she has a will of iron. Beware, a child wife may become a shrew. I will see you tomorrow after the matinee.' He smiled. 'I do not expect to be a welcome guest in the future, but I could misjudge the situation. I like to play centre stage and panache can be overwhelming. Also, I drink too much for polite society.'

The deep voice was mocking. 'Return to your scene of domestic bliss and I will away to my shabby digs in St Bartholomew's.'

Godden interrupted his reverie. 'Your carriage awaits, sir.'

Stephen strode out into the night making an exit worthy of the great Henry Irving.

★

One day Anna mounted Toby and cantered along the winding lane over the Downs towards Ditchling village. A small boy in a cottage garden was playing with pebbles and a catapult and fired at the pony's rump. Toby whinnied and reared throwing Anna over his head on to the side of the road. She struggled to her feet and caught the reins, swearing like a trooper at the child who bolted across the fields as fast as his legs would carry him. Anna turned the pony's head towards Hollingbury Copse and jogged back to the lodge.

'I have had a bad fall, Kate. Toby threw me in the lane.' She was lying down on Kate's bed when the doctor arrived.

'Mrs Donelly, you have had an abortion.'

'It must be a haemorrhage caused by the fall.'

'It is a miscarriage, Madame. I understand you did not realise you were... enceinte... as the pregnancy is only a matter of weeks, but you must take greater care if you wish to be brought to bed of a live infant. I am sure your husband will be most displeased.'

'It is my body, doctor.'

John was angry at the waste of life, especially as another child was stillborn the following year, through no fault of Anna's.

★

Anna gave birth to a live son on the 5 November, four years after her wedding. She lay in bed watching the distant glow of beacons on the Sussex hill tops and showers of golden stars from the fireworks in Ditchling. 'I am so happy, John. Shall we call the baby Guy?'

'I prefer Louis Domenic.'

His father had died the year before and Anna was too weak to argue. The name Louis always reminded her of the Empress Eugénie and her young son.

'They're going to have a bun fight for the baby's christening... real ooh la flash with a whole roast ox and fireworks. The Missus says we can ask your Mum and Dad and sister Rose and Ernie.

Some of the family are sailing from Ireland for the weekend, the Gages from Firle will be there and the gentry from the big house near Preston Park. Lots of the neighbours will come for a free meal and a booze-up. Madame Anna even wrote to Monsignor Goddard from their old church in Chislehurst. It's like the Coming of the Lord.'

'Don't be such a blasphemous little bugger, Kate. It's time they had a bit of luck after trying for four years.' All the servants knew about the stillborn infants.

The old gardener and his boy lit flares along the driveway and a bonfire on the rise behind the house, and Anna decorated every room with flowers and plants from the hothouses. Boneshakers and carriages rolled up the long steep hill towards Hollingbury Copses, blazing with light from hundreds of candles and oil lamps burning whale oil and kerosene.

Maureen and Patrick came with Declan and aunt Bridget, who spent most of the evening hovering over the sleeping child in the night nursery. Villagers brought their wives, children and dogs. Anna was drinking a glass of champagne with Stephen Phillips and did not see a black hound scrabbling in the earth near the coppice of the dead children.

'My heartfelt congratulations, Anna. You have been brought to bed of a healthy child at last. The Irish contingent will be delighted, they breed like rabbits.' He could never resist teasing her although they were good friends now. She had never encountered anyone like him before, except perhaps Robert.

'One day I shall write a play called *Armageddon* about the war between good and evil. I can envisage a scene with a hundred women on the stage turning their naked backs to the audience... but I have so many other ideas. Two Italian lovers like Romeo and Juliet, or dramas in blank verse about Herod and Nero might appeal to the British audiences. George Alexander is obsessed with Oscar's epigrams at the moment but I am sure they will soon be out of fashion.'

Patrick muttered to Brendan under his breath: 'This actor is self-obsessed.'

Uncle André smiled and sipped his cognac.

Declan and John shared a nightcap in the study talking late into the night. 'Are you happy living here, old man? You seem to be a little disillusioned. Why not come home, boy? Old Gladstone is still talking about Home Rule and a land act but there is a great deal of opposition. Thousands are still emigrating to Liverpool and the United States – I understand the conditions in steerage are appalling, but it's still better than the poorhouse. Anna could buy one of the Ascendancy houses. I am deadly serious. There is a fine one overlooking the Blackwater and another in Kinsale. I know she has money to spare.'

'My wife talks about Paris and Brussels, but I think she wants to stay in Brighton.'

'You can't waste your life clinging to a woman s skirts.' John tried to change the subject.

'I'm sorry Violet and Brendan were too short of money to make the journey. One of the boys is going to university but I feel they are using it as an excuse. Time for bed, young Declan.'

Across the water Brendan was toasting his feet at the log fire. 'It's a pity we missed the baptism and the party. The heiress is spreading her wings.'

*

Months passed and Anna was tired of waiting for another child. She wanted a baby girl. Was it a morbid fancy to bury their stillborn infants in the grounds where a fox or a badger might disturb their shallow graves?

'I think this house is unlucky, John. I loathe the peacocks screeching on the lawns like evil spirits.'

'Uncle André christened them Marie Antoinette and Louis.'

'They should be sent to the guillotine.'

'Our son is in fine fettle.'

Anna rode to hounds, and suckled her baby on horseback. Every evening John read aloud from Dickens or Walter Scott, or they sat at the grand piano playing duets, but she was becoming more and more restless. Dr Nicholson suggested it might be due to a bout of post-natal depression, but Anna pooh-poohed the whole idea.

They were driving along the seafront one morning after Mass and she caught sight of a 'For Sale' board outside number nine Brunswick Terrace, a tall Regency house overlooking the lawns. 'We should inspect the property tomorrow, John. It is in a wonderful position.'

'The price could be exorbitant, my dear.'

'You are an old skinflint, John. After all, it is my money to spend and we can afford a dozen houses if we choose.'

The estate agent pointed out the fine columns flanking the front entrance, the white stucco facade now peeling in the sea air and a rusty iron balcony on the drawing room floor, a dry basement with a good butler's pantry and attic bedrooms for the servants. Kate and Fred could live in the rooms above the stables in the mews behind the building.

'It would be a magnificent house with a few improvements, Madame.

'I am sick of living out in the wilds, John. We could be happy here... Please, darling.'

John shrugged his shoulders. 'Anything for a quiet life.'

Anna was determined to carry everyone away on the tide of her own enthusiasm.

A retinue of builders and decorators set to work on the house and 'Porky' Newman, a young second-hand dealer from Edward Street, cleared the outbuildings at the old house, lock, stock and barrel, together with all the unwanted bric-a-brac.

After the removal Anna realised she was pregnant for the fifth time, retching with morning sickness and terrified of losing another baby. Dr Nicholson's face was grave when he examined her. 'I must take a firm line, Mrs Donelly. I absolutely forbid riding or any form of strenuous exercise. If the blood pressure rises, you will be obliged to stay in bed for weeks before the birth. I could perform a Caesarean operation, and in view of your unusual pelvic formation, this might be advisable.'

'You are not cutting my stomach with a knife. I would rather die.'

Anna fancied a compote of berries laced with Cointreau and topped with whipped cream in the middle of the night,

Whitstable oysters and Beluga caviare and anchovy paste on hot buttered toast for breakfast.

John and the servants pandered to every whim, praying for the nine months to pass.

*

'Madame Anna is drunk as a fiddler's bitch!' Kate was in the basement kitchen with Fred and cook waiting for the new birth after a lapse of two years. 'Take her the chicken broth, Kate, that should help to sober her up a bit.'

There was a loud crash in the room directly above them – the master's study. 'She thinks it's a coconut shy with them French vases.'

Kate emerged from the kitchen bearing a small silver tray: soup, rolls and strong black coffee just as Anna slammed the study door and stormed upstairs into the drawing room where six pairs of eyes stared at her from behind bars. John followed close behind.

'You know Dr Hellyer says you must try to be calm, Anna, for the sake of the unborn child.'

'To hell with doctors. Babies always hurt like the very devil. Merde!'

Clutching her stomach she began to curse in the gutter French she had picked up from the French stable lads at Chislehurst. 'Shi-i-i-it! I can't bear the agony... I never want to sleep with you again as long as I live... never, never... never.' Anna snatched a glass paperweight from the writing table and flung it at her husband's head, but he ducked and it smashed to smithereens against the marble fireplace.

The Persian cats gazed out from a row of iron cages lining one whole wall of the drawing room, their pointed faces framed in aureoles of pure white or smokey blue fur. One yawned, closing her lemon eyes, and displayed sharp pointed teeth and pale pink gums.

John came towards Anna and laid a restraining hand on her arm, but she spat at him and ran out onto the balcony. He knew she might fling herself over the balustrade on to the paving stones below.

'Try to be calm, dearest, the birth will soon be over and tomorrow...'

Leaning backwards she could feel the cold iron railing giving way beneath her weight and reached out towards him, terrified of falling into the basement area beneath her. John gathered her in his arms and carried her towards the chaise longue.

'I hate you for making me suffer like this.'

'If you were not in a delicate condition, I would lay you across my knees and spank you. You are behaving like a spoilt brat not a grown woman.'

She was clinging to his hand, scared to death, weeping. 'If I die in childbirth, take good care of Louis. Promise you will remember me always, dearest John.'

Kate knocked on the drawing room door bringing the supper tray; she had been hovering outside in the corridor listening. 'Take that pap away and tell Godden to fetch champagne. We will drink a toast – to celibacy. Oh my God.' She was doubled up with pain. 'Fetch me laudanum or chloral, I have been waiting for that bloody doctor for hours. Meanwhile, you have treated me as an Aunt Sally and now I think you should retire to bed.'

'Kate, help your mistress to undress.'

'Yes, Sir.'

A gentle, maudlin Anna kissed him gently on the lips, then slowly, a few steps at a time, they made their way up the stairs and across the broad landing to the double bedroom overlooking the lawns and the sea.

Her lingering eau de cologne was sweeter than the reek of cats from the animal cages; a few droppings had spilled on to the Aubusson carpet and were trodden in to the delicate pattern of pale roses and deep-blue lovers' knots.

John sat alone throughout the night drinking black coffee laced with brandy, and waiting. The grandfather clock struck the passing hours; a painted ship sailing an indigo sea moved backwards and forwards across the dial. It was a country clock from West Cork inherited from his father. He needed Declan more than ever before. Declan with his cynical wisdom, his love of people and causes. John was roused from a deep sleep by the high thin wail of a newborn babe.

Dr Nicholson knocked and entered the room a while later.

'Mr Donelly, allow me to congratulate you on the birth of a daughter, a fine infant, three weeks premature. Mother and child are both doing well.'

The man seemed to be a little hesitant.

'Sit down, Doctor, and we will wet the baby's head.'

'You may not realise it, Mr Donelly, but your wife has a very difficult time in childbirth. She has a contracted pelvis. May I take the liberty of suggesting that you limit your family to two? I realise that this is a delicate matter for Catholics and I am treading on dangerous ground, but it would be a very wise decision.'

He paused for a sip of whisky and John came to his aid. 'We do not need to discuss the matter further. I have already decided on total abstinence if need be.'

'I must admit that I am most relieved, sir. Your wife's temperament... would not allow me to act as her medical adviser should there be another confinement. Her language can be a little offensive, even allowing for the pad of ether I pressed over her nose and mouth. She called me the scum of the earth. You will be able to see your wife and daughter when the midwife has completed her ministrations.'

Anna lay back against a pile of down cushions cradling the baby in her aims, looking a picture of calm, angelic motherhood.

John kissed her hand. 'I have not forgotten Anna. You will never endure this again.' He gazed at the little one's tiny clenched hands and pursed mouth and the light dusting of pale hair sprouting from the crown of her head. 'God bless you both.'

Next morning the doctor returned to the house carrying a large bouquet of flowers. 'Mrs Donelly, another patient of mine, Mrs Langtry, sends this sheaf of blooms and asks that you call the baby Lillie after her.' His grey beard was bobbing up and down with emotion. The Jersey Lillie one time favourite of His Royal Highness the Prince of Wales, had captured his heart with her loveliness and charm.

The heavy perfume of the flowers reached Anna's nostrils and she thrust them into Kate's arms. 'Throw them into the dustbin. I hate white flowers. They remind me of funerals.'

Kate ran down the stairs into the basement and arranged the bunch of flowers in a pitcher on the scrubbed pine table. 'They're a gift from the actress Lillie Langtry. Our missus don't want 'em and I haven't got the heart to throw 'em away.'

Anna took a long while to recover her strength. She agreed to sell all the cats save one, the Laird of Cockpen, who was allowed to sleep in a basket at the foot of her bed, and 'Porky' Newman collected the cages as scrap metal.

John moved into the dressing room and all physical intercourse was at an end. He faced the celibate life of a monk to the end of his days.

★

The long succession of nursemaids began with a Welsh dragon called Nanny Jones, and ended with a young Irish girl who ran off with the dairyman. Anna was becoming desperate. 'What on earth am I going to do, Kate? They are all hopeless, and many of them only want a position for a few months.'

'Madame Anna, you know I will never make a real lady's maid if I live to be a hundred. Thank heavens, you don't change your clothes seven times a day like some of these society women, but it's still bad enough.'

'Well?'

'I could look after the little 'uns for you. I love kids. Old Osborne always said it was the only thing I was good for; that and the laundry. Master Louis is spoiled rotten already. He'll grow into a right young devil if someone doesn't lick him into shape. Will you let me have a go?'

Anna nodded. 'I think it's a grand idea, Kate.'

That afternoon they set out together, Kate pushing Mary in a perambulator and Louis tugging his mother by the hand.

The department store in East Street had a good selection of nurses' uniforms, and Kate emerged in a long grey poplin dress that reached her ankles, a starched cap with velvet ribbons and a pair of strong black lace-up shoes. Proud as Punch, she told Fred the good news that evening, and twirled round for his inspection.

'You promise to give it all up as soon as we have kids of our own.'

'Yes, Fred, no Fred, three bags full, Fred. Give us a kiss and say you're proud of me.'

He slapped her on the bum. 'It's time for my tea, woman. I'm starving, but I quite fancy you in that get-up.'

His dutiful little wife disappeared into the kitchen to cook bangers and mash for her lord and master, cocking a snook at him on the way.

★

'John, I have an idea.'

'Jesus, Mary and Joseph, not another one, I thought life was far too peaceful.'

'Arundel House stands on the corner of Lewes Crescent. There are private gardens in the square and it is only a stone's throw from the beach, so it would be ideal for the children. If I collect the keys from the solicitor tomorrow we could view the property together. The lease is for sale not the freehold, so we should be able to make a profit on number nine.'

'You are incorrigible, Anna. That sounds like a grand illusion... I must be as weak as ditchwater.'

The rooms were elegant. The panelled walls of the drawing room inset with blue Wedgwood medallions, the marble fireplaces carved with fruit and flowers, and the plasterwork on the ceilings picked out in fine gold leaf.

'Look at that wonderful curved staircase and the belvedere.'
'What on earth is that, for heaven's sake?'

'The word comes from the Italian, bel vedere, a beautiful view. It's like a conservatory on the side of the house overlooking the Channel. I'm sure we could see France on a clear day! Let me buy this house, John, and I promise to keep the Laird of Cockpen out of the living room. He could sleep in a basket in the belvedere. (She rolled the r's on her tongue.)

'You are never satisfied, my darling,' and he kissed her. 'You know, I think English law gives me control over my wife's fortune.'

'Don't be absurd, dearest.' She brushed aside the idea.

'We can have adjoining rooms, and I will find lovely art nouveau wallpapers.

Anna was blissfully happy with their new domestic arrangement, living together as loving friends.

All the servants agreed to move a mile or so along the promenade. Only Fred was reluctant to leave the mews cottage at the back of number nine.

'You'll be past it if we don't start a family of our own soon.'

'That's enough of your lip, Mr Harris, I'm sure. I'm not ready to push up the daisies yet, but I promise you one thing… if the missus moves again, I'm leaving.'

The long lazy days of summer were sheer bliss. A zig-zag path led down to the seashore at Black Rock, and Volk's Railway ran along the Marine Parade, tickets a penny each.

Sunday was Kate's one day off, so every week Anna walked down to the beach with a picnic basket crammed with goodies, Mary and Louis in tow. She tied her hair back with a wide ribbon and her skirts were hoisted to her waist with a piece of string. Mary tucked her frock into her knickers and Louis took off his shoes and socks and wiggled his toes in the wet sand. Sometimes Anna gave two boys sixpence to borrow their shrimping net, and Louis and Mary squealed with delight as they turned over small rocks and their mother tried to catch the darting shrimps. They paddled in the shallow pools of water prodding beneath the surface, watched the fishermen digging for lugworms, then scrambled up the steep path to the house and cooked the squeaking shrimps on a gas ring in the nursery watching them turn from dirty brown to pink. They all gobbled them up with thick doorsteps of bread and butter.

Chapter Seventeen

John spent hours alone in the library or writing to the family in Ireland. It would be so easy to lose touch with his brother and sisters. Jim had died in 1890 worn out by his mission work in Southwark and Bermondsey.

Several years later the gilt was beginning to wear off the gingerbread.

'Kate wants to raise a family of her own and call the first girl Annie.'

'Poor infant.'

'I had a letter from the bank this morning, and they say the money is dwindling fast. Do you think we should move to a smaller house in the country and pull in our horns for the time being? We might even rent an unfurnished property.'

'Who on earth would buy the lease on this white elephant at the price you paid for it?'

'Hannah writes to say that her mother is looking for a residence in Brighton. She needs to take the sea air, and the old girl is rolling in money.'

Anna wrote to Lady Lansdowne with a long, highly-coloured description of Arundel House, and was summoned to visit her ladyship at Chantry House near Dorking and discuss the possibility of a sale. She knew that Hannah's mother adored cats and was highly interested in the Laird of Cockpen, champion of England in the National Cat Show, so the pedigree blue Persian travelled in style, not in the guard's van but in a large wicker basket placed on a passenger seat with his own ticket.

The carriage sent to meet them at the station climbed a steep hill out of the town along country lanes white with cow parsley through wrought iron gates to the house. Alex Lansdowne was now seventy years of age, and left the supervision of her thousand acres to the bailiff referring to her prize herd of Herefords as 'a few old cows'. Anna presented her card.

'Her ladyship is expecting you, madam. Her ladyship is with the bears, it is their special time of day. If madam will come this way?' He picked up the Laird's basket. 'Allow me,' and led her across the hall to a large studded oak door, down a wide flight of stone steps into the courtyard at the rear of the house.

'Mrs Donelly, milady.'

Crowned by a wide-brimmed hat of leghorn straw to protect the complexion, the old woman sat in a wicker wheelchair with one of the under-gardeners stationed beside her ready to push on command.

Cages encircled by iron railings stood at two corners of the courtyard, and in each of these was a small brown bear.

Her Ladyship extended a languid hand. 'A gift from Crown Prince Feodor many years ago. One of my dearest possessions. Each day I give them afternoon tea: a paper bag full of currant buns and a small dish of honey. It is their great treat summer and winter if I am not unwell. They are far more amusing than children.'

She wore a gown with lace frills at wrist and throat in the style of her namesake the Princess of Wales, and a collarette of pearls. A chinchilla wrap covered her knees, although it was a warm day. She smiled. 'So kind of you to come and see me, my dear. Hannah has told me all about you ever since your schooldays. May I introduce Catherine and Peter? You may offer them an apple if you wish.' Alex liked to drive a hard bargain in love and war, but it was difficult to assess this young woman.

'I knew your grandmother in Provence and your mother Marguerite as a young girl. I seem to remember an unhappy love affair, but that is all water under the bridge – there was never a breath of scandal. You have brought the champion to show me?'

The butler presented the cat.

'He is the most beautiful, enchanting creature in the whole world, I would be desolate without him.'

Anna braced herself to accept two hundred guineas for her favourite, and the Laird lay in all his glory merging with the soft blue-grey colour of the chinchillas covering her ladyship's knees.

Alex showed great interest when Anna mentioned Lillie Langtry and Brighton. 'The physician tells me the sea air would benefit my health and I quite fancy a second home on the South Coast. Morgan, bring a dish of salmon for the Laird of Cockpen.'

'I beg your pardon, milady?'

'The cat, you silly old fool.' She paid high wages and felt entitled to insult the servants. Alex gestured towards the Persian cat. Every gnarled finger was ablaze with diamonds and emeralds, but her knuckle joints ached as she grasped her cane. 'Would you prefer tea al fresco or shall we adjourn to the drawing room?' A few drops of rain began to patter on to the stones, so she did not wait for an answer, 'Push, boy, are you weak *and* witless? We shall be caught in a downpour, faster, faster.'

The cavalcade set off for the house, with Ferdinand pushing the wheelchair, Anna trotting alongside, and Morgan carrying the cat basket. The curtained room was kind to Lady Lansdowne's ravaged beauty. The fine eyes glittered, and her enamelled complexion no longer showed the signs of artifice that were apparent in the daylight. The rouge on her high cheekbones simulated the flush of youth. She raised a lorgnette to appraise her companion's appearance, and Anna was found wanting.

'My dear child, I think you are neglecting the essentials of life: glycerine and rosewater, cucumber on the eyelids, and oatmeal in tepid water if you insist on washing your face. Witch hazel brightens the eyes, alum tightens the skin, and belladonna...'

She encountered a blank stare.

'You must forgive my frankness, but you were such a lovely child. Now you want to live on a small broken-down farm with a dull feckless husband. Take a wealthy lover, my dear, and you could have the best of both worlds. I know about these things. I always wanted to have my cake and eat it, as Nanny used to say.'

She shivered. 'It is sad to grow old, but I have had a wonderful life. If we waste our talents, money and beauty, the end is tragedy and oblivion – a downward spiral. The death wish.'

'Your tea, milady.' The conversation was interrupted by Morgan bearing a laden silver tray. 'Do you prefer China or Indian, Madam?'

Anna was dying for a glass of wine but she sipped and nibbled and made polite conversation until she was given her congé.

'My dear, you have made an old woman very happy with the prospect of a new house in Brighton and this magnificent animal, the Laird. I shall remember your mother daily when I am living in your home.' She laughed, and for a brief moment she might have been a young girl. 'Away with sentimentality. I know we understand one another perfectly. I think we should leave the whole sordid question of money to our solicitors.'

*

John spent his afternoon at The Cricketers in good company. 'Only Anna would breed cats and babies in the drawing room.' He leaned on the bar counter and gazed at Stephen through a misty haze. 'Pedigree cats and pedigree babies too, I suppose. The Laird of Cockpen became the champion of all England, and now she may be selling him to some old biddy before he's even had time to sire a few fine kittens.' His intake of porter slurred the speech a little. 'My good lady wants to move *again*.' John was unusually verbose today. As a rule he was reticent about his private life. 'You can have your pigs at last, she says. The money's ebbing away fast, so you may as well try your luck as a gentleman farmer and breed your little piglets. Anna owns two properties now: a nursery garden run by a dolt of a manager who came to her with a hard luck story, and the house on Marine Parade, a white elephant with a belvedere.' He chuckled. 'The latest idea is to buy a semifurnished farm in Herstmonceux. Jesus, Mary and Joseph, the woman would try the patience of a saint.'

Stephen knew only one way to console him.

'Have another glass of porter to drown your sorrows. Alexander has increased the advance he paid me on the new play but Lord alone knows when I shall finish it.'

'I can tell there's a storm brewing, Stephen, and Anna's terrified of thunder. She runs to hide in a cupboard under the stairs and the servants think she is a madwoman. The train from Dorking should arrive in half an hour and I promised to meet her at the station. I know she will be heartbroken if she has had to part with that damn cat.'

He rose to his feet with dignity and screwed the monocle into his left eye. 'I'll be seeing you here next week, Stephen my boy, if I can escape the petticoat government, then I expect we shall be away to the woods to gather violets. Goodbye now.'

A faint clap of thunder echoed through the bar as he opened the door to leave.

'A real gentleman that Mr Donelly, although they do say his wife's a regular tartar.' Cissie the barmaid polished her glasses daydreaming about the tall Irishman who never even noticed her making cows' eyes at him from behind the bar.

*

'I want to give me notice, Madame Anna.'

'Nonsense, Kate, you must stay with me always. I need your help with the children. There will be a place for you and Fred wherever we go.'

'Fred's made up his mind, and you know he's dead set in his ways. We had a barney about it and then he put me in the family way. I'm happy about it really cos I'm knocking on a bit for a first baby, over thirty.'

'Poor old thing. Where are you going to live?'

'Mother Harris stayed on in the cottage after dad died, but now she's going to live with her sister and she's giving us everything, lock, stock and barrel. I know she will be as proud as Punch of her first grandchild. Fred can rent an allotment at the back of the station and keep a pig and a few chickens. He can always work as a porter on the fruit market if we run a bit short.'

'I shall be very sorry to lose you after all these years.' Anna was on the verge of tears. 'I'm happy about the baby.'

'You know where I am if you want me and I shall always turn up like a bad penny. I could stay on another month or two while you're moving house.'

'Everything depends on her ladyship. We are still waiting for a letter of confirmation from her solicitors.' 'She'd better get a move on, the baby's due at midsummer and I can't fasten me petersham belt now.'

'I thought it was the nursery food making you fat.'

'It's more than rice pud and tapioca! Where's the new abode, Madame Anna? Don't I talk posh these days?'

'I read an advertisement in the local paper about a farm house near Hailsham: forty-nine acres of land, outbuildings, pig sties and stables... and a lily pond.'

'Sounds right up your alley, Madame,' and Kate grinned knowing that she could get away with murder.

The babe was born in Martha's deep feather bed with a midwife and sister Rose in attendance.

'Easy as shelling peas,' announced the proud father.

Rose quite fancied her brother-in-law, big and burly with ginger hairs sprouting from the backs of his hands and across his chest, (she had been watching him from the bedroom window as he sluiced under the water tap in the backyard). She turned to her own bloke, little Ern. It was their last day in Brighton.

'Come on, me old cock sparrer, it's time we were off to Bermondsey and our own kids. Cheerio Fred,' and she gave him a kiss full on the lips.

'Keep your hands off my old man. I'm feeling as fit as a flea and I can see you off any time.'

'Don't worry, Ernie can still tickle me brainbox.'

Fred gazed down at his offspring in her frilly cot. 'Poor little scrap, wrinkled all over and red as a lobster.'

'She's the prettiest baby in the whole wide world and we're going to call her Annie whether you like it or not.'

That evening Fred fetched the black leather family bible from its carved oak box, opened the hasp and spread the good book wide on a bamboo table in their bedroom. He fetched a pen and ink pot and set about his task. First he sucked the end of the quill, then wiped the nib on a piece of scarlet felt and, in his best copperplate handwriting entered the birth of his daughter with slow loving care. 'Born to Frederick and Kate Harris a daughter, Anna Martha Rose, on 3 August 1895.'

Anna visited them after the accouchement bringing a pale pink matinee jacket for the baby and a pair of cut glass lustres to adorn the mantelpiece in the parlour.

'Real ooh la flash! I've always wanted a pair of jingalooters. Anna will love to play with them when she's bigger.

'She's still only ten days old so she can't smash them to smithereens for a year or two.

*

Lady Lansdowne delayed signing the contract for months on end, but arrived in the autumn to occupy Arundel House. The Laird lay in a basket lined with blue satin, a collar of fine Moroccan leather studded with rose diamonds circling his neck.

'Your husband is a very charming man, my dear. Aah! if only I were twenty years younger.' After a peck on the cheek she dismissed Anna to the railway station in a hackney carriage.

'The old lady is as cunning as a wagon load of monkeys. She was free to change her mind at any time during the negotiations.'

Mary was more concerned about the cat. 'I could not even stroke The Laird.'

'Did you leave his silver cups?' Louis broke into the conversation, but did not wait for a reply. 'I don't like cats much anyway. Mother says we shall have dogs and horses at Herstmonceux.'

Louis and Mary squabbled throughout the train journey. 'Let's count the magpies. Bet I spot more than you.

'One for sorrow, two for joy, first a girl and then a boy.'

'That's a silly girl's rhyme.'

'Mama taught me to say it.'

Their father interrupted them. 'In Ireland you spit over your finger for luck and say, 'Good morning, your lordship, and how is her Ladyship?'

'Old Wives.' Tales.' At fourteen years of age Louis was dismissive of superstition. 'I think it's daft talking to birds.'

'We could play animal, vegetable or mineral,' suggested Anna, but Louis was scornful.

'Mary can't spell.'

'She is two years younger than you, you little brat.'

The train pulled into Hailsham. A bitter cold wind blew along the platform, firethorns growing round the stationmaster's office were encrusted with snow. 'Good evening, Sir and Madam.'

The Browns, father and son, had come to meet their new neighbours at the station. Old Farmer Brown sprouted fine mutton chop whiskers, wore a hard brown hat for the occasion, a heavy top coat against the weather and a long woollen muffler wound around his neck and tied behind his back. Sam Brown's corduroy trousers were knotted with a piece of coarse string.

The old chap stretched out a hand to greet them all. 'The farm wagon's outside.'

The children had never been for a ride in the back of a cart, but they clambered aboard while Sam threw the luggage over the side. Crimson holly berries glowed in the light cast by the cart lamps.

'Hard winter ahead, God's feeding the birds.'

The slow old horse clip-clopped along the lanes, the sound of his iron hooves rang out in the frosty air. The reins lay slack on his back, he knew his way home.

Mary leaned against her father's shoulder and was fast asleep when they reached Bedlam Green on the way to Chilsham Farm.

The farm house was situated in a narrow lane leading to Bodle Street and the nearest dwelling of any consequence was half a mile away, but there were two cowmen's cottages alongside, one run-down farm on the opposite side of the road and Farmer Brown and his family lived across the fields.

'Our place is about a quarter of a mile from here as the crow flies.' The garden was surrounded by a tall yew hedge clipped in the strange shapes of animals and birds, a fat squirrel and a peacock displaying its tail in a spreading fan.

'I am sure those damn things are unlucky,' Anna whispered.

'It's lovely, father, look at the wooden bee hives in the orchard.' The moon was shining on a cluster of broken-down outbuildings and pig sties.

'I know you have bought Sliding Field, Chilsham Hop Garden Field, and twelve acres of the woodland. My Sam calls it Piggery Bottom down there. I can sell you an old sow if you've a mind to it, Mr Donelly.'

'Our first purchase should be a pony and trap in the cattle market this week.'

Farmer Brown drove his cart into the backyard, unlatched the half-door and opened it on to a homely scene. Sarah Brown came forward to greet them and bob a curtsey while three little girls stood shyly by the fire, each in a crisp gingham pinafore of a different colour: red, yellow and blue.

'Blessed is the man who hath his quiver full. That's what I always say, begging your pardon, ma'am. Sarah has given me three daughters: Mabel, Florence and Gertie, and a good son to take over when I feel the cold wind from the box. No man should ask for more.'

The long oak refectory table was laid for high tea and everyone was starving hungry.

Anna shook hands.

'Mrs Brown, you are very kind to welcome us like this. We are ravenous.' She took off her small fur toque, stole and gloves, and sat down beside her new neighbour, sighing. 'It has been a very long day and I am at the end of my tether.'

Louis nudged his sister under the table and whispered, 'Here comes the lady of the manor.'

John gave the slow lazy smile that could still charm the ducks off the water, and they began to eat after saying grace. Anna sat beside the fire toasting her hands and feet, and John read a short story to the children while Sarah cleared away and washed the crockery at the brown kitchen sink.

'I am always willing to oblige, Mrs Donelly, if you need any help in the house. The girls are almost off my hands, and you know we live close by. There is a short cut across your meadow.'

'You are a godsend, Mrs Brown, and I should be most grateful. We intend to breed pigs and keep a few cows and horses: I shall need time to help my husband on the land growing vegetables and flowers.'

Her hands were white and smooth unaccustomed to washing dishes, scrubbing a floor or grubbing in the earth, although she had learned to cook at the convent, high falutin' dishes like meringues, gateaux and souffles. Sarah agreed to work a few hours every week for a wage of five shillings.

Morning and evening Anna milked the cows, Flora and Daisy, pretending to be a dairymaid like Marie Antoinette at Le Petit Trianon. She planted vegetables and nourished them with night soil from the commodes. Louise had told her this was the custom among French peasants.

Mary and Louis were boarders, one at the Convent of the Holy Child, the other at Brighton College where he was an outstanding history student. Mama had told them so many stories over the years about life in Camden Place, the Empress Eugénie and the Prince Imperial Lou Lou.

Louis Donelly was a daredevil longing to emulate the young pretender's exploits: jumping over a campfire and falling into the flames, climbing out of a railway carriage window and riding into the next station on the roof of the train.

Perhaps some of it was hearsay, but they were wonderful tales of adventure. When he left college, young Donelly planned to join the Merchant Navy and see the world. He wasn't going to live in the back of beyond growing turnips, no sir!

Chapter Eighteen

'We owe the Browns money for cattle fodder and some old oak furniture. The school fees are overdue. I am driving the dogcart into Hailsham to call on the bank manager and ask him to extend our overdraft. Burrows has always tried to be very helpful, and of course he knows all about the trust fund from papa.'

'I am waiting for the sow to farrow then we can sell the piglets at market.'

'Mary wants to leave the convent. She is threatening to run away.' The girl was a dreamer. Anna understood Louis far better than her daughter, although he was a devious young rogue. 'That child has a voice like a nutmeg-grater. In the holidays she runs wild with the village boys. Why do you think I crop her hair and keep her in knickerbockers? I don't want her to be seduced by one of those clodhoppers.'

'Don't let your imagination run wild, Anna.'

'It could happen. She is far safer at the convent.'

Anna strode off down the garden path towards the stables, and they drove into Hailsham together. She kissed him on the cheek.

'I will meet you in The George for an early lunch if I can prise any money out of old Burrows, otherwise it will be bread- and cheese in The Crown with the farm labourers.'

The bank manager opened the door to his inner sanctum and ushered her into the 'holy of holies' reserved for important customers only, bowed unctuously and pulled out a chair.

Too much deference was ominous.

'Mrs Donelly, I regret to say that your account with us is overdrawn – not by a small amount unfortunately. Oh dear me no... perhaps one could say your overdraft is overdrawn.' He laughed at his own little joke, then came back to business. He rubbed his hands together, breathed sterterously and sucked a corner of his drooping grey moustache.

Uriah Heep. John had been reading David Copperfield aloud every evening after high tea.

'We should always be delighted to oblige you in any way, Mrs Donelly as long as the collateral is large enough – adequate. I should say. You have gone far and away beyond our little arrangement so this is not the case.' He smiled revealing bare pink gums above discoloured teeth, liking the sound of his own voice, sighing deeply as though he carried the weight of the world on his shoulders.

'I understand you are a tenant for life under the terms of a trust fund. Mr Brown has been a valued client for many years. He had a word with me about the current situation only the other day.'

She decided to take the bull by the horns. A little of the old arrogance might do the trick. 'Mr Burrows, I will not beat about the bush, you know full well that we have been farmers for over a year. We need money to pay the Brown, our grocery bill at the village shop in Herstmonceux and the school fees. A good education is expensive, as you may know; I am not raising country bumpkins.

The present situation is quite intolerable. We have a smallholding, and I think a man of your calibre should understand the situation.'

He was taken aback by her direct approach.

'My father, the late Jacques Van Maaskens, used your bank for many years, but it may be time for me to take my overdraft elsewhere. Your head office might consider this unfortunate in view of my expectations.' She rose to leave the office.

'My dear Mrs Donelly, pray be seated. Let us not be hasty. I am sure we can come to an arrangement.' She had won a brief respite in her battle for liquid assets. After agreeing to pledge more of their future income, she emerged from the bank with gold sovereigns in her reticule and a promise of more to come after he had been in touch with his head office to check the details of her inheritance.

The George was crowded with farmers who had come into town for the weekly cattle market. She passed the public bar, reeking of beer and tobacco, and found her husband waiting at a corner table in the saloon. 'We can afford luncheon and a good bottle of wine by courtesy of the bank.'

She opened her handbag and rattled the gold coins under his nose. 'Five pounds for you to spend at the sale, and the bills and the school fees. There might even be something left over for a rainy day.'

The landlord served luncheon in the coffee room. Today it was roast saddle of mutton followed by trifle and ratafia biscuits. He sent the pot boy scurrying to the cellar to fetch a bottle of the best wine for the gentry.

Anna left John to his own devices and walked down the High Street gazing at the shop windows gay with holly and mistletoe. Gas jets were burning on this dull winter's day. Plump pheasants and capons, preserved fruits, dates and puddings and mincemeat were a great temptation, but she passed by unscathed till she reached Charlie Kerridge's antique shop near The Crown. A miniature of the young Eugénie lay on a dark blue velvet cushion in the middle of his window display. The entwined N and E glittered in small brilliant sapphires. A handwritten card read:

Until recently the property of Her Imperial Highness, the Dowager Empress of France, now residing at Farnborough Hill, a gift to one of her household.

Without a moment's hesitation Anna lifted the latch on the shop door and entered. 'How much are you asking for the miniature, Mr Kerridge?'

'An elderly servant brought it into the shop. I gather he had fallen on hard times. Fifty guineas, Madame, but I could ease the price a little as I know there are connections, if I may say so.'

Anna left Kerridge's with a sadly depleted purse and a portrait of her beloved empress for old times sake. The bills could wait a while longer.

John ambled down the drive to collect the mail, expecting letters from Declan and Maureen but the post box was empty save for one long official-looking envelope addressed to Mr and Mrs John Eugene Louis Donelly.

He stuffed it in the pocket of his old tweed jacket deciding to open it with Anna at the breakfast table. A cup of strong tea to boost his courage and he slit the envelope. Due to non-payment of outstanding debts in spite of repeated applications, urgent steps would be taken to recover the total amount due forthwith. Bailiffs of the court would distrain on their goods and chattels, seizing articles to the full value of the debt incurred. The Donellys would be allowed to retain beds, a table, chairs and the tools of their trade. He handed the letter to his wife to avoid reading it aloud in the presence of the two children but she exploded.

'Merde! This is sheer madness. People know we always pay in the long run. We owe Brown a paltry few guineas. Sarah has not been to do the housework for weeks but she never comes nigh nor by when we are in debt.' John shook his head.

'Chilsham is mortgaged to the hilt. This notice says the bailiffs arrive today. The notice must have been delayed over Christmas.'

The two children were listening open-mouthed.

'John, I have an idea.'

'Jesus, Mary and Joseph, not again! We shall end our lives in a debtor's prison.'

'We need a brief respite till I can borrow from the trust or Uncle André. The bailiffs cannot distrain on fixtures and fittings so we remove all small articles and nail everything else to the floorboards or the beams.'

'That is great, mama!' Louis was excited, it was an adventure. 'Strike while the iron's hot. It is almost eight o'clock. Old Widow Jefferson will turn a blind eye to anything hidden in her outbuildings. Colonel blood and guts opposite is as deaf as a post. He will not hear a sound if we drive our animals into his empty cowsheds.'

Anna fetched a hammer and nails while Louis and Mary collected the china and glass. 'We may need some strong fish glue from the tool shed. Damn the bum bailiffs. We shall beat them at their own game.' She began to move a heavy mule chest closer to the wall, pushing and shoving it an inch at a time. 'Help me, John, help me.' They drove crooked nails across the feet and into the beams on the wall behind.

The children were yelling at the cows, urging them across the road and through Colonel Armstrong's gates with blood-curdling screams.

'Bedlam is on the other road.' John pitch-forked some fresh straw on the hot cowpats in the yard to hide the evidence. 'Conscience doth make cowards of us all. This effort is far too devious for me.'

A brown harvest jug crashed to the ground. 'Don't tell mater.' Louis kicked the broken shards under a pigsty. 'Here, catch!' and a shooting stick came hurtling through the air nearly piercing his sister's hand. 'Stuff it at the back of the widow's barn.'

Anna came out of the house with a Sèvres bowl wrapped in a pudding cloth. 'Don't forget I am putting this on a shelf in the hen house.'

John was nailing a Welsh dresser to the floorboards and gluing the feet. 'Not too fast, Louis, use the step ladder and hand everything to Mary over the fence. It's not a coconut shy at the fair. Hide the china under straw in case the men pay a visit to our neighbours.'

'My horns, mother, don't let the bailiffs take my horns!' The deer's antlers were Louis' pride and joy ever since he bought them for a shilling in Hailsham market and carried them home perched on the saddle of his rusty old bike. They were hanging in a place of honour beside the kitchen door.

'Don't worry, Louis, fetch some old newspapers and the plaster of Paris from the potting shed. Your horns will be solid as a rock, and they would need a pickaxe to remove them from the wall. I believe these men are forced to make good any damage caused in the execution of their duties.' Every piece of furniture in the house was rigid, nailed to the floor or the old oak beams striping the walls. 'We are ready for them now. I suppose they could be here at any minute.'

'Mary and I will keep cave in the lane.'

The children streaked off down the drive and crouched behind the hedgerow, ducking up and down at the sound of a bicycle or passing villager. About an hour later, hoof beats clattered down the lane and they saw a horse and cart and two men sitting up front like Tweedledum and Tweedledee.

'The bum bailiffs are coming. Run and tell mother.'

Mary scuttled off to warn her parents, while Louis ran to open the gate. 'We are looking for the Chilsham farmhouse, sonnie.'

'Good morning, sirs. If you are calling on my mother, Mrs Donelly, I think you will find her in the kitchen. Pray come round the back of the house.'

One of the men tethered the horse to a post in the silent, empty farmyard and cocked an eyebrow as they passed the deserted cow shed and hen houses.

Anna lifted the iron latch wiping her hands on one of Sarah Brown's long white aprons. 'You are welcome to share our poor meal, gentlemen, if you wish. As you can see, we have fallen on hard times.'

She gestured towards an iron cauldron of thick gruel bubbling on the range and a glutinous mess in a blue enamel saucepan. Anna had been stirring the pigswill and there was a strong smell of charred meat and cabbage.

The bailiffs showed their distress warrant and began to inspect the goods and chattels. 'That big bacon cupboard should fetch a bob or two, c'mon, heave ho!' They tried in vain to lift it from the floor. 'To me, to you.'

'There are many fixtures and fittings in the house and I would not relish any damage to them.' Anna smiled very sweetly. 'I understand it is possible to claim compensation in certain circumstances, is it not? That of course that would never do. Would you care for a glass of cider, gentlemen? Made from our own apples in the orchard in happier days.'

Louis choked knowing that his mother had bought a flagon in Herstmonceux village the week before.

'Scrumpy? Thank you, Ma'am.' He turned to his mate. 'Looks as if we shall leave here empty-handed.'

He winked at the mistress of the house. 'Some of those nails in the furniture legs do look powerful new, but who am I to say? I've never come across anything like this before, but they say there's always a first time for everything. Do you have a little hay for the horse, lady?'

Louis pitch-forked some into the yard revealing a fresh brown cowpat on the barn floor underneath, but covered it quickly with a shovel.

'Goodbye, and a very happy and prosperous New Year to you all.'

The bailiff shook his head as they drove off towards Bodle Street. 'What a woman, what a woman. I suppose she thinks she pulled the wool over my eyes.'

*

John sold his litter of piglets and the old sow for a fair price and Anna borrowed money from Uncle André to pay the bills.

'We will give a party for the village children.'

Sarah was back at work, so she scrubbed the quarry tiles in the kitchen and scoured the copper pots and pans with salt and lemon juice. The weather was fine. They spread large checked tablecloths on the grass and brought out Windsor chairs for the comfort of the grown-ups.

Kate and Fred brought little Annie from Brighton for the day. The three Brown girls were the first to arrive escorted by Charlie Kerridge, the antique dealer's son who was sweet on Mary and tried to bribe Louis with a sixpence to 'be left alone and show her my rabbits'. The cowmen's daughters wore their best Sunday frocks with wide sashes and bows. The sons' hair was parted in the middle and slicked down with pump water.

Louis took one look at the motley crew and quoted the white rabbit in *Alice in Wonderland* on his way to the party: 'Oh, my paws and whiskers.'

Farmer Brown stayed for the victuals, giving Louis a pocket knife with eight blades and an instrument for removing stones from horses' hooves. 'That Sarah has got the biggest pair of hobbledy-gobs I've ever seen,' whispered Kate to Fred.

Young Annie, wearing a bright cotton sun bonnet, sat on the grass making daisy chains, and got a clip on the ear from ma when she ate the flowers.

Sarah brought out crusty loaves, a wedge of cheese and a fruit cake crammed with cherries, peel and sultanas and laced with Anna's Napoleon brandy.

Louis had stolen some of the scrumpy, and kept a gallon jug hidden behind the earth closet for some of his cronies. The younger children played kiss in the ring and postman's knock for forfeits, but Louis suggested the Zulu Wars for those of his own age.

They tracked each other through the undergrowth at the back of the house with assegais torn from the trees. He captured Mary in the terrain of the dark continent and flung quicklime in her face, but she screamed in pain so he ducked her head in the water butt. Sarah came to the rescue and dowsed the child with flour but she was scarlet for the rest of the afternoon. Peace was declared, but a black pig was squealing after being 'stuck' as an enemy Zulu. Tired but happy, the families piled into their carts or set off on Shank's pony through the country lanes leaving Kate and Sarah to wash the towering piles of dirty crockery while Anna sat at her ease on the greensward.

The silence was broken by a 'Hullo-o-o' and the dusty figure of Stephen made an entrance up the garden path. Anna fetched a bottle of wine from the house and they sat on a mossy bank near the pond waiting for John to return after a long day at the market sale.

Stephen had decided to pay them a flying visit after the first night of his play Herod, a tragedy in the grand manner presented by Beerbohm Tree at Her Majesty's Theatre.

His feet ached after walking from the High Street to the farmhouse past The Brewers' Arms and Bedlam, right at the crossroads and down a long muddy lane.

These days there was an armed truce between them. They drank together in the twilight, a frog croaked in the shallow water, the bottle rested between them on an old wooden tray.

'We foiled the bailiff's men by nailing all the furniture to the floorboards, but John did *not* approve.'

'I could lend you money now if he would agree.'

'You know my husband is far too proud to accept charity from anyone.'

'It would be a helping hand, nothing more. John is a bright thread in the tapestry of my life. I think he might have had a glittering career in London as an academic or a writer.'

'We shall never see eye to eye Stephen. I loathe the idea of John wasting his life at a desk.'

'We are ships that pass in the night, Anna: a yacht with pure white sails and a battered man at war, all guns blazing.'

It was easy to talk in the gathering dusk.

'I am sure you are... fond of your husband, Anna. My love for John is Platonic. You must never be jealous of our comradeship.'

She blushed. 'I think I can understand your friendship at last.'

'Father was precentor at Peterborough Cathedral. I think so much godliness had an adverse affect on my character. I prefer the company of rogues and vagabonds as a rule.'

The wooden gate slammed behind John as he trudged along the garden path in his heavy boots clogged with clay.

'A glass of your own madeira, my good fellow. Anna and I are celebrating our better acquaintance,' and he kissed her fingertips. 'You have not been to visit us for ages, Stephen. I thought we were ostracised.

'The heavy burden of work, dear boy, believe it or not. I bought a cold bird in your village shop and some ham off the bone so Anna does not need to slave over a hot range tonight. Let us drink to my new play *Paolo and Francesca* and all the star-crossed lovers in the world.'

*

Sussex folk celebrated the turn of the century with fireworks and beacons on the Downs, and flaming tar barrels rolling down the School Hill in Lewes. The old Queen might yet reach her span of a hundred years.

'La vie champêtre is idyllic in novels by Rousseau, but in reality it is bloody hard work.' Anna sat bolt upright in bed and exploded. 'I am sick to death of living in the wilds on a farm at the back of beyond. I shall run mad unless we leave this place.'

'Again and again and again. Every time we move to a smaller house and there is less money to pay the bills. I have no wish to be a gentleman farmer; it was one of your high falutin' ideas. I intend to regain my independence and provide for my family. The worm turns at last. I am sick of being the consort.'

'Dear John, I know your salary at Somerset House would seem a fortune to us now.'

'I am too old to begin again as a civil servant, Anna. My own needs are few: time to spend with those I love, peace and quiet for meditation, money to buy books, food, a bottle of wine and a roof over our heads.'

She shrugged. 'Beggars can't be choosers. What shall we do now, lord and master.'

'An old scholar from St Edmunds College offered me work as an insurance broker if I would rent an office in Brighton. Perhaps we could live "over the shop"?'

He knew that Anna might be too arrogant to entertain the idea. 'I love Brighton. We could find a small place near the sea. My golden girl.'

Anna's corn-silk hair had faded to pale blonde, for she was thirty-eight years old. He kissed her gently on the lips. 'The danger of childbearing is over. Let us share a bed again for warmth and comfort and a little tenderness.'

'Give me a little more time John. I am not sure how I feel.'

The new house was situated in Middle Street close to the Hippodrome Theatre on the corner of an alleyway, with a small courtyard at the rear.

'Kate's cottage is only five minute's walk away, and she will always be there if I need her.'

John's office would be in the downstairs front rooms and the square hall was large enough to seat any waiting clients.

'What are you calling the house, father? Dun Roamin' or Mea Culpa?'

Anna cuffed her son round the ears, and he winced at the unexpected blow.

'Sorry Mater, that was in rather poor taste.'

'I suggest The Laurels, for there are two sooty little shrubs in the backyard.' She went out into the kitchen slamming the door behind her, trying to hide her tears.

John sighed. 'Life with your mother will never be peaceful, my boy. One can only look forward to eternity.'

*

Alexander was urging Philips to finish the tragedy he had commissioned for the St James's Theatre, so the playwright was burning the midnight oil in London. He wrote to invite his friends to the first night on 6 March 1902.

> *My Dears,*
>
> *It will be either a triumph or a disaster. Who knows? I may be forced to tour the provinces again or join a fit-up company in the wilds of Ireland, a fate worse than death.*
>
> *I am asking you both to join me. There will be a reception after the play and I have booked you a room at the Cavendish Hotel in Jermyn Street at my expense. This new establishment will soon rival Walsingham House and The Savoy.*
>
> *Please accept this small offer of hospitality, I cannot survive without your presence John to give me moral courage.*
>
> *Poverty has forced me to complete this story of the phantom lovers at last. Heaven protect me from the critics, although William Archer compared me with Milton after the production of Herod. He has a great admiration for George Bernard Shaw and Henrik Ibsen so I am surprised the man has a fancy for blank verse.*
>
> *Henry Ainley, 'the most beautiful young man in London' is to play Paolo. I am disintegrating, but I know that I will see you both at the theatre on the night. Do not desert me by all that we hold dear.*
>
> *Your loving friend,*
> *Stephen*

Anna bought a new gown of dark blue velvet sewn with paillettes to celebrate the occasion after visiting the pawnbroker with a few ornaments from the house.

A cavalcade of carriages and hansom cabs made its way up the Haymarket carrying theatre-goers to this fashionable first night. A heavy mist shrouded the passers-by but a few 'ladies of the town', painted and bedizened, plied their trade in Piccadilly.

A giant figure of a woman bearing a torch aloft, illumined the staircase leading to the auditorium. Stephen was waiting in the foyer and kissed them on both cheeks.

★

A crescendo of sound like a gathering swarm of bees spread from the pavement into the foyer and auditorium. The playwright was almost at the end of his tether after drinking heavily throughout rehearsals. His hands trembled and a slight nervous tic was apparent at the corner of one eye.

Paolo and Francesca, those phantom creatures of his imagination were leading him to the brink of success or despair.

'Come and drink in the Green Room. The curtain goes up in half an hour.' He clasped John's hands. 'I could not survive this evening without you to give me strength. I am terrified of failure. Elgar is here for my opening night and so is Laurence. You remember our book of poems *Primavera*?'

He added in a low whisper, 'Pray for me, John.'

The first bell rang for the audience to be seated, while the orchestra played a haunting overture.

'Our stage box is by courtesy of the management.'

A dowager bore down on him like a galleon in full sail. 'My dear Mr Phillips, we are all awaiting your new tragedy in fear and trepidation. Herod was magnificent! Arrivederci!' and she sped away to join two jeune filles à marier and their escorts.

'The duchess is an outrageous lion hunter, but kind at heart and she keeps one of the best tables in the West End. One entertains in order to eat. It is a boon for hungry artists, and a stone's throw away from my lodgings.'

'Mr Phillips, do you remember me? I was your fag at Oundle School.'

The eager young man was brushed aside by the crowd.

'Good evening, Phillips, was it Archer who hailed you as the new Shakespeare? I always thought his tribute a little fulsome.'

'Tonight the vultures gather to pick the bones white. The Marlborough set is in evidence, and I understand Shaw is somewhere in the audience. Max Beerbohm was kind to Herod, but of course it was in the family – Beerbohm Tree is his half-brother. Odious man.'

Stephen took Anna by the elbow and ushered her through the crowd. 'John, for God's sake let us get out of this crush. I have not eaten for days and the heat is overwhelming. Come, we shall soon know my fate. The public is a fickle jade.'

A call boy plucked at his sleeve. 'Please, sir, Mr Ainley would like to see you in his dressing room: it's about his speech in the last act.'

'Tell Mr Ainley I am very tired and a little drunk, so he may stand on his head in the death scene if it pleases him.'

They reached the box at last. Anna glanced at her programme. 'The scene is Florence in the Middle Ages.'

Stephen looked green under the house lights.

The Duchess raised her opera glasses, quizzed the audience and bowed to her new lion, Mr Phillips.

The painted safety curtain rose to a hushed audience. Red and gold velvet parted to reveal the opening scene, the Malatesta Palace leading Francesca into the golden sunlight.

A latecomer disturbed an entire row. A man coughed, feet shuffled and the play began.

The footlights cast strange shadows on a story of passion and murder. The poet's work enchanted the audience, and by the first interval everyone knew that Stephen Phillips was the darling of polite society. He was called on stage after the final curtain with cries of 'Author, Author!' to receive a standing ovation, and was bereft of words for once in his life.

George Alexander and the company, toasted him in champagne again and again, then a cab took John, Anna and Stephen round the corner to The Cavendish.

Stephen was exhausted and maudlin. 'My dear John, you were the only one to believe in me. I shall remember that as long as I live.'

'A crying jag, sir,' murmured the night porter as he helped the playwright to his rooms on the first floor.

The following morning Stephen was dead to the world, so they caught an early train to Brighton to relieve Kate from her chaperonage of the young people.

Louis was furious that he had missed such a grand occasion. 'Next time it will be our turn, Mary, and we shall not take the parents with us. Just you wait and see, my dear mamma.'

Royalties from the play provided Stephen with a subsistence allowance for years, and he could afford to visit Brighton as often as he pleased, staying in his old theatrical lodgings. He was still drinking heavily. John and Stephen roamed the streets for hours arm in arm, after a night on the tiles. A strangely ill-assorted couple, one in a voluminous cloak and a broad brimmed hat, the other in threadbare tweeds searching for his door key with a monocle.

Stephen confided his latest plot to John after a few pots of ale in The Cricketers. 'It will be an epic drama about Nero and Ancient Rome, and dear old Laurence wants poems for a new review, but I lack inspiration.'

Chapter Nineteen

Louis had spread an old copy of *The Times* across the scrubbed kitchen table, and was polishing his one and only pair of black shoes till they shone like a mirror. 'I'm going to see the show at the Hippodrome tonight, second house. It was a circus for years, but now they have some of the top acts from London.'

'Louis, please take me with you, I've never been to a music hall.'

'Don't be daft, girl. You can't go up in the 'gods', it's only fellows and a few tarts.'

'You know I can always pass as a boy. No one will ever guess.'

'Alright,' Louis grinned. 'Pin those long golden tresses on top of your head and make sure they don't fall down in the middle of the performance.'

'How can we get out of the house without being seen? You know the parents lock up and retire for the night about eight o'clock.'

'Don't worry, big brother has everything under control. I took a wax impression of the back door key and bought a duplicate from the ironmongers, so now I'm free to roam the streets at any time of the day or night. The curtain goes up at eight, but it's a long haul to the gallery, and we shall have to queue. See you about 7.45 p.m. I'll leave some of my old clobber in your bedroom so you can have a dress rehearsal.' Louis strolled away.

Mary was far too excited to eat her high tea. She borrowed one of her father's tweed caps from the hallstand, bolted upstairs, coiled a plait of hair on top of her head and fixed it firmly in place with thick hairpins filched from mama's dressing table drawer. Louis had left a pile of his castoffs under her bed, including a shirt, trousers and a Norfolk jacket.

His figure was long and slim while Mary was short and rounded. She pulled on the trousers, and the crutch was almost down to her knees, so she rolled them over and cinched the waist with a leather belt and safety pins. The fly buttons were a problem. She had forgotten that everything would be back to front, the boy's way. She looked at her reflection in the mirror. At fifteen she seemed to stick out in all the wrong places. Rummaging through Anna's underwear she found a bust bodice, a long strip of linen with tapes sewn on the ends, and lashed herself together with this. She could scarcely breathe, but at least she was as flat as a board. Thrusting her hands into the trouser pockets she found a dog-end, and cramming the large cap on her head, set out to find her brother. Mary knocked and Louis opened the bedroom door to be confronted by an apparition with an unlit fag dangling from the side of its mouth.

'Bet you can't smoke it without being sick. You look a scruff, Mary, but you could pass for a young bloke out on the town. Come on or we shall miss the first turn.'

The key creaked in the lock, and they crept out of the back door, across the yard and into the alley beside the house then sprinted the last few yards up Middle Street to the Hippodrome Theatre. Garish pictures announced the star turns appearing that week. People were milling around the front of the house. Louis made for the gallery doors and, after queuing for a few minutes, handed over a few coppers at the box office, and they began to climb a steep flight of stairs past the dress circle and the upper circle to the 'gods'.

Mary was breathless and clutching her trousers to stop them falling around her ankles. The house lights were still on when they found seats on a hard wooden bench.

'Hello, Bessie, this is my kid brother, Marius.'

'Pleased to meet you, I'm sure. You're the spittin' image of Louis only smaller. Here, budge up a bit then I can sit in the middle – a rose between two thorns.' She giggled.

They were lucky to have found places in the front row.

'I met your brother on the pier when he was out skylarking with some of his pals.'

A whiff of cheap scent tickled Mary's nostrils and she sneezed. 'Bless you!'

The orchestra was playing a selection from *The Merry Widow*. The musical director received a polite round of applause then the music changed to a rumty tumty tum, and the curtain rose on the first act: A red-nosed comedian, a long-boot dancer, a row of chorus girls decked in lace and spangles, tunics and tights and thigh boots.

Madame Fifi's troupe of French poodles walked on their hind legs and jumped through paper hoops. Mary's favourite rode a unicycle. The top of the bill was a woman who brought the house down with her risqué songs. At one moment during the show she felt Bessie's hand on her knee, but brushed it aside and leaned forward to watch the motley audience. In the interval they nibbled chocolates, and Bessie rolled her eyes at Louis. Mary was the only fellow in the 'gods' wearing a cap.

'It's ever so hot up here. Why doesn't young Marius take his cap off?'

Louis whispered in her ear. 'The poor kid's got alopaecia you know, the hair falls out in tufts and you get bald patches. Don't say anything, he gets very upset, but it's not catching like ringworm.'

They stood on the pavement after the curtain fell. 'Let's walk home with Marius in case he gets led astray, then I'll take you back to Oriental Place, Bessie.' He gave Mary the key. 'Leave the door on the latch, and I'll see you in the morning.'

She crept into the back kitchen. There was still a glow from the kitchen range. She picked up the poker to rake the coals, turned and saw her father sitting very quietly by the table drinking a cup of tea.

'I am glad you have come home at last. I have been waiting up for you.' His voice was low and gentle. 'Where have you been at this time of night?'

'Louis took me up in the 'gods' at the Hippodrome, father.' Thank God, this was a harmless escapade he could understand.

'You look like a scarecrow.'

Mary took off the enormous cap and scratched her head loosening the hairpins. Her long fair hair fell almost to her waist.

'Poor little ragamuffin... Come here.' He held her close to his heart for a moment. 'My darling girl, I would kill anyone who harmed you.'

'Louis took care of me. He said the gallery was too rough for a girl so I borrowed his old clothes, but Bessie wore a blouse and skirt. It was a wonderful show, father. We should go together one day. Mama would enjoy the dog act.'

'Bessie. Where is your brother now?'

Mary had been dreading this question. She did not want to split on Louis, but she was too naive to lie. 'He walked home with Bessie as it was getting late.'

John kissed his innocent young daughter. 'Go to bed now. We will not tell your mother about this adventure; she is sure to make a scene. Goodnight, God bless.'

Louis came home at one o'clock in the morning to be greeted by his father waiting patiently by candlelight. He tried to brazen it out. 'I went for a moonlight walk along the prom with a few of the boys from college. We forgot the time.' He was floundering.

'Do your friends wear cheap scent and face powder?' John brushed some white dust from his son's lapel. 'Sit down Louis and do not insult my intelligence.'

'If you must know I walked a girl home and she asked me in for a drink. Is there anything wrong with that?'

A long pause followed the insolence.

'Don't preach to me, father. I know you haven't slept with a woman for years, not even mother. You have separate bedrooms.'

John slapped him across the face with the back of his hand. 'Say that again and I'll leather you.'

'I'm sorry, that was unforgivable, but life is not black and white, father, there are shades of grey. Should I remain a cock virgin, live as a celibate priest or indulge in 'the love that dare not speak its name'? No one talks about the sins of the flesh in this age of hypocrisy. Tell me the answer.'

'You could be riddled with syphilis after one night with a prostitute.'

'I shall risk lying with Bessie and other girls and feel their warm rounded breasts and thighs.'

John wondered if he should thrash the boy or lecture him. The moment of decision was lost.

'Poor father, shall we forget all about sleeping with men, women and pigs? Have you read the *Marquis de Sade*? He had some very strange ideas. At the moment I could murder a cup of tea.'

John smiled, and it took twenty years off his age. 'Sit down at the kitchen table, boy, and I will put the kettle on the hob. Perhaps you should talk to Father O' Shaughnessy on Sunday.' He tipped a dram of whisky into each cup.

'I think my greatest danger is the Irish sickness – fancying a drop of the hard stuff.'

'At least I shall not end my life as a lonely wizened old man playing with myself under the bedclothes. 'For this relief much thanks!'

The boy was incorrigible.

'Pax, father?'

'I shall be leaving home in a few months anyway. I've applied to join the Merchant Navy.' He reached out to his father and smiled. 'I really am sorry to shock you, Dad. Tonight was the first time.' They clasped hands across the table.

'You are right, it is a terrible pong. God, I'm tired.' Louis turned back when he reached the foot of the stairs. 'We read Swinburne at College, long erotic poems, and I dreamed of lying naked with a beautiful woman, but I think Bessie drops her drawers to anyone for a tanner.'

He met Mary on her way to the bathroom the following morning. 'Did you enjoy your nightcap with Bessie?

'Stop being so bloody naive, little sister. I got into trouble with the old man and endured the full catechism.' Later he made for the nearest pub on the sea front to celebrate the loss of his virginity with a double Scotch.

*

Mary collected lame ducks: a baby hedgehog to be fed with raw eggs and cat's meat, a thrush with a broken leg she tied to a matchstick as a makeshift splint, and Tibby a jet-black kitten retrieved from beneath an area grating. Gyp the Airedale was a birthday present from her father: pure pedigree with a head shaped like a brick.

There were many beaux: Alfred a poetic sentimental bank clerk who taught her the language of flowers; Charlie O' Byrne a wild Irish boy who ran off to join the navy when she refused him; and Giuseppe, a waiter from the Café Royal who serenaded her with Neapolitan love songs beneath the bedroom window.

'I want our daughter to make a good marriage, but there are no suitable young men to be found in Café The Mikado, and your friend Julien must be over forty.'

John ignored her. He was engrossed in a book by Purcell about Cardinal Manning. 'Listen to this extract... I think Thomas Doyle was a distant relative. You know I was baptised in the Cathedral at Southwark in 1855. "The funds for the erection of the Catholic Cathedral in London were collected by Father Thomas Doyle, head priest of a little chapel in the London Road and afterwards canon and provost of St George's Cathedral, Southwark." It goes on to say that during the outbreak of cholera in London in 1833 he administered the last sacraments to the dying and lifted the bodies of the dead, Catholic and Protestant alike, into coffins or carts. He travelled throughout Germany and Austria and received large donations from the King of Bavaria and the Emperor of Austria towards the cathedral. I think he might be an uncle. I must ask Declan. I know the Doyles and Donellys living in Southwark intermarried.'

Chapter Twenty

André wrote from Brussels in the spring of 1908 asking his great-niece, Mary, to spend a long holiday with him in the Avenue Louise.

I am sure you are lonely now that Louis has joined the Service and it would give me great pleasure to entertain you with a visit to Bruges, nights at the opera, perhaps a little flutter at the casino in Ostend. Your reputation will be safe with such an elderly relative, and Mademoiselle Ernestine Dupont acting as housekeeper and chaperone. I can assure you the lady is as incorruptible as Robespierre! Remind your father that travel broadens the mind.

The invitation was accepted in spite of John's reservations. André was a very wealthy, ageing bachelor and Anna thought it would be improvident to refuse. The ladies agreed to dine at Claridge's on the eve of departure.

'Her wardrobe is deplorable, John.'

Her husband provided the wherewithal for a new day and evening gown, fripperies and fol de rols, and two first class tickets to Victoria.

André waited with a glass of cognac on the table beside him. He cut a very distinguished figure at seventy years of age, with his iron grey beard and sidewhiskers. His dearest wish was to adopt Mary. He was tired of living alone waited on by a housekeeper.

Anna had frittered away her inheritance and her charming Irish husband would never be a worldly success.

André appreciated the quiet luxury of this elegant suite once occupied by Napoleon and Eugénie. His own dearest possessions were his library, a collection of fine antiques and his lovely house. He still had a vivid memory of the days when he pushed a handcart round the back streets of Brussels collecting scrap metal and old rags for his father. One day when he was eleven years old some rich kids spat in his face, it was anexperience he would remember always.

Anna was late as usual. When they arrived he rose to greet his guests, kissing Mary on both cheeks. The girl was shy and so was he, under the urbane veneer. He intended to leave her his entire fortune: the House of Van Maaskens could be directed by a woman now that he had diversified from scrap metal to fine arts.

The servant took the ladies' cloaks, and Mary sat beside her great-uncle on a low stool. Her gown was simple and inexpensive but becoming. 'Well, my dear Anna, it seems a long while since we met. How is your good husband?'

'Fatigued with the day-to-day business of making a living.' This was not the bland reply he had expected.

They dined well, and Mary retired early to rest before the journey. 'You know that I have travelled to England with an express purpose, my dear?'

'I think you want to adopt our daughter, uncle André, but I am sure my husband would never agree – he is devoted to the child. I expect her to make a good marriage on her return from Brussels.'

He shrugged impatiently.

'Le folies de grandeur. Let us be honest with one another. Your husband is an impoverished gentleman struggling to earn a living in the back streets of Brighton. Your daughter cannot be presented at court because you do not have a penny to bless yourself. There are many beautiful American heiresses on the marriage market hoping to catch an English lord. I suggest we discuss the affair in six months and if Mary agrees, I will leave her my entire estate, you understand.'

'You cannot expect me to barter, uncle.'

Anna's lips were set in a fine line.

'I understand Mary left the convent at fifteen, but she will soon learn the social graces.'

'The considered opinion of a scrap merchant or a connoisseur of the arts?' He smiled wryly at the deliberate insult, and Anna raised her glass in a toast.

'To the Van Maaskens and the Donellys... Long may they survive and flourish against all the odds. God bless them all!' She tossed the wine glass over her shoulder into the fireplace where it shattered into a myriad pieces of crystal.

Mary wrote to the family every week.

> *My Dear Father,*
> *We landed safely after a very rough crossing, and you can imagine my amazement as the train steamed into Brussels' Midi Station to see a giant painting on the side of a house: André Van Maaskens – Scrap Metal Merchant! I am ashamed to admit that I was a little embarrassed by the sheer enormity of this advertisement; it seemed a little vulgar.*
> *I picked up the courage to mention it to Dé-Dé at the dinner table but he only shrugged and said 'Les Affaires. It was a long time ago and it achieved results.'*
> *I am looking forward to this holiday in Belgium, but I will not stay... not even to live a life of luxury as uncle André's adopted granddaughter. I want to be in England with you and mama and Louis. I know we never talk about money but I do understand the situation. I am determined to find work when I return: maybe selling flowers, with an antiquary, or in a kennel caring for small animals.*
> *Here in Brussels people seem to talk a great deal about the Jews, the Kaiser and the Entente Cordiale, and there is a strange feeling of unrest. I do not understand the conversation very well because it is usually in French or Flemish, and you know I was never good at languages when I was at the Convent of the Holy Child. This is a dull letter, but I will write again in a few days. All my love, and a kiss for mama and Louis, the sailor home from the sea.*
> *Your devoted daughter,*
> *Mary*

> *Dear Louis,*
> *What devilment are you engaged in at the moment? My own life is pure as the driven snow. I am spending a wonderful holiday with Dé-Dé (he says he feels old if I call him uncle André, but he must be seventy years of age if he's a day).*

I am acquiring a new wardrobe from the finest salons, visiting the Opera and the Plage at Ostend. You will not recognise your little sister when she returns to her native land, a young lady of quality educated on the continent! We might even aspire to stalls at the Hippodrome when you are on shore leave.

Take care, Louis. Be good. God bless.
I miss you all desperately,
Mary

Dear Kate,

We are staying in a beautiful white hotel beside the sea at a place with a very funny name – Knokke-le-Zoute. The old women make lace in the streets of Brussels, and you would love the mannekin pisse – a little boy fountain who does a wee-wee all day long.

Take great care of the family until I come home in September or October.

Best wishes to you, Fred and Annie, Gyp, Daisy and the cat.
Mary D

Dear Mama,

I will answer the burning question once and for all. I will not spend the rest of my life in Brussels with Dé-Dé, although he is a darling man. Mademoiselle Dupont has been very kind to me, but I am sure she would resent another female in the household after so many years. I would not stay here for all the tea in China. I want to live at home until I marry a chimney sweep or a road sweeper for love.

Julien, father's friend from Lyons, came to visit us and was most attentive, but he is rich and old and very, very dull. I met a young artist in the gallery who is 'trés sympa' but do not worry, dear mama, I have not lost my heart. I shall be home in a few weeks to plague you.
Your loving daughter,
Mary

After a lapse of two months she received an epistle from her brother.

My dear little sister,

I rejoin my ship in September when doubtless you will still be cavorting around the continent. I find the uniform has a devastating effect on young ladies although Dorothy has left me for another.

The father is still beavering away to no avail. Mother had letters from three old school friends, and she was over the moon for a while. I suppose they find this little house oppressive after Marine Parade and the farm at Herstmonceux.

Jo your pet rabbit is poorly, but I stuff him with lettuce leaves and he sleeps for hours. I suspect he is pining for you like the rest of us.

All good wishes from one fortune hunter to another.
Your loving brother,
Louis

There were a few letters from her father concerned for her welfare.

My dear Babs,

Try to be patient and study while you are in Brussels, remember your schooling at the convents was all too brief.

I am sending you some pocket money, five shillings in a postal order to be collected as from J L E Donelly. Next week I will forward extra money for milk which is essential for your health. You know the doctor thought the gland in your neck might be tubercular.

Your mother and I went to Worthing on the motor bus yesterday, and it was a very pleasant afternoon.

Do write to your brother. He is somewhere off the coast of New Zealand at the moment on the way to Australia. I will enclose the address later.

All my love. Try to be good, my darling girl.
Your devoted father

His last letter remonstrated with her.

André writes to tell me that you are staying with him in Belgium, then I receive a telegram to say that you are leaving at the end of the week. It is all most confusing. I have sent a postal order for the fares and a wire to let you know the time of arrival. If this is insufficient I am sure you will be able to borrow the balance from André or Mademoiselle Dupont.

The boat trip from Ostend to Dover costs eleven francs, but I am not sure about the train. Your mother will meet you at Dover, so remain at the point of debarkation. I shall be very happy when you return safe and hope you have learned something from your visit.

All my love,
Father (Drink your milk.)

They were sitting tête-à-tête after dinner with the curtains drawn against the night air, when André decided to plead his case. 'You do not understand why I want to adopt you as my granddaughter, Marie. It is not the whim of an old man trying to recapture his lost youth. Listen, and I will tell you a story.

I fell in love when I was nineteen years of age. Because I am a bachelor many people think Dé-Dé is a secret roué or a pédé... what do you call a gentleman of the green carnation in England?' He flicked the fingers of his right hand in the sir like a puff of smoke disappearing in the breeze. 'A Pouf! They suggest I like süsse knabe – sweet boys, yes?'

He chuckled and his accent became stronger as he told her the story of his love affair. 'Remember, I was a rag-and-bone man at eleven years of age. A very poor little boy with no arse to my trousers. The Revolution in Belgium was over at last.

Every Sunday after Mass I walked in the park with my older brother who had left home to work for a wine merchant. He knew a thing or two my Jean Jacques – it was the only trade acceptable in society.

One day we met a young lady taking a promenade with her governess, and her little pet dog bit me on the ankle as an introduction. I still have a small scar on my leg after all these years.' There was a long pause as he recalled the past.

'What happened, Uncle André?'

'There is not a great deal more to tell. We met every day and fell in love but her grandmother, the countess, would not consent to such a marriage. Jean Jacques made his way in the world and became a tolerable suitor. The lovely girl in the park was your grandmother, my beloved Marguerite.'

There were tears in his eyes. She put her arms around him.

'I have waited for her all my life.'

'Dearest Uncle, you know I love you so very much.' She kissed him on both cheeks.

'Don't cry. I must go back to father. His birthday is in November, and I have a strange feeling he is unhappy and needs me, you understand. Mama would not care if I lived at the ends of the earth – Louis has always been her favourite. Perhaps I could stay with you every summer and winter for long holidays?'

'Bless you, my child. Sweet dreams.' André knew it was pointless to argue with this girl. She adored her father and would never leave him.

Mary came down the gangplank to find her mother, cold and disapproving, her hands thrust into a astrakhan muff and a second-hand fur stole round her shoulders. 'Your father insisted that you were in need of a chaperone on the train journey back to Brighton. I think you must be mad to leave a warm comfortable home in Belgium for this.'

'It's lovely to be in England, mama.' She kissed Anna and wanted to cry at such a cool welcome.

John's face lit up at the sight of his daughter. 'I was sure you would be here in time for my birthday.' He clasped the girl in his arms and led her into the study. 'A pot of tea and a plate of Bath buns: how's that for a home coming? Take off your coat and hat and warm yourself by the fire.'

Gyp the Airedale pushed his warm muzzle into her hand, and the marmalade cat jumped onto the arm of her chair. 'A cosy picture of domestic bliss.'

'I will bake a cake for your birthday father, and stuff it with sultanas, raisins and cherries. I bought you a present in the Avenue.'

A pure silk, olive green cravat lay at the bottom of her trunk, achieved with the remnants of his postal orders and francs from Uncle André.

'I want to see it now.'

'No father, you must be patient for three weeks.' She crossed to her father's chair. 'You look tired, I am sure you are working far too hard, but I can help now. I will bring you both breakfast in bed.' She ran out into the yard to fetch some coal. Flakes of snow brushed her cheeks, and she held out her hands to catch them as they fell.

★

John puffed on his meerschaum pipe, gazing at pictures in the fire. His study desk was strewn with long overdue accounts waiting to be dispatched to clients the following day – 'An early settlement would oblige' written in copperplate handwriting at the foot of every one. Full of aches end pains like an old carthorse at the day's end, he rose to throw a log on the dying embers and caught sight of the heading on a sheet of writing paper: 'J L E Donelly – Ocean Insurance, etc. etc. etc. Tax Recovery Agent.'

Louis should be home on Christmas leave. The house was quiet in his absence. Three photographs stood on his desk: Louis in naval uniform, Mary with the white rabbit Joe and Anna as a young girl in a riding habit.

John cleaned his steel-rimmed spectacles with a large pocket handkerchief and fixed them on his nose. (The monocle on a black moire ribbon was a relic of the past). He picked up a pen, wiped the nib on a piece of red felt, dipped it in the ink well and set to work again.

The mail thudded on to the coconut mat inside the front door: several brown manila envelopes, a circular and a long white letter with a foreign postmark. John recognised the flamboyant handwriting of his friend Julien Lenotre, a silk merchant who wanted to marry Mary, although he was old enough to be her father. This might be another proposal of marriage.

He slit open the missive with a small carved ivory paper knife and began to read.

My dear John,

> *I leave Ostend on the 4th November and after spending the night in Dover, hope to be with you on Guy Fawkes day. Perhaps we shall celebrate en famille with fireworks and a bonfire?*
>
> *It will be a great pleasure to meet your charming wife and daughter once again. You are aware that I called on dear Miss Pink in the Avenue Louise, and she received my attentions with great courtesy. Dare I hope for my future happiness?*
>
> *I will call at your bureau to claim the hundred pounds left with you for safe keeping on my last visit before I travel to the Macclesfield silk mills.*
>
> *With all good wishes for your health and prosperity,*
> *I remain your friend as always,*
> *Julien*

John's hands lay still in his lap. The letter fluttered on to the carpet. The fire crackled and the grandfather clock ticked away the minutes.

The hundred pounds had been frittered away to pay fares to Brussels, buy dresses, litres of milk, a few bottles of cheap wine, and dinners for Anna at the Café Royal. Julien had promised to return in the spring, and John used the money intending to repay it from his fees. He had trespassed against his own code of honour by embezzling funds entrusted to him by a friend. The bank account was grossly overdrawn and Stephen was almost penniless praying for royalties from his new play 'Faust'.

John closed his eyes and saw Anna dancing along the Strand in Ireland, with her pale golden hair flying loose in the sea wind; the Tinker family giving the carven cherrywood doll as a fertility symbol on their honeymoon. 'There's nothing half so sweet in life as love's young dream.'

John rose very slowly and placed his old red leather slippers side by side next to the armchair, put on down at heel brogues, took the Inverness cape, hat and gloves from the hallstand, and walked out of the house locking the door behind him. He had a slight cold and the autumn mist swirling along the promenade and over the dark indigo sea caught him by the throat.

John turned left towards Kemp Town and after a while became aware of light footsteps following close behind him. A girl laid a hand gently on his arm.

'Good evening, my fine gentleman, would you like to come home with me for a bit of comfort? I only charge a shilling.' She had been leaning on the rail as he passed by. It was early evening and there was time to kill.

In the lamplight he saw a girl of about sixteen years of age, with a pair of bold, laughing eyes set in a dark gipsy face, and the sight of her awakened a sudden longing for tenderness and relief after so many years of celibacy. He wanted to lie naked on the beach under the stars and sleep, all passion spent.

A small, slender hand brushed lightly against the front of his trousers, either by accident or design. The muscles in his loins tightened and he was aroused.

Her voice came thin and clear on the night air as she drew a bright woollen shawl across her shoulders. 'It's cold out here, guvnor, and foggy. I'll make it a tanner if you're a bit short.'

He laughed out loud. Thank God she had broken the spell that bound him. He hesitated then reached into the inner pocket of his cape, drew out his last remaining guinea and held it towards her.

'Here you are, child, take it and promise me that you will sleep alone tonight. Your need is greater than mine. God bless you my dear.'

'Gawd, I picked a ruddy priest. Say a prayer for me, father.'

The girl bent down and kissed his hand then, clutching the piece of gold turned and ran off along the seafront.

Dark shadows loomed out of the clotted mist. Footfalls echoed on the pavement, the sea and strand were almost invisible. A cab passed on the King's Road and a ghostly-white horse glowed for a moment in the gaslight.

'We are all in the gutter, but some of us are looking at the stars.' It took a long while to reach his destination, the presbytery of St John the Baptist in St James's Street, where an austere housekeeper answered his knock at the door.

'I wish to see the father.'

'The father is at dinner and would not care to be disturbed.'

'Pray tell the priest in charge it is a matter of some importance.' She came back a few moments later and he was sure the whole affair was a pretence. 'Will you call again in the morning? The father will be here all day long tomorrow. Perhaps you would care to make an appointment. What name shall I give?' Her voice was grating and staccato.

'Tell him an unknown man came to make his last confession.' He turned on his heel and walked away with the woman gazing, bewildered after his receding figure.

Father, forgive me this mortal sin. I lack courage. *Mea culpa, mea culpa, mea maxima culpa.*'

A basket of violets lay on the pavement outside a greengrocer's shop. He bought a bunch, then made his way to the pharmacy on Marine Parade that had served them at Arundel House in he old days. The pharmacist looked up from hi accounts as the shop bell rang.

'Well, bless my soul, how good to see you again, Mr Donelly, it must be six or seven years since you left the area. You know her ladyship passed away? She left your house to an elderly Russian gentleman, Prince Feodor. I understand he had been an admirer... for many years, although he was considerably younger than her ladyship. Anyhow, enough of my chit-chat. What can I do for you, Sir, now that we have the pleasure of your patronage once again? More trouble with the pests, I suppose, or is it the lawns this time? Rather late in the gardening season.'

'We have a problem with rats, so I need Prussic acid, potassium cyanide, a small quantity will suffice. Do you wish me to sign the poisons book?'

'I am sure that will not be necessary, sir. You are not the kind of gentleman to murder your wife in cold blood.' He sensed an adverse reaction to this merry quip. 'Forgive the pleasantry, I'm sure.' He dispensed the white powder into a small paper cone, wrapped this carefully in a blue bag and handed it over the counter in exchange for a shilling, bade his customer 'good night' and locked the shop behind him.

The chemist reported the incident to his wife over high tea. 'He used to be a jolly cove, that Mr Donelly, when they lived in the big house up on the corner of Lewes Crescent. I thought he looked very tired tonight, not himself at all, too much gardening I suppose at his time of life. He's no spring chicken, must be knocking sixty.' Then he dismissed the whole matter from his mind and retired into the parlour behind the shop to rest his feet after a hard day's work.

The house in Middle Street was quiet. John took off his tweed cape, lit a candle, picked up a chamber stick and mounted the stairs. He placed the bunch of violets outside Anna's bedroom door, then sat down to write a brief letter.

My Dearest Anna,

I have always loved you more than anyone else on earth but a great deal of our life together is beyond my understanding. We might have been happy in a world of everyday things, loving one another, caring for Mary and Louis, living in a small country house full of books with a few animals in the yard, buffeted by the wind and the rain. I suppose this is all I ever wanted. I never had any delusions of grandeur.

Now you are free to be alone and the choice is yours. Remember, I kept the promise I made on the hills above Chislehurst: to love you as long as I lived.

Adieu.

God bless you all. Pray for me.

John

Shadows flickered on the worn Persian rug where he knelt every night to say his prayers.

Slowly he poured the dull water from the carafe beside the bed into a glass and emptied the powder into it. 'Holy mother, pray for me. Mother of God, pray for us sinners now... and at the hour of our death...' The low voice trailed away, lost in the silent night. He drained the liquid and lay down upon the bed fingering his beads. Death from cyanide should occur in one to fifteen minutes. His whole body was wracked by convulsive pain, and he saw a blinding light at the end of a tunnel. 'Anna, my dearest Anna.' He reached out to touch her, but she vanished, and he fell backwards, his body writhing in agony. The cyanide burned the flesh around his mouth, and turned his lips a deep purple.

A street musician was playing 'Vilia' on the violin as Mary returned home from the Theatre Royal. She went to into the study to kiss her father good night; his body was cold as marble, eyes wide open gazing into eternity.

A piercing scream rent the air. Anna woke, reached for the garter pistol that lay in the drawer of her bedside cupboard, and listened to the heartbreaking cries echoing across the landing. She threw a shawl across her shoulders, and padded towards the door on her bare feet, still clutching the weapon between her hands, terrified of intruders.

Gyp the Airedale was lying on his rug outside Mary's door, rough brown hair bristling the length of his back. 'Here, boy.' He came to heel, and they crossed the landing, following the sounds. A faint light was flickering under the bottom of John's bedroom door, and she beard a woman's hysterical weeping. Anna flung open the door, levelling the pistol.

Mary knelt sobbing beside the bed, clasping her father's hand, chafing it between her own in a last desperate effort to warm him. The dog nuzzled her arm but she brushed him aside.

Two women alone in the house with a dead man. Anna met death face to face for the second time in her life. The bittersweet smell of cyanide tainted the air.

'For God's sake, be quiet girl.' She slapped her daughter round the face. 'Your father is dead. We cannot get help till morning. All we can do is pray.'

'Close his eyes, mama, please close his eyes.'

'I don't know what to do.' Anna burst into floods of tears. 'Bring candles and a cloth to wipe his face, then at daybreak you can fetch the priest and the doctor.' She bent over to kiss John on the lips. 'God bless you, my dearest love.'

Part Three

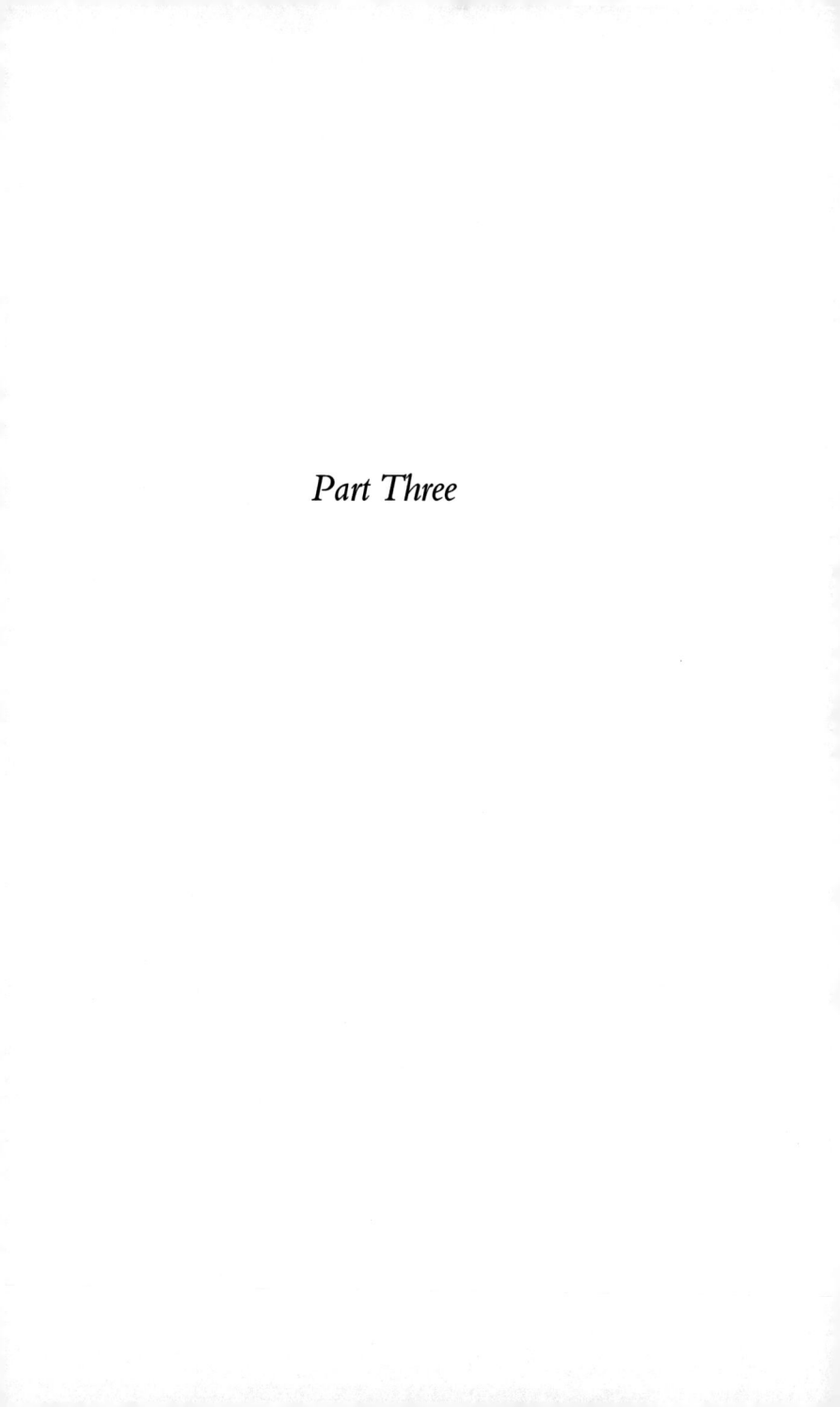

Chapter Twenty-One

'The blinds are down, Joxer, the blinds are down.' Sea green light pierced the old wooden shutters, and cast eerie shadows on the face of the dead man. Lighted candles flickered at his head and feet.

Brendan, Violet and Maureen knelt beside the coffin fingering their beads, the women keening like banshees in the wind. Anna stood alone, blind with tears, frozen in grief. There was a wild rush of air as Maureen rustled to her feet and pointed a long bony finger at the widow. 'That woman killed this man.'

One by one the Donellys filed out of the bedroom along the narrow passage and down the stairs. Only Declan paused for a brief moment to clasp Anna in the old bear hug. 'Remember that John loved you with all his heart. Dear John, may God forgive him.'

Anna's wreath of lilies and Parma violets lay on the coffin beside Stephen's white roses, inscribed, 'To my dearest friend with love always.'

Stephen rode in the carriage with Anna, Mary and Louis to the Church of St John the Baptist in Kemp Town, where the priest spoke of John's many fine qualities and his tragic death.

The hearse and mourners stopped outside the little house in Middle Street for a last blessing, followed by prayers at the graveside, earth shovelled on the coffin, a few Hail Marys, and the service was over at last. Darkness fell. Kate lit the oil lamps and brewed the tea in Anna's old copper samovar; a bottle of sherry, ham sandwiches and homemade cakes were laid out on paper doilies in the sitting room of number forty-three, Middle Street.

Louis stood in front of the fireplace to read his father's last will and testament, made at the time of Mary's departure for Brussels. His voice was husky. 'I understand that Kate has wrapped the small bequests so you may take them away when you leave this house.' Louis cleared his throat and began.

I, John Louis Eugene Donelly being of sound mind… bequeath my worldly goods as follows:

To my son Louis, a silver medal of St Christopher carrying the infant Jesus across a river. May the patron saint of travellers keep him safe on his journey through life.

To Mary, the Louis Wain picture of manic cats in a school room that she loved as a child.

Violet will receive the family photographs in my bureau; Maureen a silver christening spoon by a Cork maker, and my old monocle on the black moire ribbon as a keepsake.

The father, Aunt Bridget and Jim have all passed away, so I bequeath a Waterford glass dish to André Van Maaskens, giving thanks for his many kindnesses. My dear friend Stephen will flourish my malacca cane with his usual panache.

To my dearly beloved wife Anna, I bequeath my dearest possession, my two children, my gold signet ring, and the cherry-wood doll carved by a tinker in Ireland that she lost many years ago, together with all my remaining worldly goods.

Alone at last, Anna broke down and wept crying for John and all the wasted years. She had driven him from happiness and piety to death and disillusion and the ultimate sin.

His mind was as clear as a bell when he made the final choice between death and dishonour.

Anna remembered looking out at the night sky from their bedroom window at Hollingbury Copse when they were first married. 'Take him and cut him into little stars and all the world will fall in love with night and pay no worship to the garish sun.' Dear God, how she loved him twenty-six years ago. A brooch of French paste fashioned as a dragonfly glittered on her black dress, John's last gift for her birthday in April – the dragonfly symbol of the resurrection.

'Lay me in the good earth. I am sure there will be no wake to celebrate my death.' The Irish contingent left without a backward glance or a swift goodbye.

Stephen got drunk in The Cricketers, then fetched his Gladstone bag from the old digs in St Bartholomew's, and tottered up West Street to the station.

Urchins in a shop doorway were singing:
'Christmas is coming and the geese are getting fat,
Please put a penny in the old man's hat.
If you haven't got a penny a ha'penny will do,
If you haven't got a farthing, God bless you.'

He fumbled in his pocket, and flung sixpence in the battered topper lying on the pavement.

The last train had pulled out long since, and the waiting room was pitch dark apart from one corner dimly lit by a gas bracket. Wrapping his long cloak about his person, Stephen stretched his length on the slatted wooden seat and fell into a deep sleep to be wakened the following morning by the stationmaster shaking his arm. 'The early train for New Romney leaves in a few minutes. Do you have a ticket, Sir?'

He could not bear the thought of his old surroundings in London or the pro digs without John as a drinking companion. 'I will take a first class single ticket.'

'The driver stops at Ashford, Appledore, Lydd and New Romney. How far are you travelling, Sir?'

'All the way.' On the spur of the moment, he decided to evade his creditors and disappear from the face of the Earth for a few months.

The salt wind blowing across the marshes almost took his breath away when he left the train at the deserted country station, and he decided to take the Pilgrim's Way and walk to Rye. Stephen bought a stout pair of walking shoes in the men's outfitters near the church and a knapsack and ash stick in the village store.

'Porter and a hunk of bread and cheese, if you please, Landlord.' His head was clearer when he left The Star and set out westwards, the bland faces of bumbling woolly sheep gaping at him from the marshes and bleating as he passed by. 'Mary had a little lamb' – poor Mary, a lovely golden girl left alone at the mercy of that ghastly tough old mother. Yet Anna must be grief stricken in her own way.

He might stray from the footpath at twilight and fall into a muddy dyke and blessed oblivion, but a passing carter offered him a lift, and they reached the lovely old medieval Cinque Port by nightfall. The lights of The Mermaid Inn were tempting but he settled in favour of a fisherman's cottage near the harbour recommended by the driver. Almost penniless, but thank God he was miles off the beaten track and alone to work out his salvation.

He walked for miles beside the harbour and along the cobbled streets and after a while resumed work on his new play, and wrote brief notes to George Alexander and his cousin Laurence.

Dear George,
I am working again but I need money to survive in very straitened circumstance. An advance would help.
Stephen

Laurence came in person and found him propping up a bar and reciting the Sonnets to a bunch of yokels in exchange for pots of beer, playing the actor laddie.

'Laurence, old fellow, how good to see you. I am incognito. This is a poor house, but needs must when the devil drives. George Moreland painted prize pigs in exchange for ale. I too bring culture to the masses in my own crude fashion. God bless the Bard and dear old Frank Benson for his tutelage. Do you remember the time I played Acre in *The Rivals* at Oundle School? The yahoos prefer light entertainment, so I give them "Dangerous Dan McGrew" and "A Little Yellow Idol to the North of Katmandu".' There was a brief pause. 'Can you run to a double Irish whisky?'

They left the inn arm in arm, and Laurence insisted they return to town after Stephen had spent a bucolic weekend. In the Mermaid he was becoming a little maudlin.

'Take me back to Brighton first Laurence, but I must stay away from Anna otherwise I might wring her neck.'

A cab took them to the house in Middle Street where an estate agent happened to be on the premises awaiting a prospective tenant. I understand the Donellys are staying at the Royal Albion Hotel near the Palace Pier. I hear on the grapevine that Mr Donelly's insurance company paid out about five thousand pounds after the coroner's verdict decreed 'suicide while the balance of his mind was disturbed. Can I interest either of you gentlemen in this desirable property?'

'Thank you no, we prefer to live in London.'

Laurence rented a warm comfortable garret off Old Compton Street from a motherly Italian woman who agreed to cope with Stephen's cooking and laundry. Money would be made available to pay for a daily carafe of Chianti and spaghetti ad infinitum.

'I want you to edit the 'Poetry Review'. We can discuss the sordid details once you are on your feet again.'

'Soho is an ideal milieu for me, dear boy. You know May has left me and taken our son with her? I was at the end of my tether in Brighton.'

'You will feel better after a good night's sleep and a few days on the water wagon.'

'Do you remember my poem 'Christ in Hades'?

'It is the time of tender, opening things.

Above my head the fields murmur and wave,

And breezes are just moving the clear heat.

O the mid-noon is trembling on the corn,

On cattle calm and trees in perfect sleep,

And hast thou empty come? Hast thou not brought

Even a blossom with the noise of rain

And smell of earth about it, that we all

Might gather round and whisper over it?

At one wet blossom all the dead would feel.'

Dear God, it is all so long ago,' and he broke down in a paroxysm of weeping.

*

Anna was holding forth in the back kitchen about the future of the family, while Percy Newman loaded their goods and chattels on to a horse and cart having bought everything at a knock-down price. All John's clothes were thrust into battered cardboard boxes; even the Inverness cloak, a bowler hat and a tweed deerstalker, his last Christmas present from Declan. The house was nearly bare.

Mary felt sick, but Louis was trying to keep up a brave front as Anna discussed her plans.

'We could have chosen the Grand or the Metropole, but the Royal Albion is more Bohemian and cheaper. The insurance money should last a long time.'

Kate snorted in the background as she tried to clear up the mess left by Percy and his henchman. 'I am sick to death of living in a doll's house. We should be able to stay in the hotel until Mary makes a good marriage.'

'I am sure this is a sick joke, mama.'

'Listen to me, baby, I no longer believe in the coup de foudre when love at first sight strikes you like a thunderbolt. I fell in love with my father's secretary when I was seventeen, and it was a disaster. I still bear a few scars on my back to prove it: papa lashed me with a horsewhip, and he was right not to give us his blessing.

I am sure Louis will make his own way in the world.' She smiled fondly at her errant son. 'He talks of a rich merry widow and a castle on the Rhine or a brownstone house in Manhattan. You Mary are living in a fairy tale world of amorous chimney sweeps, a thatched cottage and six children.'

'You disgust me, mother. I shall never understand you. You talk of money, money, money and an arranged marriage, your marriage of convenience, while father lies in the cold ground.'

'Let us break open a bottle of vin ordinaire, Louis. We are talking about survival, courage and honesty.'

'You could teach music or languages. You never tried to help father when he was desperate for money. The priest's housekeeper told me that father went to the presbytery to make confession on the night he died. I am a lapsed Catholic. I shall never go to Mass again as long as I live.'

'The girl is hysterical, give her a glass of water, Kate.' The children must not be allowed to pierce her brittle veneer. It was her only strength, but she was longing to tell them of her loneliness and sorrow. An only child is vulnerable. 'To hell with water, let us all get drunk and forget. What do they call it, the Irish sickness?'

Mary raised her glass. 'We drink to oblivion. Schlainte!'

Chapter Twenty-Two

Life at the Royal Albion was luxurious after the farm at Herstmonceux and the house in Middle Street. Anna was in her element, looking out of her bedroom window at the old familiar scenes: the Palace Pier, the fish market, the changing colours of the English Channel.

Mary received several proposals of marriage over the next few months but refused them all with great charm and a sweet smile: here was a Spanish prince, a wild Irishman, and the son of a South African diamond millionaire. 'I'm not on the shelf at twenty, mama.'

One afternoon before their second Christmas in the hotel, Anna was taking afternoon tea in the lounge as usual: Earl Grey, tiny meringues light as air, coffee and chocolate éclairs, and cucumber sandwiches. Anna nibbled, gazing absent-mindedly across the promenade and decided she must remember her waistline.

'Good afternoon, Mrs Donelly, it has been a very pleasant afternoon, has it not? I have been enjoying a breath of sea air.' A tall, grey haired, distinguished man stood before her, his hands resting on the chased silver knob of an ebony cane.

'How good to see you, Sir Charles. Will you join me in a cup of tea?'

He sat in one of the gilt fauteuils, crossed his silk-clad ankles and surveyed the scene.

A large fir tree by the entrance to the foyer was surmounted by a fairy doll with long blonde ringlets. Tinsel garlands of gold and silver hung from the branches, and all the sporting prints were festooned with bows of crimson and emerald green velvet. Holly and mistletoe wreathed the ceiling lights.

'You admire Harry Preston's decorations?'
'I prefer something a little less ostentatious.'
He nodded. 'My sentiments exactly.'

Sir Charles had retired from the diplomatic service, and now spent his time between Paris, the Riviera, Brighton and Ireland, where he owned a property near the Duke of Devonshire's place in Lismore. 'I was in Monte a few weeks ago and travelled on to stay at the Villa Cyrnos with the Empress Eugénie. She is in fine fettle now, but it has taken years for her to recover from her tragic losses. She spends most of her time at Farnborough Hill where she built a mausoleum in the grounds in remembrance of the emperor and her dear Lou Lou. Four monks keep vigil day and night praying for the souls of the departed.'

He rose to leave after a little more light conversation. 'I shall look forward to seeing you and your charming daughter at the dance tonight, dear lady. Your son is on shore leave for a week or so? Good, good. A tout a l'heure.'

That evening the manager was waiting at the foot of the staircase to present each of his lady guests with a single rose. 'Red for Madame and white for the young lady. A pleasure to meet you again ladies, Sir Charles.'

His bald pate gleamed in the artificial light as he moved swiftly on narrow patent leather dancing pumps from one resident to another. 'Mrs Donelly, I trust our guests will not prove too boisterous during the festivities, but as you know we entertain many of the theatrical profession and the boxing fraternity.'

'Thank you for your consideration, Mr Preston. I am greatly amused.'

'I sincerely hope you are right,' whispered Sir Charles under his breath.

Everyone adjourned to the ballroom after dinner. Louis was immaculate in his dress uniform, the widow wore black satin and pearls, while Mary's gown was pale grey chiffon with a short train and a butterfly brooch in sapphires and diamonds pinned on one shoulder.

A dance programme embossed with gold lettering hung from a ring on her little finger.

The palm court orchestra opened the ball with 'The Pink Lady Waltz' and Sir Charles bowed to Mary.'

'May I have the pleasure?'

Louis was whispering in the ear of a chocolate box beauty, so Anna was happy to sip her champagne and rest awhile.

Suddenly there was a fracas in the middle of the dance floor and several couples nearly collided: the cord on Mary's programme had become entangled with a button on a man's tailcoat. 'My deepest apologies. We were destined to meet.'

Mary gazed up into a pair of dark brown eyes, dilated in the lamp light. This was a man, not a callow youth; tall and handsome with black curly hair flecked with grey, a high forehead and a flashing smile. He might be forty years of age.

Sir Charles grasped her by the waist and sailed across the floor. 'Stupid fellow, doesn't know how to waltz in reverse.'

She danced an exhibition tango with Louis, and waited for the next move. The figure of a young man loomed over their table. 'You may not remember me, Mrs Donelly. George Yeats at your service. My father acted as your solicitor some years ago but I was only a boy at the time. May I present an old friend, William Lester? Mrs Donelly and family.'

'How do you do.'

'Good evening.' He bowed to the matriarch.

'I think another bottle of bubbly is on the cards. May we join your party?'

'By all means. I remember your father well, Mr Yeats, an excellent lawyer; he negotiated with Lady Lansdowne on my behalf, and she was quite a termagant.' She turned to his companion.

'What is your profession, Mr Lester?'

Nosey old cow. 'I am a building contractor, Madam. The family business was founded by my father in 1871. I left school at twelve and worked as a bricklayer carrying my victuals wrapped in a red and white spotted handkerchief.' That should give the old girl something to mull over for the next half hour or so.

She realised the man was a rough diamond, but thought he was pulling her leg.

William decided the mother was a real battleaxe, but he could not place the distinguished figure watching him from the opposite side of the table with an air of faint amusement.

'May I introduce Mr Yeats and Mr Lester – Sir Charles Palin.' She turned to Yeats. 'One of King Edward's daughters lives in Arundel House now – the Duchess of Fife.'

'One of the Three Hags.'

'Sir Charles tells me the Empress Eugénie visited Buckingham Palace and stayed in the suite she once occupied with Napoleon. The King was too sentimental to change the décor, but she took one look and murmured, 'Encore ces affreux rideaux!'

Anna laughed. 'Her English was always erratic, although she went to school in Bristol for a while and tried to stow away on a boat to India. She scattered her h's willy-nilly. She gave permission for her neighbours to course hares on her land at Farnborough Hill and said, "I 'ope you catch the 'ares in front of the 'ouse." Sir Charles tells me these stories now that I am out of touch. I understand the Winterhalter painting of the empress and her ladies hangs in the entrance hall, and Lou Lou's perambulator lined with faded pink satin stands nearby.'

William rose to his feet. 'Will you do me the honour, Miss Donelly?'

'Is a two-step or a cake-walk safer than a waltz, Mr Lester?'

'It is naughty to tease a poor middle-aged man with two left feet.' William circled the parquet floor and finished with a flourish under the mistletoe. 'May I steal a kiss from a lovely young lady? After all it is the festive season.'

Mary extended her hand and gave him an enchanting smile. 'You may kiss my little finger, Mr Lester. This is our first meeting.

'Mary must be stark raving mad to consider Lester as a suitor; a middle-aged married man with an estranged wife and five young children. Apparently the brats live with a housekeeper in a flat in Woldingham, and he is supposed to be a wonderful father. The woman is flying her kite somewhere in the West End. I expect the whole story is a pack of lies.'

Kate was washing knickers and stockings in a hand basin of the hotel bedroom and trying to turn a deaf ear to the tirade. 'You should be glad that Miss Mary has found a nice young man.'

'Lester is an arrogant sod and I can't bear the sight of him.'

'He's not in love with you.'

'William, William, William... every other word is William. I am sick to death of the name. He is a detrimental. Sometimes he reminds me of Robert Feldmann.'

Kate gave a wry grin. 'I can see what you mean.'

'I am fond of young Willie O' Malley. He is amusing and well-bred, and his uncle is T P O' Connor; Michael Leverson is the son of a diamond millionaire. They have both proposed marriage, but she is obsessed with a man old enough to be her father.' Anna shrugged her shoulders. 'The girl drives me crazy. I could understand Mary being a suffragette and chaining herself to railings outside the Houses of Parliament, or breaking a few windows, but this is crass stupidity.'

'Oh Gawd, you're not becoming a "new woman" now!'

'I want money and freedom to live as I choose for the first time in my life. I am certain I shall die a wealthy woman, but only God knows how.'

'There's always Charlie. You say he fancies you. Yes milady, no milady. I reckon you'd be a real pain in the arse with a handle to your name.' Katie blushed like a kid.

'Sorry, I've gone a bit too far this time.' She changed the subject.

'I'm as happy as a sandboy living in a back alley with my Fred and Annie, food on the table and a new frock every Easter regular as clockwork. We still make love on Saturday night.' She grinned.

'Don't forget we're knocking on a bit now. Rosie tells me that Ernie is a bugger for his greens, but I expect she learned a trick or two up West in her palmy days. Butter wouldn't melt in her mouth now.'

*

Anna enjoyed the little luxuries of life: a tortoiseshell comb that did not scratch her scalp, emerald green bath oil by Floris of Jermyn Street smelling of stephanotis and rose geranium, the services of a court dressmaker or Barrance & Ford's emporium on the King's Road, and Katie's nightly visit to dress her hair before dinner. It was three years since John died, and she might be reconciled to sleeping with a man if he were docile and considerate. She had already decided to marry Sir Charles when he screwed his courage to the sticking point and asked for her hand. The insurance money had dwindled and there were a few outstanding bills for a black sable stole and a violet satin gown by one of the fashionable new designers, Edward Molyneux.

Sir Charles Palin had reserved a suite on the first floor of the hotel since leaving the diplomatic service. It was a convenient pied-à-terre where both the staff and management turned a blind eye to his peccadilloes.

He paid court to Anna for months on end. 'I am a lonely man, and the passing years make it increasingly difficult for me to meet anyone with whom I have a certain rapport. At my age, the heyday in the blood is cold... I have no illusions.'

Anna walked along the hotel corridor to their first assignation à deux, wearing a becoming gown of dove grey satin with a bunch of violets on one shoulder. Sir Charles bowed to kiss her hand and she was aware of tiny brown liver spots on the skin and ridged fingernails where the years at Chilsham Farm had taken their toll. Her vanity was returning with a vengeance.

His personal manservant waited at table: Whitstable oysters served with wedges of lemon in silver tongs, and seasoned with paprika followed by salmon en croute and raspberry Pavlova.

'You may leave us, Vittorio. I will pour coffee myself.'

Charles had brought a few pieces from his exquisite collection: an Impressionist painting of a water garden by Monet, a marqueterie étagere and Fabergé bibelots, enamel eggs, and a Russian cigarette box of dark grey slate inlaid with a diamond sword.

Anne sipped her liqueur and waited. She appreciated good breeding in men and horseflesh. A marriage of convenience to Palin would be preferable to life in reduced circumstances, and she was fond of the man. She rolled the cognac on her tongue.

'Another cup of coffee, Anna? I may call you Anna after waiting so long?' She saw the world through rose-coloured spectacles... couleur-de-rose, couleur-de -rose.

'I think we speak the same language, my dear, you are a woman of the world.' He crossed the room and sat beside her on the settee taking her hand in his for a brief moment, then rose abruptly and crossed to the window.

She knew his pale grey eyes were watching her reflection in the small Georgian looking glass hanging above the mantelpiece.

Only the clip-clop of horses' hooves on the seafront broke the silence. Through the long balcony windows she could see the moonlight shining on the water. His fingers began to drum on the pane of glass.

'My dear Anna.' The man was as nervous as a young boy, it was rather endearing. There was a slight pause.

'My dear Charles.' Her voice was a little husky.

He was finding it difficult to come to the point, but this must be a proposal of marriage. She glanced away from him and was still, her hands folded in her lap. Even at their age he had chosen a romantic, intimate occasion to declare himself. His voice became clipped and precise. 'I have a proposal to make and as you are a widow I am sure you will understand what I am about to say.' He twisted the stem of his brandy glass between long slender fingers and leaned towards her, his eyes translucent under the artificial light, and she was afraid.

'Anna, it is difficult for me to begin. I know that you have been left without resources, an impoverished gentlewoman. I am glad your son has returned to sea. I fear he might not appreciate my intentions. Louis is a charming young man, but I think we should have very little in common. Your daughter Mary would be enchanting if she were educated a la Parisienne.' He sighed. 'You are a woman of the world, Anna. I must confess that I like the company of beautiful young men in the bedroom. Dear Oscar was persecuted because of his liaison with Alfred Douglas and, en passant, with a waiter called Hyacinthe. What a lovely name for one's amour. My own tastes are a little more catholic... I like a young woman to be involved in my affaires... it adds a certain je ne sais quoi.' There was a long silence.

'I am a very wealthy man, and would pay well to satisfy my desires. If Mary learned to pleasure me, you would receive a generous allowance for the rest of your days. Allow me to show you a work of art.' He lifted the small carved mirror from the wall and pressed a secret catch hidden in one of the gilt flowers, to reveal a picture of two young men in tight Georgian breeches exposing their private parts. A serving-maid lay on a chaise longue clothed in period costume, her skirts lifted and her legs spread wide apart. 'It always reminds me of a girl dancing the can can in Paris sans culottes. I have a fabulous collection of erotica that I am sure would amuse you. We are all voyeurs at heart.'

She sat immobile. He learned over her, his warm foetid breath fanning her cheek as the fingers of his right hand caressed the picture.

'My dear Charles,' she caught her breath, 'I am not a procureuse.' Raising her brandy goblet in the air, she smashed the glass on the picture to smithereens. A splinter caught one corner of her mouth and a thin trickle of blood ran down her chin. 'You can go to hell in your own way, but stay away from my daughter. You should be castrated like a bullock.'

He stood transfixed, eyes staring, mouth agape, but as she moved towards the door he caught her arm and she felt a jagged spear of glass piercing her throat. She tried to wrench herself from his grasp and suddenly he thrust her away. 'You are a jealous, embittered old woman. Get out of this room, you bitch, before I kill you.'

In the cruel glare of the electric light she saw the enamelled maquillage: pale rouge flushing the high cheekbones, and turquoise shadow lining the heavy eyelids.

Slowly the door opened and Vittorio stood in the corridor where he had been waiting throughout the evening. 'You are leaving, Madame?' The young man's voice was insolent. She looked into his face for the first time: smooth black hair, a swarthy complexion, and a straight cruel mouth.

He bowed from the waist in mock deference, then turned to enter his master's rooms.

She could hear him addressing his master in sibilant tones as she walked away. 'It is Vittorio, Sir Charles. I am here if you need me.'

Anna lay awake all night sniffing her smelling salts and weeping. In the morning, she knelt to say her prayers, ate her simple breakfast of croissants and honey in bed, felt sick and then suddenly, she had an idea.

The manager was hovering at the foot of the stairs when she came down with Mary later in the day. 'Good morning, ladies. The weather is clement for the time of year. I am sorry to say that Sir Charles left the hotel early this morning, and he does not appear to be in the best of tempers.' His expression was louche. 'It is sad... one had certain expectations.'

'It is of no consequence whatsoever. I consider your manner presumptuous. My daughter and I will leave the Albion at the end of the week.' She swept into the dining room like a ship in full sail.

Mary was puzzled and disappointed. 'I thought you and Sir Charles had an understanding, mama?'

'We are living in the twentieth century, child. His decadence is... fin de siecle. Our friendship is a thing of the past.'

Anna decided to sell the sables, a tea gown of coffee lace, and a costume with a hobble skirt to a wardrobe dealer from Kensington Gardens, and settle their hotel bill.

'Stop fussing like a mother hen. Lester would visit you in the workhouse. I am not going to die in a seedy boarding house on Brighton front or teach French to scruffy brats. I would rather sell flowers on the pavement outside the Hotel Metropole. We shall survive. I have told Lester to behave like a gentleman, but I doubt if he understands the meaning of the word. You know the church will never marry you without a dispensation from the Pope?'

'We are loving friends.' Mary tried to change the subject. 'You say the money is running out, so where on Earth shall we live now?'

'Wait and see. I have a brilliant idea to tide us over.'

Kate came to tidy her wardrobe that afternoon. 'Do I hear wedding bells?'

The answer was a four-letter word. 'I think Sir Charles has a few strange habits.'

'You mean he's a dirty old man? Well it's better to find out now than later. My sister Rose knew a very funny old boy up West, who did strange things with sausages.'

Anna laughed. 'You are incorrigible, Kate.'

'Didn't you notice Charlie's pale pink rouge under the electric light? I could still put you wise about a thing or two, Madame

Anna. I saw him on the prom one night talking to a young man who was "working the rail" and I was sure he was *one of them*.'

'Why on Earth didn't you warn me?'

'I never thought you might go the whole hog and marry the man.'

The whole episode was falling into perspective, and losing its outlandish quality. Katie was like a breath of fresh air blowing away the dark cobwebs.

'How about a nice cup of tea?'

'I need strong black coffee and a dose of chloral to forget that abominable man. I know you have a spare room in the cottage. I thought Mary and I could be temporary lodgers, and pay you a fair rent. What do you say?'

Kate took a deep breath. She had been dreading this suggestion for months. The only way out was to be honest. 'Fred might not be too keen unless he got the spondulicks every Friday on the dot. He puts the money away in little tin boxes and in the old brown teapot on the mantelpiece, same as his mum and dad before him. So much for the talley man, pennies for the gas meter, and a bit put by for a rainy day. Creature of habit my Fred. He's even saving up for Annie's wedding, and she's not even walking out yet. I'll see what he says.'

Fred was willing as long as the Donellys did all their own cooking and cleaning. 'You didn't marry me to work as a skivvy for nothing.' Anna was full of enthusiasm. I can make wonderful bouillabaisse, fish stew. We learned to cook at the convent: meringues, omelettes, sole béchamel.'

'You'll stink the house out. There's only a kettle and a gas ring in your bedroom. I think you're safer with eggs and bacon, sausages and black pudden.'

Chapter Twenty-Three

William kept his horseless carriage in stables at the back of the Grand Parade, and travelling at a speed of four miles an hour they could motor to Stanmer Park and back in time for supper with mama. Mary usually wore a dun-coloured topee with a motoring veil tied under the chin, while William sported goggles, knickerbockers and long woollen socks, thinking he was a helluva lad.

One afternoon they sat in the car watching the rabbits at play and talking about the future. She told William the truth about her father's suicide not Anna's garbled story of death by misadventure. 'Your mother is a terrible snob. She hates the sight of me because I'm what she calls nouveau riche.'

'You are a married man, William. Mama is a Catholic… a mongrel, half bourgeois and peasant, half aristocrat. She is very proud of her Bourbon ancestors on grandmother's side of the family, and says we are related to the royal house of France.'

'Thank God for the Revolution. Now I've fallen in love with the daughter of this paragon of virtue.'

Mary changed the subject, moving his roving hand from her knee at the same time. 'Why are you estranged from your wife?'

'She was the ironmonger's daughter who lived nearby when we were children. We made love in the loft above the builder's yard, and married when she fell in the family way at seventeen. It wasn't a shotgun wedding, but my mother always called her a flibberty gibbet. She left the new born baby with her family for days on end, and ran off to the West End to fly her kite.'

'You were in love with her?'

'Years ago. Now I want to marry you more than anything in the world.'

'There are so many young children.'

William evaded the issue. 'Ellen was renting a room in Bayswater and drinking in tarts' parlours like Verrey's and the

Leicester Lounge. She came home from time to time, but the relationship was doomed from the start. Now I live with the children and a housekeeper. I have hired a private detective, and I intend to divorce Ellen as soon as I have the evidence of adultery.'

'Is she very beautiful?'

'Dark as a gypsy with a cloud of black hair, a milk-white skin and flashing eyes. You are as different as chalk and cheese.' He took Mary in his arms and kissed her. 'Ellen is a nymphomaniac who sleeps with taxi drivers.'

He thought it strange that he was still angered by the thought of her infidelity. Perhaps it was wounded pride.

William had a roving eye for a pretty face and a shapely ankle. He had slept with one of the little typists from the office, and a wealthy American widow adored him, but now he was madly in love with Mary and it was a hard life. 'Marry me, dearest girl, as soon as I am free. I will love you till I die.'

'Mama will scream for the sal volatile and have a fit of the vapours, but I can decide for myself when I am twenty-one. I want to be your wife William, although we shall be living in sin in the eyes of the church unless we get a dispensation. I have not been to Mass or Confession since the day of my father's funeral, so I am a lapsed Catholic.'

'I am a Protestant for weddings and funerals. Mother emigrated from West Cork after the hunger and went into service with a family in Lewisham. Dad was working nearby as a master carpenter. She left Clonakilty on the carrier's cart with just enough money for a steerage passage to Liverpool and the fare to London.'

'I think we should tell mama the truth when the divorce is granted but not before. Louis has guessed already.'

'A divorced self-made man is hardly a good catch in your mother's eyes.'

He climbed down from the running board and cranked the engine. They drove a few yards and the automobile spluttered to a halt. The tank was empty, so they walked all the way to Moulscoombe to buy a gallon of petroleum spirit.

★

'Take the hors d'oeuvres trolley to Madame la Comtesse at the window table, and be quick about it. You know she does not like to be kept waiting. The guinea fowl is excellent tonight.' Francois bustled around his small kitchen stirring a sauce, or tasting his soupe a l'oignon, and basting the game.

Madame Donelly, la Comtesse, was his favourite customer. She appreciated his culinary art and sent her compliments to the chef with a small douceur every week. 'The English do not understand good food. Marcel go go go!'

The patrons of the Café Royal near the Hippodrome were mostly petit bourgeois, shopkeepers from the Lanes and Duke Street, with well-rounded bosoms and bellies – a certain embonpoint.

The young French waiter was standing at Anna's elbow, napkin folded over his sleeve, waiting to take her order. 'Shall I serve now, Madame, or would you prefer to wait for Mademoiselle Marie?'

'Bring me a bottle of vin ordinaire, Marcel. I do not intend to wait.'

They met in the Café Royal every Friday evening at precisely seven thirty. Her daughter was already ten minutes late.

She chose sardines drenched in fine olive oil, crisp spring onions, egg mayonnaise sprinkled with chives, salami and black olives.

Anna savoured her hors d'oeuvres followed by the guinea fowl, game chips and slivers of emerald green haricots. There was still no sign of her daughter when the crêpes Suzette were flaming in a silvery pan beside her table. Anna sat watching the café door for almost an hour.

She knew it was William's weekend in Brighton. The horseless carriage might overturn and Mary could be lying in a ditch with a broken neck like her parents. 'Strong black coffee, Marcel.' She took a Balkan Sobranje cigarette from her case and put the gold tip between her lips; her hands were shaking with nerves. The waiter lit a match and bent forward as Mary walked into the café wearing a gown of pale lilac with a bunch of sweet peas at the waist. 'Mama, I am so sorry to be late but the automobile ran out of petrol, and we walked for miles to find a garage. I went home to change because I was so hot and dusty.'

Mary bent to kiss her mother on the cheek, but Anna brushed her aside. 'I have been out of my mind with worry, and you tell me this cock and bull story. Where the hell have you been? Did your amour seduce you in a private room or under the Palace Pier?' Anna rose to her feet and spat in the girl's face.

'I think you are a liar and a whore'

Deadly silence in the restaurant. The other diners stopped eating to watch the peep show. A man at the next table sat open-mouthed with his knife and fork propped up in front of him.

Mary wiped the slime from her cheek and tried to fight back the tears. 'I am telling you the truth, mama.'

Marcel pulled out a chair, flicked the seat with his napkin and bowed. 'If Mademoiselle would care to be seated…'

'Thank you, no, Marcel. I have lost my appetite.'

Mary walked blindly out of the Café Royal leaving Anna alone to repent her foul temper over a glass of cognac.

The next morning breakfast was eaten in silence. 'Are you still a virgin?' The mother's query was met with a blank stare. 'I am asking you a simple question, and I am entitled to a straightforward answer.'

'The reply is yes, mama, but I do not intend to make a marriage of convenience to satisfy you and replenish the family coffers. After last night I refuse to be tied to your apron strings any longer. I am going to work and make my own living.'

'Doing what, may I ask?'

'I am afraid you will have to wait and see.'

William had gone back to town so Mary agreed to meet Michael 'Baby' Leverson for tea at The Mikado Café. 'I want to ask you a favour, Baby.'

'Fire away, old thing.'

'You told me about Cedric Ferley the painter who had executed some commissions for your father. Does he still need a model?' She blushed. 'Perhaps he wants a raving beauty. I might not stand a chance.'

'My dear girl, don't be absurd. I will arrange an interview first thing in the morning. I think our Cedric has a roving eye, and his wife is a bit of a gorgon, so beware.'

Ferley opened the door himself: a tall man with black curly hair and classic features, wearing green corduroy trousers and a peacock blue cravat tied loosely round his neck. 'Miss Donelly? Do come in.'

She followed him into a large studio where the north light fell on the figure of an old woman sitting on the model's throne draped in a Paisley shawl. There were dark blue curtains, an oak cupboard with copper hinges, Kelim rugs on bare boards stripped and painted emerald green, and a heap of pictures stacked against the far wall, including portraits of naked young women.

He paid the model and dismissed her. 'My wife and I offer one shilling an hour for head and shoulders, or half a crown for the altogether. The choice is yours.'

He smiled. 'I know some young ladies are a little squeamish about posing in the nude. Will you at least take off your hat and coat?' He watched her fluid movements as she crossed the room and nodded. 'Painters see the body in three parts. You are rather thin, my dear. Would you like some tea?' He rang a small hand bell and demanded, 'Tea Martha, with muffins if you please, very hot and soused in butter.'

After a while his wife came into the room, an intense-looking female with thick eyebrows and dark hair caught in a bun at the nape of her neck. 'You must be Mary Donelly, Michael told us all about you, I think the poor young man is besotted. He was sure you would refuse to sit for the *tout ensemble*, but we both need a young model who will not faint after posing for an hour or two. Can you start tomorrow? Three hours in the morning for Cedric and two in the afternoon for me... five shillings a day and there is usually a frugal meal at midday with bread and butter and jam in the afternoon. Are we agreed?'

The work was a godsend. They should be able to survive, pay Fred's weekly rent on the dot and keep the wolf from the door. Anna still received a few pounds every year from the firm of solicitors in Bromley, the dregs from Southwark and Bermondsey.

*

Cowley's Olde Bunne Shoppe in the valley near the Palace Pier provided Chelsea buns and cups of strong sweet tea or chocolate for tuppence, and this was Mary's great extravagance after a week working for Cedric and his wife. She sat down in one of the old farmhouse chairs, stretched her hands towards the glowing fire and arched her back like a cat. Her body ached from holding the same pose for hours.

The latch on the shop door was raised, and Mary looked up to see a tall figure leaning over her, holding a wide brimmed hat in both hands. His eyes gleamed like coals in the firelight, the shadow of a faint beard blurred his chin and upper lip.

'Mary, my lovely Mary, may I sit down and join you in a dish of tea?' He drew out a silver flask from his hip pocket and poured whisky into the second cup brought by the waitress. 'I was walking past on my way to The Cricketers as is my wont, cast an idle glance through the window and saw my girl!' There was a long pause.

'This is my evening constitutional from the theatrical digs in St Bartholomew's, along the seafront then a short cut towards Prince Albert Street and the Lanes. What are you doing these days, my dear?' A slight hoarseness marred the rolling cadences. Stephen cleared his throat, flicked an imaginary crumb from his trousers and looked away from her, out of the window at the narrow alley outside. The girl's clear blue eyes and wide forehead reminded him of John as a young man.

'The money's all gone, uncle Stephen, we are staying in Crown Gardens with Fred and Kate. I am working as an artist's model for a shilling an hour in costume, otherwise the father would turn in his grave… just head and shoulders.'

'You know I disappeared for six months after John died. I could no longer write empty tragedies in blank verse. John still lives in my head and my heart. May left me in 1908 and took our son with her. I was blind drunk for days but Laurence took me back to London. I can still afford a glass of porter and tea in a bun shop. Waitress, may I have the bill if you please.'

He took his companion gently by the elbow and ushered her between the tables and out on to the pavement. 'Let us walk together along the promenade.'

Stephen offered his arm, and she placed a gloved hand on his sleeve. 'How fares, Madame Anna?'

'Mother is well. I think idleness becomes her. She misses the countryside from time to time, riding to hounds, life at the Albion. She still talks about the first night of Paolo and Francesca, and your standing ovation from the audience.'

'I am writing a trivial play which is to be presented at a little theatre near Victoria Station – The Studio. I think it is involved with the Women's Institute – Jam and Jerusalem You should come, but I am no longer in a position to offer the railway fare. For years I received handsome royalties, about one hundred and fifty pounds a week from my Italian tragedy, but now the well is dry, and I am out of fashion.' He quizzed her in the failing light. 'Have you been swept off your feet by a knight in shining armour astride a milk-white stallion?'

'We-e-ell, there's young Willie O'Malley and Mike Leverson and William Lester and a few other beaux.'

He knew from the tone of her voice which man she favoured. 'William? A sound old English name.'

'The cards are stacked against us, uncle Stephen. He's a married man with children, living apart from his wife, but he's suing for divorce on the grounds of adultery.'

'My poor Mary, a cradle Catholic guilt-ridden by generations of Celtic priests, not to mention your dear mamma in the background. I should write a lament for the swans of Coole and their lame ducklings. A legend of Ossian says the gods were transmogrified into swans with the feet of human beings. I suppose we are all crippled in one way or another.'

Somewhere in the distance a clock struck six times. 'I must away to drown my sorrows… and yours dear child.' Stephen doffed his hat, kissed her lightly on the cheek, and walked away into the shadows. She never saw him again.

Chapter Twenty-Four

'1914, the years are racing by and I shall be an old spinster, Kate.'
'Stuff and nonsense. You could twist any man round your little finger.'

The Entente Cordiale was broken, and the country was at war, with young ladies giving white feathers to men out of uniform. Louis enlisted as a lieutenant and Anna dreaded a yellow envelope, and scanned the lists of war dead in the penny papers.

Daily life in Brighton was almost unchanged apart from long queues for food, especially bread and meat, and whisky at three shillings and sixpence a bottle.

William was not called up as he was in a reserved occupation building army barracks. His children stayed in the country away from zeppelin raids, and he kept a bachelor flat in town. 'Cedric says he has fallen in love with me, so I shall leave. I don't worry, his wife hovers over us like an avenging angel.'

'You earn a pittance modelling for the Ferleys, thirty shillings a week at most.' He clasped her hand across the tea table. 'We need a young lady to train as a telephonist, and you could soon learn to operate the switchboard. The job carries two pounds a week, and you would escape from the clutches of your dear mamma!

The new offices are in the city, but there are plenty of cheap rooms near Victoria Station. No strings, I promise.'

'On your word of honour?'

'Cross my heart and hope to die.'

'Stephen Phillips wrote offering me a part in his new play *Armageddon*, as one of a hundred naked backs. It is about the war between good and evil, to be presented at the New Theatre in 1915. It is a great temptation but the father always said he would shoot me if I went on the stage.'

'Ellen still refuses to give me a divorce. As the guilty party she is afraid of losing touch with the children. You know that we have been apart since Patrick was born.'

'Poor William, the celibate monk.'

'You are a wicked flirt to keep me dangling like a puppet on a string. When are you going to take pity on me?'

'I am not very close to my mother these days. She behaved outrageously that night at the Café Royal. I agree to take your job on trial, but there will be a dreadful scene.'

William found her a clean comfortable room with a Mrs Donovan in Wilton Place for ten shillings a week. The Irishwoman was a wise old bird. She eyed the tall good-looking man about town from head to toe.

'This is a respectable house, Mr Lester. Men are not allowed in the rooms at any time, night or day.'

'We understand one another perfectly, Madam.'

An iron bed with a spotless marcella coverlet stood in one corner of the room, and an aspidistra blocked out most of the daylight filtering through the fine dust outside the window.

'She's a dear woman, William, what father used to call 'lace curtain Irish', as opposed to bog trotters the Ascendancy and the natives who live beyond the pale.'

'My mother came from a bardic family in West Cork but you know I am only Protestant for christenings, weddings and funerals. I might be an atheist.'

'Sitting on the fence as usual admiring the view.'

'I can't believe in God with a woolly beard floating on a cloud, or hell and damnation for all sinners.'

*

Mary soon learned to work the switchboard, and they met every day in the office often dining together in a small Soho café or Frascatis, as a great extravagance. His only romantic progress was a chaste goodnight kiss on Mrs Donovan's doorstep.

William avoided Bayswater and the tea dance at the Piccadilly Hotel like the plague. He did not want to meet Ellen with Mary on his arm.

The private detective was charging a small fortune, without results. 'The lady in question does not spend the night in hotels with her companions, so we cannot bribe the chambermaid to lend us the key of a bedroom door and catch the couple in the act. We need to provide hard evidence of adultery in court.'

Mary wrote to her mother every week, enclosing a few shillings, and describing her new life in London... a visit to Harrods as a sightseer, daily trips on an omnibus between Victoria and the city, and the day her umbrella blew inside out. 'It was a disaster, I could not afford to buy a new one for a fortnight.'

William had delusions of grandeur. 'I want to buy a Georgian house in Sawbridgeworth. I first saw it when I was a kid of ten. The asking price is twenty thousand pounds. Your mother could live in a cowman's cottage on the estate.'

'You must be joking, she would raise hell if you were brave enough to suggest it.'

*

William's estranged wife, Ellen, remembered her old Gran cackling. 'Wash your face and hands gel and your arse and pockets. We don't want them calling you kipper-knickers up the board school.'

Ellen dreaded the thought of ending up in the clap hospital in Lisle Street with half her nose eaten away. She was getting maudlin. Thank God there was always a bottle of cheap port stashed away in the cupboard near the gas ring, although she had drunk enough to sink a battleship that afternoon. The soldier boy she had picked up in The Windsor Castle was Irish – her old man William was half and half. His ma was a dragon with green eyes and red hair and a temper to match. They had never spoken to one another since her mother-in-law Helena railed at her, 'You're little better than a hoor.'

The bloody corkscrew had disappeared, she found it in the wastepaper basket with some old discarded letters. The next thing would be snakes crawling out of the plughole – DTs.

Ellen was very drunk. She lay half naked on the bed, the lawn camisole top straining across her dark nipples, a light fuzz of hair sprouting under her armpits.

A moth flew round and round the white paper lamp shade hanging from the middle of the ceiling. The glaring orange light hurt her eyes like hell. She rose stretching her arms wide, took a deep breath and crossed to the chipped enamel wash basin behind a screen in one corner of the room, and splashed her face with cold water.

Bayswater was quiet at this hour of the night. She pulled back the curtains and looked out across the cobblestones. A tall man stood in the shadows near a lamp post on the other side of the road staring up at her window. He pulled a cigarette case out of his pocket, drew out a fag and lit it, looking a bit like the young soldier she had taken back to her room that afternoon. Mrs Higgins the landlady would be waiting outside her bedroom door tomorrow morning waiting for a handout as usual. 'Man in the bed, a shilling extra.'

All the kid gave her was an hour's pleasure and a packet of Woodbines! Poor Mike, he was so young, lonely and scared of the trenches. They were passing strangers in the night. She would never see him again. They say all cats are grey at night, but she was nearly old enough to be his mother. Every morning she pulled out a few silver hairs from her long black tresses, and peered at the crow's feet beside her fine dark eyes. God how she dreaded the future as a sad, lonely old woman on the game. William wanted a divorce, and she would be barred from seeing the children.

She could still pick and choose her men in a bar or at a tea dance: officers and other ranks. She was never a snob with her favours. If a man was attractive, she took him to her bed. Whenever William lost his temper, he called her a nymphomaniac who slept with taxi drivers.

She sat down heavily at the bamboo writing table, poured another glass of port to steady herself, and left the bottle at her right hand. 'My dear William,' she began to write in her large sloping handwriting, but the room was twisting and turning around her. William... William as she remembered him making passionate love in the loft above the carpentry shop in his father's builder's yard, and out in the fields at midsummer.

She was crying now. It must be the booze, or perhaps she was a sentimental old cow? Ellen still fancied the man. Her husband had become a respectable pillar of society sitting on the local council and the hospital board, joining the freemasons. On the square? My aunt Fanny.

William was a wonderful lover, but now the old devil wanted his freedom. They both had a roving eye in the past, but she was determined to resist all his pleas and offers of money in exchange for evidence of her adultery. Ellen didn't give a damn about the cash.

She took another swig of port, refilled the tooth mug and began again. 'How are the children? Do they miss me? I want to come home for Christmas.'

The youngsters were old enough to resent that clergyman's daughter who ran the household in her place; a martinet with high moral standards who looked down her long nose at Ellen.

The girls still loved her. 'When are you coming back to live with us, mummy?'

Ellen was crying drunk now. The tears trickled down the sides of her nose and across her chin, and she could taste the salt on her tongue. She wiped her face on her sleeve, but her eyesight was blurred, and her writing slanted backwards across the page.

She could tell him about Mike who was on his way back to the horrors of war after a little comfort from that old tart in Bayswater. He would have a story for the other lads.

She was hungry, and fancied oyster pudding and champagne with the toffs in Verrey's.

'This room is very poor... I miss you all so much... I want to live at home. Sack the old grey mare.

Her head was throbbing hammer, hammer, hammer. Tell him the truth for once in your life. 'I am drunk as a fart... drunk and lonely... pissed as a newt in paradise every night of the week.'

She pushed the letter away, and began to sob at the utter futility of life.

Bobby, the nancy boy in the next room, was knocking on the wall and calling out, 'Be quiet Ellen, you old soak, I can't sleep a wink with your sodding noise.'

She raised her hands to cover her ears and shut out the world and a large black hairpin like a stick insect fell onto the white notepaper. Waiting for it to move Ellen scratched her scalp and a mane of wavy hair cascaded down her back.

'Sod William.'

Reaching for another swig of port, she knocked the glass sideways against a tall brass candlestick standing on a corner of the table. It smashed into long jagged shards, and a spear of glass slashed her wrist as she fell forward in a drunken stupor. A string of artificial pearls embedded in the folds of her neck broke, scattering the beads like hailstones across the bare floorboards. Ellen's face and hair were mottled with blood and wine, and five blood-stained kisses sprawled across the page.

Bobby found her body next morning when he knocked on the door to borrow a cup of sugar, screamed like a woman, and ran all the way to the police station.

'Gawd gel, I never saw so much blood since Ma had a miscarriage after the second house at the Hackney Empire! I'll have another port and lemon.' He was in their Notting Hill local chatting up the barman, Limping Ada. 'What a gel. Different chap every day of the week. I met her old man once on the stairs: six foot tall and lovely brown eyes, dear... Bona. She wasn't really on the game, just willing to be kind.

She always went out to post a weekly letter to the kids, regl'ar as clockwork. It didn't work out for poor old Ellen. I suppose she was around for about five years on and off. I shall miss her in the room next door, although she could be a pain in the arse.

"Monday I go out with a soldier

Tuesday I go out with a tar..."'

He turned to the other drinkers in the bar:

"'If you will take a shilling

I'll make a man of any one of you."'

He paused for breath. 'Come and give us a tune on the piano, Khaki Gel.' Bobby crossed the room to confide in a bit of rough beside the fireplace. 'You remember poor old Ellen? She fell off her perch last night, and I called the cops. I think they suspect foul play.'

*

Mary was sitting on her bed wondering whether to cook black pudding or sausages on the hissing gas ring, when the telephone rang in the hall.

She could hear Mrs Donovan's low brogue, then the landlady knocked and poked her head round the door. 'It's a gentleman for you, Miss Donelly. Sounds like Mr Lester, he seems very upset.' Mary picked up the receiver.

'It's William. I must see you at once. Something terrible has happened. I'll take a cab and be there in about ten minutes.' He rang off before she had time to reply.

William strode into her room, white as a sheet, took a long gulp of whisky from his hip flask and began to tell her the whole story. 'We are not allowed men in the rooms, Mrs Donovan is very strict, but she might make an exception.'

'Don't be a bloody fool, Mary. Ellen is dead. It happened around midnight, but the police only got in touch with me about an hour ago. She spent the evening at Verrey's, then went back to the boarding house in Bayswater. The police think she was drunk. They say she was writing a letter to me when she died. There was broken glass and an upturned bottle of port. The wine seeped through the plaster ceiling of the room below. I don't know what to do... they want me to identify the body in an hour's time. There will be a post-mortem.' He cupped his face in his hands, his body shaking. 'God alone knows what she wrote in that letter. The police may think I killed Ellen because she would not agree to a divorce.'

'We are not lovers.'

Mrs Donovan was standing in the doorway frozen-faced. 'No men allowed in the rooms.'

'Mr Lester's wife has had an accident. Will you bring us a pot of tea in the front parlour?'

'Oh, the poor dear man.'

She came back with a tray, placed it on a low table in front of the chesterfield and whispered to Mary, 'Is the good soul still alive?' Mary shook her head and the Irish woman crossed herself. 'May she rest in peace.'

William gulped a cup of hot sweet tea. 'God knows I wanted my freedom but not like this. The police think it could be suicide or death by misadventure. They seem to have ruled out murder. I feel so bloody guilty... I haven't seen her for weeks, and I knew she was hitting the bottle. I'm worried to death about the letter. It could be a suicide note incriminating me. I can prove I was with the children at the time.' William broke down in a flood of uncontrollable weeping. Mary had never seen anyone so shattered and defenceless. She cradled him in her arms, and he slept like a child, only waking in time to leave for the mortuary.

The coroner's verdict was death by misadventure, caused by loss of blood due to the accident with the glass, and a very high alcohol content in the body. William was exonerated from all blame, and the letter was not produced in evidence.

'I think we should wait a year before marrying. The children will need time to accept the idea of a new mother.'

'I suppose it is only common decency.' Mary had never envisaged a future with five young stepchildren.

'I might buy that country house in Sawbridgeworth, you know I was born nearby in Waltham Abbey.'

'Mama could rent a cottage in the village to be near us.'

The older woman was adamant. 'I want to stay in Sussex, Mary, my only roots are here.'

William and his family would remain in the apartment with the redoubtable Miss Wooderson for the time being.

'These days I can afford lunch in the Grill Room at The Savoy, the theatre, punting on the river at Maidenhead... the business is doing well. I have tendered for an army contract today to build some new married quarters, and there's a masonic hospital in the pipeline.'

Her girlish dream of a thatched cottage with roses round the door was fading into oblivion.

'Come to supper tomorrow night. I know a little restaurant off the Haymarket. Wear the blue dress, it matches your eyes.'

'Now who's kissed the Blarney Stone?'

William came to Mrs Donovan's in a hansom cab, and the landlady watched them leave from behind the lace curtains. 'They would make a fine couple now that his wife has passed over, God rest her soul – like two lovers you might see at the flicks.'

William was strangely silent as they drove past the walls of Buckingham Palace and Apsley House. Street lamps in Piccadilly cast a soft glow over the trees in Green Park, and as they neared theatre land, she thought kindly of Stephen Phillips. The papers had printed a short obituary earlier in the year, and the total value of his estate amounted to five pounds. She remembered Laurence Binyon's poem *To the Fallen*: 'They shall grow not old as we that are left grow old.'

The new statue of Eros rose above the crowds around the Circus, and Cockney flower girls were selling roses and bunches of violets on the steps below. One of them poked her head through a window of their cab.

'Buy a flower for the young lady, guvnor?'

William handed over a few coppers for some Parma violets; his manner was sheepish.

The cabbie turned into the Haymarket, then veered left into a dimly-lit side street, where he pulled up outside an Italian restaurant, Julio's, got down from his box and handed them on to the pavement. William opened the stained-glass door. A few diners were scattered around the marble-topped tables, and an Italian maître d'hotel bearing a large tasselled menu, bore down upon them near the entrance.

'A-aaah, Signor Lester, so good to see you again. It has been a very long time since your last visit. Signorina...' he bowed from the waist. 'I can recommend the Beluga caviare and the oysters. They are a delight.' He touched the tips of his fingers with his lips, and blew a kiss into the air. 'As you say in England, one should never eat them when there is an r in the month.' He wagged a finger. 'Your usual table, Signor?'

'Thank you, Giorgio.'

The head waiter moved towards the back of the restaurant, where a long curtain of black and yellow beads concealed a winding staircase. 'The first door on the right at the head of the stairs, Signor. I am sure you will remember it well.'

They mounted in single file. William's hand urging her forward. The door opened to reveal a small room with a table laid for two, and a bottle of 'The Widow' resting on a bed of ice in a silver-plated bucket. Gilt chairs, gold-plated cutlery, an enormous chaise longue covered in rose pink brocade – a touch of vulgarity everywhere.

'A cold collation. Perhaps you would prefer to serve the young lady yourself.' Without waiting for an answer, the maître d disappeared. William had nodded before the door closed on the Italian.

He lifted the bottle of champers and, without a word, began to pour the wine. Golden bubbles sparkled in the hollow stems of the cut crystal glasses.

Like Alice in Wonderland, Mary opened the small door at the far end of the room, and saw a giant bed with red curtains, heavily embossed wallpaper, and a fat carved cherub hanging by a gilded chain from the ceiling. A vast mirror was suspended over the four-poster, and a screen partly concealed a washstand and a bidet. She was frightened and very, very angry. Then she began to laugh till the tears ran down her cheeks. 'You sly old fox, William. Did you hope to seduce me in this maison d'assignation? I suppose tired business men bring their mistresses here for love in the afternoon, une heure bleue.' Mary sat down at the supper table and dried her eyes. 'It would be a pity to waste the food, I'm starving.'

The deflated William kept his distance and did not look at her. 'How many girls have you brought here, William? They seem to know you very well in this establishment. The food and wine are good but that love nest is hideous.'

'I must have been mad, Mary. I want to make love to you so much, but we are never alone together. Your mother sits in Brighton like an old spider spinning her web and Mrs Donovan is determined to protect your virginity against all comers.'

'You poor lonely widower.' She loved this man but he was like a small boy determined to have his own way.

'You know I am ashamed of myself.' Fumbling in his pocket he brought out a small blue velvet box containing a large square cut sapphire ring. 'Give me your hand. I want it to be our engagement ring.' He slipped it on the third finger of her left hand. 'I can't ask you to marry me yet because of the children. It is far too early to give them a stepmother. They would never accept the idea. It will be easier when they are at boarding school. Besides, I am terrified of marrying again after my life with Ellen.'

'You want me to be a rich man's plaything. "She was poor but she was honest. A victim of the squire's sin."' Her voice trembled as she sang the old music hall ballad.

'You are asking me to be your mistress, William, although Ellen is dead and you are free? You know you are offering me hell and damnation. I need a breath of fresh air. Let us walk along the Embankment after supper. It will be almost midnight.'

'We are only talking about a scrap of paper.' He kissed her on the doorstep of Donovan's lodgings. 'I do love you, Mary.'

'I love you too, William. Good night, God bless.' Mary sank to her knees beside the narrow iron bed to say her prayers. If only the father was alive, she would know how to behave. He would have gone stark raving mad at the idea of his daughter's seduction and a life together out of wedlock. William would have been powerless against his fury, but he was not afraid of Anna who could be manipulated by her own determination to survive...

She fell asleep at last, dreaming of the crackling flames of everlasting hellfire, and the stink of sulphur. Hellfire and brimstone, into eternity for all sinners.

Chapter Twenty-Five

Anna was sitting in Kate's kitchen feeling irritable after drinking a whole bottle of vin ordinaire with her bread and cheese. Her mouth felt like the bottom of a parrot's cage. A cassoulet was simmering on her gas ring for the evening meal, but beans gave her the wind, and it was a very strange colour.

She began to pick on Annie who was peeling vegetables at the sink and enjoying her half day at home with the family. 'Why don't you work in a factory, girl? You are old enough, and they pay very good money.'

'I don't fancy it, M'm.'

Kate joined in the conversation. 'You know very well that your Dad would never see you in a place like that. When you finish in service at the end of the month, there's a job going for a young waitress to train at Sweeting's Restaurant, bottom of West Street. Quite genteel!' We can't have you working at Dival's, can we love?' That evening Kate grumbled to her husband.

'If Madame Anna starts ordering our girl around, she'll have to go.'

'The worm turns at last. Don't forget we must always protect Lady Muck of Turd Alley.'

'Fred, you've gone too far as usual.'

'It's true. You've been at her beck and call for years.'

'She was very kind to all of us when we were young.'

'I know, but that's a long time ago and she can't dine out on it for the rest of her life.'

'Don't worry, I'll tell her a long-lost cousin from down under wants to come and stay for a month or two, so she must be on her way.'

Anna was devastated. 'I thought it was a longstanding arrangement until Mary comes back to Brighton, at least.'

'Sorry I'm sure, but she's a relative from Fred's side of the family, so I can't argue.'

★

Mrs Pearl Saunders was Anna's guardian angel; a plump lady with tarnished hair, and a large single stone diamond ring on her marriage finger. In her prime, she had bestowed her favours on a few gentlemen, and a grateful, slightly disreputable, major, bought her a pretty terrace house in Ivory Place. Her lodgers were hand-picked. The current amour was a gentle blackmailer, who sadly returned to a cold cell in Lewes Gaol whence he came.

Anna met her in Kensington Gardens, where they were both ferreting through the bead necklaces and furs. It was a cold day and they adjourned to the Duke Of York's for a pick-me-up, where, after two glasses of port and lemon, Pearl realised that her new-found friend Mrs Donelly, was a real lady in distress. Two gentlemen of her acquaintance nodded and winked from the bar.

'I used to be well-known in here, dear.'

Kate came to meet her old mistress in the snug, and was surprised to find her in the public bar with Pearl Saunders. She whispered in Anna's ear. 'You know that she is an old pros.'

'This lady has kindly offered me lodgings for five shillings a week. I am sure Fred would prefer my room to my company, so I shall leave your cottage at the end of the week. They say the Lord will provide.'

Kate breathed a sigh of relief, and decided not to argue the toss.

★

A letter came from Ireland.

My dear Anna,

It is sad to know that we shall never meet again. The doctors in Dublin have diagnosed a cancer (thank God it does not affect my heart or my head for the time being) and predict my death in a few weeks.

The consulting rooms are in St Stephen's Square, a few doors away from the hotel where we celebrated your wedding so many years ago. 'Nymph in thy orisons be all my sins remembered.'

My life may not be a failure after all. I have loved my family, the school children and my country. Collins is dead, but Dev will try to build a new Ireland on the ashes.

God bless you now and always,
Declan Aloysius (the name is a well-kept secret!)
'Captain Moonlight'

*

Mary kept all her letters in a large hat box on top of the wardrobe in her bed-sitting room away from prying eyes. They were dated from 1908 to 1915, written by a wide variety of pals and suitors: Billy from India, Arthur Knight on board HMS Caernarvon anchored at Plymouth or Bantry Bay and Willie 0'Malley who said he would cheerfully throttle her if she were as cruel to him as to some of the other beaux.

Billy wrote a long diatribe about 'the diabolical labouring classes' and 'the Germans who are worse than Cannibals'. He was addicted to capital letters and to his mother who was 'jogging along although she is very feeble these days'.

One of the earliest letters from Arthur was written about the episode with Sir Charles Palin.

Beautiful Lady,

Do write and tell me more about your mama's matrimonial ventures. Think of it, you might be able to cut the umbilical cord at last and escape into the free world for the first time in your life. Will you meet me at the Prince's in Piccadilly for luncheon at 1 p.m. if you are able to flee from the clutches of your dear parent?

I enclose a photograph of myself taken by a bald little man with fuzzy hair in a bad light, six for 2/6. The homburg was chosen with great care and I hope you consider it fetching.

I did not fancy a visit to The Quaker Girl, so life has been very dull. Don't forget 1 p.m., post meridian not midnight you featherbrained creature. I know you have no sense of time whatsoever.

With all best wishes,
Arthur

Those from Willie were in a different vein altogether.

14 September 1914
My dearest Mary,
You will be glad to know that I got a commission in the Territorials as Second Lieutenant, so in a few days I will be a full-blown army officer. I don't think I will die when I hear what you are going to do, unless it is to become a member for the prevention of flirts.
Yours Affectionately,
Willie

My dearest Mary,
You do not say anything about William. We are having a hell of a time here working like blazes. On Wednesday last we were up at 4.30 a.m. and out by 7.30 a.m., all guns etc. and were not back till 8 p.m. That means we were in the saddle for about eleven hours and it was raining hard all day. We have an awful lot of work to do as we are training for the front. We are all under canvas which is very nice in fine weather, but awful in wet. We have a full compliment of horses (about four hundred). In my section I have eighty men, fifty-six horses, two guns and four wagons. Some looking after. Altogether not an easy job.
When I see you I shall tell you all about my little love affair. I am still… you know! I don't think I shall be long now.
All the best,
Willie

Officers' Mess

My dearest Mary,

I was going down to Brighton on Saturday last but was bagged! Met a very nice girl at Westminster Cathedral and was hauled on the river. Wait till I tell you all about it. Very rapid progression. Please write. We haven't moved yet. Spoke to Kitchener about it yesterday, but he was rather rude to me.

Best love, yours affectionately,
Willie

3 August 1915
My darling Mary,
Of course by all means tell anyone you like to go to hell. I think I am getting over my last love affair. So you are properly in love now, I should like to meet him.
Have been trying to injure myself by riding wild horses, but I have had no luck. You see, if I get a broken collar bone or something like that, I shall have a nice holiday.
With love to mum and also to self,
Yours affectionately,
Willie

She had written to ask his advice about living with William without the blessing of the church, then tried to make her own decision.

22 April 1915
2/6 London Rifle Brigade RFA, 105 Holland Road.
My dear Mary,
I received your letter this morning with great pleasure. I was very bucked to think that you had a little thought for me at last. I am very glad indeed that you have decided to chuck the wretched affair. (I mean wretched from one point of view you understand.) My mother has often said to me that she would rather starve in the gutter than do a dishonourable thing. This is no idealistic preaching but for a girl of your refinement and character, a practical point of view. I have never done anything in my life that I knew was wrong, but I suffered hell's own remorse for it after. There is only one way and that is the way of purity and self-restraint. Your argument that it is selfish to be so anxious about one's purity when the lack of anxiety may do another material good, is both wrong and pernicious.
Must I steal and murder to get money for a starving woman? Perhaps you are wondering why I am at last taking up the right and strong attitude in this matter. I will tell you. I always had a

strong objection to this proposed step of yours but I think I must have been carried away by your impetuosity and spirit.

I must ring off now. Give dear old mum my best love.
With love to your sweet self.
Your affectionate friend,
Willie

P.S. Saw Dolly last night. She said she would like to live with me. Hot stuff, eh! (Pip-pip.)

12 August 1915
RFA Much Hadham.

I went up to town for a few hours to see my Agnes off to Ireland. Hope you are getting along well with 'Villum'. I wish I could have a straight talk to him about you. I think I would open his eyes a bit.

Don't be afraid to put private things in your letters to me as I shall destroy them if you wish.

P.S. I am very sorry to hear that the dear old girl is unwell. I sincerely hope she will soon be quite recovered.

Willie O'Malley was killed in action at the Battle of the Somme, and Mary lost her dearest friend. His mother wrote from Ireland.

Willie was a lovely lad and I know his dearest wish was to marry you after the war. He told me how you met in a newspaper office in Brighton: you were writing an advertisement for a lost bird, nibbling a pencil and trying to spell Norwich Canary. He always called you his sweet innocent Mary.

Let us remember Willie every night in our prayers.
Catherine O'Malley

Chapter Twenty-Six

Mary wore the sapphire and diamond ring on her engagement finger out of office hours, taking afternoon tea in Gunter's or punting on the river at Maidenhead every Sunday afternoon. She tied her long golden hair with a ribbon and wore a straw boater to save her complexion from the rays of the sun, but William rolled up his shirt sleeves and was as brown as a berry. They often lingered over strawberries and cream on the terrace at Bray, before driving back to London and the parting of the ways. Every Saturday Mary sent Anna a postal order for fifteen shillings. William had given her a rise after the first few months work.

'Will you come to Clovelley with me for a week's holiday? I can book a double room at The Crown Inn and no one will be any the wiser. You see I am being straight with you this time.'

'Will you buy a brass curtain ring to make me an honest woman? It might turn green overnight! "With this ring I thee wed, with my body I thee worship."' There was a catch in her voice. She resented the idea of an affaire, but she loved the man. 'I will ask mama's advice.'

'That old harridan would sell her soul to the devil.'

'I can't see the horns. I love my mother although she can be infuriating at times.'

'I hope you love me more.'

'Sometimes you are like a great selfish child, William, demanding your own way. I want a simple life. Yesterday I was happy.' There was a long pause. 'I will write to mama tonight.'

Brighton, September 1915
My darling Mary,

Just received your two letters, and I am grieved and joyed. I will do as you say and hunt up anyone likely to employ you at a minimum wage of a pound a week.

In answer to your query of course we could exist the two of us on a pound a week and pay our rent perhaps out of it. Five shillings weekly is not much, but does your experience of bills give you a clear vision of a balance of fifteen shillings a week to live on? If we are to keep clear of livestock, we must put down two shillings weekly for washing, sixpence to bath our bodies etc. so, to cut it short, we should only have with the utmost care, five shillings each weekly out of which we must save for shoe leather, clothes etc. You will have to face all weathers and risk pneumonia.

Inevitably the time must come when acting like this we will both be shoeless, homeless, poverty-struck, sick and dying, wanderers and tramps on this earth. True for a very short time for we should both die in the gutter. Thank God, so far you and I have escaped. Dear heart, you say you feel you would be unhappy living not maritally with WL, but would you be happy seeing us shrivel under the storm of life? I have courage, or rather did have, but you will get older and the five shillings subsistence and clothing allowance is a pittance. You will not get the chance again... even of living with WL. and with the possibility of his marrying you at the end. You will be less unhappy and perhaps more holy and good too. If offered to God in a spirit of sacrifice and hopelessness of us both, never can He blame you.

You could get a home, a little house or a flat. Your mother in her declining years would be spared the misery and shame of the workhouse. As a mistress you are free, free as the birds of the air. I personally would prefer it. I have been a wife for twenty-eight years and, my God, how have I wished myself free. Free beloved! He wants to remain so, take it from me, make your bargain like a holy good little Jew. Offer your sacrifice, make rules of life for yourself in the new calling, stick to them, boss yourself and him too. Don't ask too much at first. Say you've thought it over. Ask him to show you the flat he proposes, the style of furniture and the rooms. You want one for your mother and one for receptions occasionally. How often would he see you? Don't refuse, don't be a fool, chances do not occur daily. Fix your weekly allowances at least for twelve months on trial and no children. There will be no marriage at the end of this in my book. This is if you wish to lose your freedom and make him keen... 'women's trickery'. You are a damn fool and would have the best time of your life.

Now Mary, you say you would be unhappy, and so you would, and I too on five shillings weekly. It seems to me either way there is some unhappiness and sacrifice.

I am willing to come to London and live with you or remain here. Kate would be only too pleased to work for you and keep her mouth shut. In fact you could tell her you were married.

My dear, be careful and weight weigh, weigh before you murder us both. I may tell you I pawned various odds to have a dinner at Edlin's to try and get you a barmaid's job. I offered your services free while you learned your business. They are sacking all their women as things look bad for the brewers and distillers. Women may be debarred from earning a living in licensed houses.

Dear old girl, I was a bleeding fool to instill so much good in you but I suppose I was such a heroic angel myself and did not know the terrors of want and misery. I will be your guardian angel and take great care of us both.

I wrote to Louis, but he never answered. I hear he is often in The Clarence tippling, and there was a deadly fight the other night. Well now I'm off out of bed, eleven o'clock this morning, (looks like work, don't it?). I will read the dailies for work, and go to the Labour Bureau. It does seem hard Mary, with your beauty and chances that you do not have the brains as well to manoeuvre a good home for both of us.

I must be off and see if I can get some work.

Have you seen Uncle André?

Your affectionate mother

Kate has no money yet and I have nothing, and we owe altogether to Mrs Saunders: rent £3 10s, including old balance £1 7s 3d; Louis 11s 6d; Me 4 weeks, 12s 6d.

I will have nothing to eat today, so see how I feel in summer time. That should give me a pretty good idea what it will be like next winter on five shillings weekly, That's a good plan is it not?
I think I will take all my clothes off and ribbon them a bit, and see the effect on Brighton just before you refuse the offer. And I'll try to

sell some laces in the gutter to see how much I can earn. I might sell crochets or try bloody fortune-telling to the poor skivvies in the areas. Now think before you refuse. You are taking on too much for both of us spiritually and temporally. I tell you honestly I am not a saint and I have not the physical strength to face it. If you do not take this offer, he will never make it again.

Mrs Saunders says you are a cat.
Good-bye and God bless you.
Mother

Her mother's letter came by return of post. The die was cast. Mary dreaded an illegitimate baby, but she was ignorant of Marie Stopes' advice on birth control. Instead, she read a woman's magazine and visited the pharmacist to buy a small safety sponge and a bottle of quinine. She understood the sponge should be soaked in a solution of crushed aspirin, or quinine and water, inserted and left in position all night.

The chemist showed her a wicker basket full of bath sponges. 'These are imported from Egypt, and I have some excellent loofahs if you prefer one of these, Madam.'

He brandished a fine specimen about a foot long, and Mary blushed to the roots of her hair. 'I need a very small sponge for bathing the eyes, a bottle of aspirins and some quinine: I think I am sickening for a bout of influenza.' To hell with precautions.

Long ago she had dreamed of walking down the aisle on her father's arm, a virgin in a long white velvet gown wearing her mother's veil of Brussels lace. Now it was time to tell Mrs Donovan a tissue of lies.

'I shall be leaving in a few days and going back to live with my mother in Brighton.'

'I shall be sorry to lose you, my dear, I thought you might wait a while out of respect for the dear departed then marry your man. We could have had a lovely wedding in Westminster Cathedral.'

A fortnight later William and Mary drove through Devonshire stopping for a picnic by the wayside. 'I've brought smoked salmon sandwiches and a bottle of bubbly.'

'Mrs Donovan gave me some of her soda bread for mother.'

William was like a small boy on a day out in the country. Mary twined fuchsias into her corn-silk hair. 'Our Lady's earrings.' She remembered her father saying that in Herstmonceux.

The road fell away as they approached the village, where shaggy donkeys shambled up along and down along the street of Clovelley.

The Crown Inn was a backwater smelling of sawdust, beeswax, beer and roasting meat.

Love making was swift and lusty. A warm animal experience, unlike her romantic dreams of a mystic sacrament. She wondered if the act itself merited the reams of paper wasted by Willie and her mama. The first night was the worst, a sad mixture of pain and guilt. Afterwards, they made passionate love rolling in haystacks, romping on the sands in secret rocky coves, and lying in their downy bed with the casement windows flung open to the sea air and the night breezes.

Sometimes William put on his dressing-gown and smoked a cigarette looking down at his lovely girl, a skein of golden hair spread across the pillow, and one arm outstretched seeking the comfort of his shoulder to lie on.

Mary lost Mr Clarke's safety sponge either down the water closet or hidden away in some crevice of a lavender scented drawer.

Throughout the mock honeymoon they fought like Kilkenny cats about everything under the sun: Ireland, religion, her mother, and where they should live together in the future.

'I suppose I could stay on at the lodgings, but Mrs Donovan would demand to see our marriage lines.'

'Your mother's friend, Mrs Saunders, must be an old pro and I would not leave you with her for all the tea in China. To be honest, I rented a furnished flat in Brighton when you agreed to come away with me. It was meant to be a surprise at the last minute.'

'I might loathe the place.'

'There is a spare room for your mama, and she can act as chaperone when I am away in case you get up to mischief.'

There was a blazing row on the journey home, and he dumped her by the side of the lane, and drove away faster than she could run, watching her standing there through the rear window and roaring with laughter. She trailed behind him along the dusty road, then as soon as she gained a few yards he trod on the gas. William pulled up at a tea garden and wound down the car window. 'Pax?'

'Yes, but I'm not sorry for anything I said. You are a horrible man. I love you, but I don't like you.' She climbed on the running board, and he stowed her dressing case in the boot.

'I may not be an educated man, but I shall always remember a line from one of Shakespeare's sonnets: "He mounted her but would he manage her?" As Bernard Shaw wrote in Pygmalion: "Not bloody likely!"'

★

The flat in Devonshire Place was a stone's throw from the sea, shabby but adequate.

'I will open an account in your name at Hannington's, and you can tart it up a bit with new curtains and a few knick-knacks.'

Anna was already ensconced in her room (by prior arrangement with the bricklayer) so they met for a house-warming drink in Edlin's Bar near the Aquarium, run by two brothers, Lloyd and Tubby. Lloyd was a ladies' man, tall with fair curly hair and laughing eyes that crinkled at the corners, Tubby a comedian. Later he played the Tommy in a tour of *Alf's Button*.

'One or two drinks to celebrate, then we can all go home together for the first time.'

★

One Sunday morning they were lying in bed together while Anna prepared coq au vin in the cramped little kitchen. William was smoking a cigarette, while Mary read the latest romance from the lending library.

'You will get as fat as a pig if you eat so many chocolate creams.'

'I fancy smoked salmon, peach melba and some ripe camembert.'

'My God, you're pregnant.'

'Three months, isn't it wonderful? I am going to buy two layettes: one pink and one blue in case of emergency.'

'Don't be a sentimental idiot, Mary. I thought you took precautions.' He was very quiet for a few moments. Another child would be a millstone round his neck. 'I know an old woman who would adopt the baby for a hundred pounds or I could arrange an abortion.'

A blazing virago slapped him around the face. 'I don't want some filthy woman in a back street operating on me with a knitting needle! Kate told me about the laundry girl's friend years ago and death from peritonitis. I am going to keep our baby and you can go to hell.' Mary broke into a fit of hysterical weeping, and he held her in his arms.

'Will you marry me when all the children are at boarding school?'

She nodded, sniffing into his linen handkerchief.

'Six is a round number… I'll back it on the roulette table at Monte Carlo when the war is over.'

'How shall I break the news to mother?'

'She is a tough old bird. Just tell her she will be a grandmother in August.'

Anna was furious, and threw a dynamic scene. 'How on Earth could you be so stupid? The man will have to marry you now.'

Mary only left the house after dark. The days lay fallow, and the two women endured the loneliness of living together through the long hot days of early summer.

In spite of Anna's blandishments, Mary refused to see a priest or talk at length about the birth and the possibility of marriage in the near future.

Kate thought it sad that Miss Mary's child should be a by-blow. 'You know where I am if you need me. There's a phone in the pub near the station where you can leave a message for me or Fred any time.

★

'Pray to St Anthony, pray to St Anthony. I can't find any of the baby's clothes. What on earth is a swaddling clout? Holy mother of God, I don't even like tiny babies!'

'Don't be so melodramatic, mama, everything we shall need is in the chest of drawers outside in the passage.' Mary was trying to rest quietly on the bed with a large box of chocolate creams on the table beside her. 'The contractions are coming every five minutes now, so I think Kate should run and fetch the doctor. Oooooh!'

She lay back on a heap of feather pillows and stroked her stomach. No one had warned her beforehand and she had never known any great physical pain.

'Mum hung on to the bedpost when us kids was born.' Kate remembered Anna's first stillborn child so many years ago and now she was still here repeating the same words. She had left Fred and Annie to cook and clean for themselves, and moved in to the flat for the accouchement; sleeping on a rug in the hallway.

'Tell the midwife I'm in agony, and call the doctor at the same time, and hurry!'

Anna was scrabbling around dropping odds and ends on the floor in her excitement. 'It could be a false alarm. This place is a shambles.' She looked at her daughter. 'I think you are going to die. Where is the bricklayer? He should be here for the birth. This is the last time I help to bring one of his bastards into the world.'

Mary caught her breath in pain.

Anna lit the gas jets above the fireplace, and the yellow light flickered.

'Nurse Perello will need a length of cloth for the baby's navel, some safety pins and an old cocoa tin. Don't ask me why. They are in a cardboard box on top of the kitchen cupboard to keep them clean.'

Mary touched the huge pink satin bow on top of the chocolate box for luck, it was William's last present before catching the London train. 'He knows the baby isn't due till the weekend, so he plans to leave town tomorrow.'

There was a loud knocking at the door. Anna nearly jumped out of her skin, then opened it a few inches. Louis stood on the threshold in his officer's uniform looking tired and dishevelled.

'Good Evening, Mater, the return of the prodigal son.' He kissed her on both cheeks. 'May I come in?'

'Louis, how wonderful to see you. Are you on leave?' Mary flung her arms around her brother and gave him a big hug. 'Dear Louis.' It was so good to see him she was almost in tears.

'It is a long story my dears.' He sat down on the edge of the bed and rubbed his eyes. 'May I take off my boots? Have you got a drop of the hard stuff in the house? I'm dog-tired.'

Anna was clucking round him like a mother hen, and came out of the kitchen with a tumbler half full of William's malt whisky, topped up with a little water.

'It's a bit stiff, even for me. I shalt be blotto. Still, who cares?' Louis had deposited his boots in the middle of the floor and sat wiggling his toes in the thick khaki socks. 'Well...' there was a long pause for the full dramatic effect of his story. 'Louis has been a naughty boy. There was a large mess bill so I gave a cheque as usual but the bank refused to honour it – insufficient funds in the account. There had been a few gambling debts as well – poker games to while away the time. The straights and the flushes were not coming my way: too many people 'seeing me' when there really wasn't very much to see. The luck of the Irish ran out after a while, and it was considered to be conduct unbecoming of a gentleman.'

He stretched his long legs and took another swig of the whisky. Mary's contractions were coming every two or three minutes now, and she was trying to camouflage the pain.

'Actually it's worse than it sounds. The mps want to arrest Louis and take him back to barracks to be court-martialled and cashiered. But I am determined to give them a run for their money.'

You could have heard a pin drop.

'Thank God father isn't around to see it, talking about his code of honour. I'll join up again in the ranks. They can't keep me out of this scrap whatever they do. "Keep the Home Fires Burning." Jingoism stirs the entrails, but it gives you the shits too.' Breathless, Kate ran into the room.

'The doctor will be here in a few minutes, Miss Mary. I ran all the way but I'm knocking on a bit now. There's two soldiers on the doorstep asking for Lieutenant Donelly. I told them we hadn't seen him for ages, but they won't go away till they've had a word with you, Madame Anna. Oooooer!' As she turned away from Anna she saw the young master standing in a dark corner of the room.

'Get into the wardrobe Louis and hide behind my evening dresses; they will never find you there. We'll bluff it out.'

Louis grabbed his boots and dived into the tall oak cupboard. There were muffled snorts of laughter as he became entangled with silks and sequins, then all was silence.

'You can let them in now, mother.'

Anna drew herself up to her full four feet eleven inches, and opened the front door.

A tall figure in sergeant's uniform stood to attention. 'Sorry to disturb you, ma'am, but we are looking for Lieutenant Donelly. We followed him as far as Brighton Station, but he managed to give us the slip. We were given your name as next of kin.'

'My daughter is about to give birth to her first child in this room, Sergeant, and I regret I cannot help you in any way. We are expecting the doctor and midwife. I must ask you to leave this apartment immediately.'

The sergeant hesitated.

There was a dramatic groan from the bed. 'Thanks for your help ma'am. Can you suggest anywhere else he might be in hiding?'

'Some fancy woman's apartment perhaps.'

The sergeant and private turned away, but as they were about to leave the premises, there was a great cracking of timber, and Louis' feet appeared through a hole in the bottom of the wardrobe. The oak door burst open and he lay in a heap on the floor rocking with laughter and festooned with pink, blue and lilac gowns.

'You never knew I was a transvestite, mater dear.'

Mary collapsed in a fit of helpless giggles, while her brother staggered to his feet and divested himself of the silks and satins.

'May I suggest you men wait outside in the corridor till after the baby's arrival? Then I will go quietly, and in the meantime, I promise not to escape by the lavatory window. I am sure my mother will provide chairs for your comfort, and we can all wet the baby's head in a drop of Scotch.' He won his point, turned to his sister, and gave her a slight bow. 'After all this excitement, uncle Louis must know if it's a boy or a girl before he is dragged away in handcuffs.'

'Louis, you can't possibly sit there getting sozzled while the baby is delivered. Go into the kitchen and boil a kettle of water, or help Kate till the midwife gets here. Four of us should be able to manage, with two mps camping outside the door.'

Dr Hellyer arrived in a flurry. He knew the mother-to-be was unmarried, and expected grandma to be practical in an emergency or collapse in hysterics. She was a lady given to extremes of temperament.

Kate acted as general dogsbody. She plied the military police with food and drink to keep them quiet, and scurried hither and thither with hot water and towels.

A fine baby girl was born to Mary without mishap. Mary had sworn like a docker after a whiff of ether, and called for William again and again.

They all toasted the mother and child. Then the soldiers escorted Louis Donelly to Brighton Station on his way back to barracks, to face the charges against him.

★

Some weeks later the postman brought a letter addressed to Anna.

My dear mother,

Everything went according to plan after our last meeting, and I am now somewhere in France serving king and country in a new capacity. The flowers here remind me of the lanes around Herstmonceux in high summer.

I met a terrific girl on my last leave, she's dancing in a show with Jack Buchanan and Elsie Randolph. Don't worry mother, she's not a tart, she's even got an auntie Clara in Devonshire with a few quid in the bank. Great Expectations... What larks, Pip! I know it's a bit of a comedown after the fantasies of a rich American widow and a brownstone house in Manhattan, but I couldn't be happier. I think I'm in love for the first time in my life and I wanted you to know how happy I am. (It makes a change from the stews of Suez and Marseilles.).

Kiss the baby for me and big hugs for you and Mary.
See you all soon, God willing.
Love Louis

A brief note followed about a month later.

Dear mother,

I've bought one. Don't worry unduly, it's only a wound in the calf of my left leg but it's put me out of action for a while. The doc says it's peppered with shrapnel, and I was livid when they told me the news in hospital, but now I am quite reconciled to the idea, especially as I may be up for a medal. I expect to be discharged at the end of the month.

Catherine's show is playing the Manchester Opera House and we intend to marry in a registrar's office with a couple of chorus girls as witnesses.

We might have a church wedding later, but Cathy is a Protestant. Forgive the unseemly haste, but we are very much in love. (No, she's not in the family way, before you ask.)

I want to open an antique shop in the Lanes, and lead a quiet life. The council should grant me a tenancy as an old soldier, and is Cathy quite happy to give up her career on the boards to share my life. Did I tell you she is only seventeen and very naive, so please be kind to her?

See you all very soon as an old married man.
Your ever-loving son,
Louis

A few weeks later the young lovers stood together hand in hand in the shabby living room of the Brighton flat. Cathy wore a straw boater, a white blouse and a navy jacket. Anna gazed into a pair of deep blue eyes and knew the poor child was terrified of meeting her new mother-in-law. 'You are lovely, my dear. I am sure you will both be very happy.'

Louis whispered encouragingly in her ear, 'I knew you would come up trumps, mater.'

★

'We are never alone for two minutes in this flat. It's far too small for three grown-ups and a baby.' William peered over the top of his evening paper to watch Mary's response to his grumbles. Anna was cooking in the tiny back kitchen, an omelette aux herbes de Provence, but he fancied steak and chips or even bangers and mash for a change. This new-fangled continental cuisine gave him the collywobbles, and he delighted in playing the rough working man just to annoy her.

'There's nothing like a good blow-out.'

Anna shuddered at the British vulgarity.

'I have an idea Mummy if you will only sit down and listen to me for two minutes instead of playing with the baby.'

'I'm only giving her a cuddle before putting her to bed.'

Sometimes William was jealous of all the love and attention lavished on his infant daughter.

Mary brought two glasses of chablis, and sat beside him on the worn sofa, a spring pinged as she lowered herself on to the moquette upholstery. 'Every damn thing is falling to pieces. I want to tell you about my surprise. There is a small villa for sale in Hove. It's in Langdale Gardens, just off the seafront. It's not jerry built and the price is about right – six hundred and fifty pounds, but I reckon the man would take six hundred. He's a bit short of the readys.

Spider Woman could live with us and help with the baby if you insist, or we could afford a maid. Money's always safe in bricks and mortar. Will you come and look at it with me tomorrow afternoon?'

William bought the house, and put the deeds in Mary's name, which reassured the 'tarantula'.

'Perhaps you are not on approval any more?'

★

They visited Hannington's Department Store as a trio and bought a red Turkey carpet and brocade curtains for the dining room, a brass chandelier for the hall, chintz cutains and covers with blowsy pink roses to adorn the drawing room, and a tall mahogany double bed for the first floor front (with a balcony).

Marianne's room was pink and white with tiny bluebirds on the wallpaper and, a porcelain holy water font to hang beside the bed.

They left the flat in Kemp Town without a backward glance. Only Mary would remember it with love as her daughter's birthplace.

★

'Your grandfather was baptised in Southwark Cathedral when he was five days old. Have you decided on a date for Marianne?'

'We are leaving it in abeyance, you know I have not been to confession since father... killed himself. The priest will tell me I am living in sin and should marry for the sake of the child.'

'You would never forgive yourself if the baby should die young and you had thrust everything to one side for the sake of William.'

Anna raised the lid of a domed trunk standing in a corner of her bedroom disclosing documents, birth and wedding certificates of the whole family, yellowing parchments. 'These could be our inheritance one day.'

'You remind me of Miss Flitt in that book by Charles Dickens.'

Anna drew out a small package wrapped in black tissue paper. 'It is the only thing of value I possess now: a gift for Marianne with my love. God bless you both.' Her voice was husky with emotion. She was offering the child her last remaining treasure.

Mary tore away the cover and held the miniature of Eugénie framed in sapphires and rose diamonds. She gazed at it for a moment in silence then thrust the velvet bag into her mother's hands.

'You should sell it mama and buy some new clothes. I know you have cherished fond memories of the empress for years, but it is all a nostalgic illusion.' She turned away from the trembling woman and left the room. Was this a thrust to kill or lack of understanding?

Anna was heartbroken. She drank like a fish for days, seeking oblivion, anything to kill the pain. When she was not drinking, she locked herself in her room and slept. Boozers in a pub near Portslade Station thought she was an old soak but it was the first time in her life that she had entered a bar room.

One night a cabbie took pity on her, and drove her back to the villa in Langdale Gardens free of charge.

'There you are mother, we were lucky to get past the curfew without any trouble. You should stay at home for a few days and lay off the booze.' Anna had lost her door key. She banged on the door again and again but there was no answer. 'Bastard. Your baby is a basta-a-a-rd!'

William raised himself on one elbow to look at the bedside clock, then climbed out of bed.

'The old woman is drunk as a fiddler's bitch.'

Anna woke with a fuzzy head, rubbed her eyes and looked out at the bleak grey world. She could remember being dowsed with icy water, and William frog-marching her up the stairs. So this was the end of the affair as far as she was concerned she never wanted to see the man again as long as she lived. Mary was sure to give her a subsistence allowance. She would go to Louis and appeal for help in finding somewhere to live.

'Perhaps it is all for the best, mama. Dolly won't put up with your interference in the kitchen, and I've lost one mother's help already.'

'I shall go to Louis. He told me once, "You may be irresponsible, mother, but you are never boring".'

'I will pay the cab fare, mama, and give you a weekly allowance out of the housekeeping money. William refuses to contribute a penny towards your upkeep.'

'Scum of the earth,' and she swept upstairs to pack her few belongings in her trunk together with the miniature of Eugénie. She looked out of the window at the smug suburban street and remembered the wonderful houses in the past: Hollingbury

Copse, Brunswick Terrace and Arundel House – tall and elegant with high ceilings, long Georgian windows, wrought iron balconies and the belvedere.

'One day, maybe... when my ship comes in, and I am a wealthy woman again.' Talking to oneself was said to be the first sign of madness.

The shop bell rang and Catherine peeped through the glass door leading from the parlour. 'Your mother's waiting outside, Louis, with a taxi driver and a pile of luggage. I think she's moving in.'

'Over my dead body.' Louis hurried to investigate.

'Mary paid the cab before I left. Good riddance to bad rubbish as far as that man, William, is concerned. Tip the cabbie, Louis, I do not have any small change.' She stood squarely inside the door waiting to be invited into the sitting room.

'My dear mater, are you going on safari? Come inside, have a cup of coffee, and tell us all the news from the front.'

She subsided into an armchair, and took a deep breath before launching into an embroidered version of her story. 'Your sister's paramour has thrown me out of the house at a moment's notice. He can stuff his bijou residence. I need to find lodgings. Can you suggest anywhere for me to stay?'

'Have a drop of brandy in your coffee, it might serve to calm the nerves.'

Anna leaned back against a pile of cushions and closed her eyes.

'Do you remember "Porky" Newman, the second-hand dealer? He's come up in the world, a property man with rooms to let in most of the back streets of Brighton. You stay here with Catherine, and take a dose of sal volatile, while I go round to his office in Prince Albert Street. I shan't be long.'

He returned about half an hour later. I think the randy old devil fancies you. I said you would go round straight away, and his piggy eyes were glistening when I told him your name. The rent is ten bob a week, but I'm sure he will make a special reduction in your case.

Louis, you are beyond the pale.'

They set out together, but Louis abandoned her on the threshold with a promise that old Sam, their odd job man, would deliver her skips and the domed trunk on a hand cart later in the day.

'Good luck, mater.'

A large sign painted in bottle green and gold announced: *Percival Newman, Property for Sale and to Let.*

Anna caught sight of herself in a small mirror hanging in the outer office. A trim figure in a dog's tooth costume with a black felt hat set at a slightly rakish angle on short, bobbed silver curls, carrying a small ebony cane. She was still a beautiful woman despite her age. An office girl ushered her into the sanctum without delay. Porky sat at a vast desk with a plate full of bread and cheese in front of him, a copy of *The Sporting Life* and a pint tankard of ale at his elbow.

He rose as she came into the room, and held out a pudgy hand in greeting. The man had put on weight since removing her surplus goods and chattels from Hollingbury Copse, number nine and Arundel House with a horse and cart. 'Mrs Donelly, it is a great pleasure to meet you again after so many years. Take a pew.'

Porky was wearing a loud tweed suit and brown boots. 'I hear your daughter went off the rails with a married man... living over the brush, as they say. Ah well, these things happen in the best regulated families. The sins of the flesh. The sins of the flesh, as you might say, and very nice too.' He leaned back in the chair and his pot belly shook. A thick gold albert jiggled up and down.

Anna knew she would slap his face at any moment, but she was trying to hold the candle to the devil. He took a swig from the pewter tankard. "In the mouth and round the gums. Look out stomach here it comes!" That was a saying of my old dad's when we were kids.'

He bent forward, piggy eyes gleaming, holding something in his fat little trotters. 'Your rent book and key, dear lady, or may I presume to call you Annie? A special price, not ten shillings a weeks as I told your son. Ho no, but seven and sixpence, all signed, sealed and delivered. Nobody can turn you out of your little nest, a cosy dry basement if ever I saw one.' His pupils narrowed like the dark slits of a parrot's eyes, as he looked her up and down. 'You're still a damned fine woman, Annie, if you'll forgive me for saying so, in spite of the ravages of time. My own good wife is a very prepossessin' woman, very prepossessin', but she doesn't understand me. She's a good plain cook, but no imagination, if you get my meaning.'

He stood up behind the broad pedestal desk, and she saw his fly buttons were undone, his trousers gaping wide. He was wobbling a large pinky-beige sausage under her nose. 'Put your hand in here, my darlin', and you can live rent free for the rest of your life. I'll not ask anything more for the time being. I'm not a mean man, we could have a lot in common.'

Anna felt as sick as a dog. She had never seen a man's private parts. Slowly she moved closer and closer towards him, his whole body was shaking as she extended her gloved hand towards his nether regions. He closed his eyes in expectation. Pale sunlight filtered through a window on to his rampant manhood.

'Thank you, Mr Newman, for your kind offer.'

'Call me Perce.' The man was grunting like a hog.

Anna picked up the tankard and poured the cold beer straight don the front of his trousers, picked up the rent book and swept out of the office, leaving a howling Porky behind her.

'You cow... you've ruined me bloody new suit.'

Anna climbed down into the basement, one mossy step at a time, and nearly tripped over a loose slab of stone near the front door. It was painted a sickly lime-green. A tom cat had sprayed the area to mark his territory, and a pile of rubbish and leaves blocked the drain.

The first room was furnished with a single iron bed, washstand and deal cupboard and a square of yellowy linoleum. The walls were veined with a fine tracery of mildew, and sparkling crystals of frozen damp like a mosaic of diamonds. The back kitchen held a table, painted Windsor chair, and a ramshackle chest of drawers. In a cupboard under the sink, she found a scabby blue enamel saucepan and a frying pan. She sat down on the bed and waited for Sam to bring her belongings on his barrow.

A text over the bed announced, "The Wages of Sin are Death". She thought of the revolting Porky and his sausage daring to offer her this mouldy apartment in exchange for her favours! Anna began to laugh for the first time in days, and the tears streamed down her face. Sam heard her roaring fit to bust as he rounded the corner and thought she must be stark raving mad but she looked sane enough when she answered the door and gave him sixpence for his trouble. 'Thank you, my man.'

Bloody airs and graces, but you could tell Mr Louis' ma was a lady.

Chapter Twenty-Seven

One of Porky's rent collectors called for the seven shillings and sixpence every Saturday morning as regular as clockwork. Anna had been a tenant for about six months when she found a note pushed through the letterbox. (She had been hiding behind the milkman's horse and cart to avoid the man.)

Mrs Donelly,
    Four weeks rent now overdue: thirty shillings in all, (underlined in red ink). If payment in full is not received immediately, I shall take out an eviction order.
    Percival Newman Esq.

Anna made a cup of strong black coffee and sat down at the kitchen table. 'Pray to your patron saint pray to St Anne,' she murmured. She had an idea, took a sheet of writing paper from her old leather case, and began to compose a letter to the Empress of France.

Her Imperial Majesty, the Empress Eugénie, Farnborough Hill, (How did one address an expatriate dowager empress, should she write in French or English?).

Your Majesty,
    For many years I have tried to emulate your great courage in adversity. You may still remember your Christmas child, the little girl with violet eyes in St Mary's church, Chislehurst: it was the bitter winter of 1870.
    My beloved husband John could not face debt and dishonour and committed suicide, I shall never know if I drove him to his death.
    My son has a young family to support, and my daughter does not love me. I am living in a basement flat in Brighton, in arrears with the rent, and the landlord threatens eviction.

> *I need one hundred pounds to begin life anew, and I appeal to you for help. I shall never be able to repay you as I have squandered my inheritance.*
>
> *My lifelong devotion to you, ma'am, and sincerest wishes for your well-being.*
>
> *I remain, as ever, your devoted servant,*
> *Anna Marie Rose Donelly (nee Van Maaskens)*

Anna read through her begging letter and shrugged her shoulders it was *une blague*, a sick joke. She was far too proud to post it. There must be another way out of this impasse even now.

She threw the letter into the waste paper basket, crammed an old fur felt hat on top of her head, buttoned her coat against the cold, and set off down the street.

It was a bitter day, and she was at the end of her tether. She stopped for a moment at the corner of North Road, took a deep breath before wrapping the muffler tightly round her mouth and turned towards the sea. The rotting skeleton of an old dwelling place was being pulled down to make way for a new block of flats. She peered through the slats of wooden fencing erected to keep out children and trespassers at the demolition site, strewn with flint stones and rubble. 'Jesus, Mary and Joseph, I have an idea.'

There, within feet of the barrier, lay a dead rat. Rigor mortis had set in, and the animal's sharp pointed claws stuck out towards her. She was terrified of vermin and the bubonic plague but, prodding her walking stick through a gap in the fence, she could almost touch the dead body of the rat with the metal ferrule.

Anna reversed the stick and managed to hook the corpse and pull it towards her by the crook. It was almost within her grasp. She shuddered and braced herself, reached the dead rat with her gloved hands and dropped it into her shopping bag.

This was a battle for survival; the creature might decompose. She walked quickly through the back streets to the town hall where a notice board directed her to the sanitary inspector's office.

Anna knocked on a door marked 'Enquiries' and said she had an urgent problem she wished to discuss with the sanitary man. A few moments later a girl showed her into the inner office. 'A Mrs Donelly to see you, sir.'

Anna held the carrier at arm's length and with a gesture worthy of the divine Sarah, flung the offending creature on to his desk. 'This, sir, is my problem.'

He opened the bag, accidentally touched the fur, and recoiled. Wiping his fingers on a large spotless white handkerchief, he listened to her pathetic story.

'I am a widow, my name is Donelly, and I rent two rooms near the Clock Tower from a certain Mr Percy Newman. I dare say you know his reputation of old. He calls it a basement flat. He is always pressing me for the rent and I am almost out of my mind with worry. This cr-r-r-reature was found under the floorboards in my kitchen after I noticed a terrible smell.' (She kept her fingers crossed in her lap as she lied.) ' See the dust and rubble on it's whiskers, it has been dead for weeks. It is decomposing It might carry any disease, typhoid fever, anything.' She began to cry.

The sanitary inspector thrust the bag to the far end of his desk. 'There are cockroaches under the kitchen sink, sir, great black beetles...' Her upper lip trembled. She must not be tempted to embroider the story.

The Inspector sneezed. 'That animal stinks. Poor Mrs Donelly. No one can expect a lady to live under these conditions. Mr Newman could be prosecuted under the Public Health Act. I am sure he would offer to pay compensation if you do not press charges. Perhaps the whole matter could be settled out of court; otherwise he would be liable to a very heavy fine. However there is still the matter of suitable lodgings. Under the circumstances I am sure the council will take emergency steps to offer you alternative accommodation.'

Anna sank back into the chair and dried her eyes; this was beyond her wildest dreams. One must not appear too eager. 'I have set my heart on a little shop where I could sell antiques, in the Lanes perhaps. I think I might be able to earn a modest living.'

He listened to her ideas. 'If you could persuade Mr Newman to pay me a small sum of say one hundred pounds, I might be able to forget the whole terrible experience and start afresh.' She trembled in anticipation and he thought she was shaking with fear.

'If you care to wait a few moments, I will ask the office girl to make you a cup of hot sweet tea while I have a few words with my colleague. Only yesterday one of the councilors mentioned a small shop with living accommodation that had fallen vacant in Union Street, the lane running from Ship Street towards the meeting house. Rent to be in the region of ten shillings a week. Would that be agreeable to you, Madam?'

He left the office carrying the corpus delicti at arm's length, and came back a while later to say that everything was arranged for the poor lady. A distressed gentlewoman could not be expected to endure such horrific conditions.

'If you would be kind enough to make all the necessary arrangements? I could not bear to face the humiliation of dealing with Mr Percy Newman myself.'

Anna moved into the Lanes a fortnight later after prising up a floorboard in the kitchen as evidence of the rat's last resting place. The obscene bladder of lard knew when he was beaten, and paid up like a gentleman.

'One hundred smackers to that old bird. What a conniving cow.'

In exchange, Anna consented to sign an undertaking that she would not take proceedings against him for contravening the Health Act.

Chapter Twenty-Eight

'William is to get a knighthood in the New Year's Honours List.'
They had just finished the Sunday roast beef and Yorkshire when Mary dropped her bombshell.

Anna roared with laughter. 'You are joking! That must have cost the bricklayer a packet.'

'You are horrible, mama. William has given a great deal to charity, works hard on the local council in Hertfordshire, and sits on the hospital board. You know he is a Justice of the Peace?'

'So you are the only skeletons rattling in his cupboard? I am sure it would be very easy to leak information to the papers... Grand Master of his Masonic Lodge has secret love nest in Brighton, and a little bastard child. Even Lloyd George might not be so enthusiastic!'

'William always had the idea you might blackmail him.'

'So why the hell doesn't he do the decent thing and marry you if only for the sake of the child? You know her name could be altered on the birth certificate if you were to marry, as you were both free when she was born? Are you still teaching his eldest son to swim and visiting the girls at Roedean with cream cakes on their open days? Under an assumed name of course. I believe you are a war widow with a small child whose husband was killed in the Royal Flying Corps? It's time you came to your senses instead of playing charades.'

'You are a heartless cow, mama.'

'I am trying to be realistic for Marianne's sake.'

'William has decided to move. We are letting this house in the autumn and renting a large flat on Brunswick Terrace, the drawing room floor for eight pounds a week, number twenty-six, near the house where I was born – so the wheel has come full circle.'

★

The Armistice was signed at last, and the newspapers heralded 'Peace in our time and a Land fit for heroes'.

Mary invited mama to lunch every Sunday because William was away in the country with his other children, but there was always a blinding row by the end of the afternoon, and Anna was banished to the Lanes in a taxi cab.

In peaceful interludes, Anna and Marianne escaped hand-in-hand down the garden path through the wooden gate and across the allotments to a secret garden. 'I will teach you to speak French, little one. *Attrape jolie mouche. Natalie, Natalie, elle est toujours très jolie.* Perhaps we should sing together *Sur le Pont d'Avignon...*'

Anna bought her little granddaughter a black and white rabbit, and on hot summer afternoons they sat on the back doorstep near his hutch making wet mud pies in a couple of flower pots. 'I pretend to be as tough as old boots, but the little one is enchanting.'

*

The Spanish flu epidemic spread across Europe from the rotting corpses on the battlefields and the mass graves; people were dropping like flies. Anna took heavy doses of quinine and became a recluse refusing to open the shop door to anyone. One afternoon she could not ignore the heavy-handed rapping on the glass. Lucy, Mary's 'maid of all work', stood on the pavement outside.

'The missus sent me to fetch you, she's desperate. Miss Marianne's been taken bad with the flu and the doctor says we need help night and day. There's a taxi waiting on the corner of Ship Street. Will you come?'

The child lay in a crumpled heap under the bedclothes breathing heavily. Anna took her hand. Marianne blinked, opened her eyes and looked at Anna. 'Grandmama,' then she fell asleep again.

'The crisis will be tonight. Her temperature was over one hundred and four degrees and rising. I can't take it now, she is breathing so badly and I don't want to disturb her by putting the thermometer under her arm. Her night gown was wringing wet from the fever. The doctor is coming back later tonight. He says all the hospitals are full of the dying and it is impossible to save them.' Anna handed her coat and hat to Lucy.

'Tell cook to make tea for your mistress, and fresh iced lemonade for the child if she wakes. I will take a glass of dry white wine now.' She sat down beside the bed to keep her vigil.

'Drink your tea and lie down for a while Mary, you must be exhausted. There is nothing more you can do, and I will stay as long as you need me.'

Anna bathed the child's burning forehead with tepid water.

Lucy brought a carafe of wine and a goblet on a tray. 'Now that your mistress is in bed, I think it is time to call the priest.' She took out her rosary. 'See to it, girl.'

The hours dragged by. Around midnight the child was gasping for air, the body shuddered and was still. Anna crossed herself. Tears pricked her eyelids. The child's hand was still warm in hers. They were alone together in the darkness with only the glimmer of a nightlight. Lucy had not brought the father in time for the last rites. The hand fluttered like a small bird in her grasp. The girl was alive. Her prayers were answered.

Kate died of influenza while Anna was nursing Marianne, and Fred buried his wife in the churchyard of St Nicholas where they were married. Fred, young Annie, Rose, Ernie and two of their children, stood at the graveside with a cluster of friends and neighbours behind them. No one could find the mistress in time for the funeral.

The clergyman droned on and on about 'Our dear sister, Kate'.

Fred thought he could hear Kate's voice saying, 'Silly old sod. I'm pushing up daisies now so you will have a bit of peace and quiet, Fred. Don't keep me waiting too long.'

Everyone gathered in the cottage parlour after the funeral. Fred poured glasses of ale for the men, and port and lemonade for the ladies while Annie made a big pot of tea in the kitchen for those who had signed the pledge. The doorknob rattled, and Cecil brought a few empties to the kitchen sink. 'Come on, girl, perk up!'

They were walking out. He worked behind the haberdashery counter at Leeson and Vokins and Mum always thought he was a bit of a nance, but Annie found him a tower of strength.

'We must keep an eye on your dad, he's found a bottle of rum at the back of the cheffonier, and I'm afraid he may get plastered and show himself up. Here, let me carry the tray.'

'If you get sick of Brighton you can always come and work for me, gel. We've got a nice little wet fish business in a posh part of Surrey, Epsom, not far from the race course, eh Rosie? We go to the Derby every year and take all the kids. It makes a great day out, with chunks of pineapple and a glass of whatever you fancy.' Rosie had filled out and forgotten her days of wine and roses in the Haymarket brothel. She was a comfortable little body now with twinkling eyes and a ready smile, well corseted in a new black suit, wearing a hat with a veil and a cock's feather at the side to cheer it up a bit.

Katie always said she wanted us to have a bun fight when she passed over. My kid sister hated a load of old misery guts.'

Fred rose to his feet with Annie and Cecil on either side of him. He was swaying slightly as he stood to attention and raised his glass. 'To my Kate, the best little wife in the whole world, God bless her.' They drank the toast, munched their way through the ham sandwiches and seedy cake, and drifted away to their own homes, leaving Fred and Annie alone in the cottage.

Fred had not been able to find the missus for days because she was staying at the villa in Hove. He called at the shop in the Lanes, cap in hand, holding a small parcel and shifting his weight from one foot to the other, blurted out the news.

'Kate's dead, Madame Anna. I think she caught the flu looking after old Granny Lewis in Terminus Street. I'm lost without her after all these years. Annie s a very good girl and she'll stay and look after me for a year or two, but she's courting a young man.'
'Come in, Fred.' Anna remembered him best as a freckle-faced lad working in the stables. 'Sit down and I'll make you a strong cup of tea. Three spoonfuls of sugar? You see I remember.' She

wanted to cry, but brushed away the tears for his sake. The poor man was sick with grief. 'Why can't Annie marry her young man and share the cottage with you? That would kill two birds with one stone. I'm sure it's what Kate would have wanted. The girl can't stay an old maid looking after her father for years.

He gulped the strong sweet tea. 'I never thought of that.' He held out the brown paper parcel. 'Kate always wanted you to have this if she went first.'

She took the package from his big, red hands. It was tied together with a neat bow of string.

'Kate wrapped it herself in bed the day before she died.'

Anna opened the paper. Inside lay the black and white china dog she had bought for threepence at the Fair on the common and given to Kate when they were both young girls.

'It's the comforter, ma'am. She always said you called them spaniels comforters.'

There was a note from Kate written on pink notepaper in her best handwriting, very neat and upright.

It read:

Dear Mrs Anna,

Please take care of my little dog. I don't think I shall need him any more. Keep him in your room for luck. His name is Sam.

Good-bye. God bless.

Love Kate

There was a big kiss scrawled across the bottom of the page.

Anna picked up the black and white dog and stood him in a place of honour on the mantelpiece, between her photographs of John and Louis.

Fred put his cup and saucer down on the table, and she shook hands as he was leaving the shop. 'Good day, Ma'am. You know my Katie always loved you better'n me or Annie. It hurt sometimes.' He shuffled off down the cold dark street, a broken old man still dressed in his best Sunday suit with a black armband on one sleeve.

Anna was bereft. She had no real friends only a few acquaintances among the totters and the old women with a pitch on the stones in Kensington Gardens Market. Hannah, Mimi and Maureen had faded into oblivion.

There was no rapport with Mary these days. Freud might have said the mother felt guilty about her past influence. Dear Louis was a different kettle of fish altogether. She doted on her son.

Sam sat on the mantelpiece gazing down, black boot-button eyes and shaggy hair covering his ears, looking like Kate as a girl. Anna remembering her swinging on the orphanage gate the first day they met, dancing the tarantella with the organ-grinder, polishing Fred's old brown boots in the scullery of their little cottage, pushing Mary's bassinette along Marine Parade with her uniform starched to the eyebrows and trying to look fierce like a 'nanny from hell' to intimidate young Louis.

Anna put on her old furs, locked the shop door and walked through the Lanes for a cup of strong coffee with her son and heir: Catherine and the boys.

Chapter Twenty-Nine

One day early in 1926, Anna was sitting at an iron table in the bar of The Seven Stars waiting for her daughter to bring the weekly remittance money, and buy a round of drinks, the usual ritual every Friday. The double doors opened to reveal Mary, a fashion plate in a fawn cloche hat, knee-length broadtail coat with a fox collar, and beige glace patent shoes. Her fair hair was shingled to a point at the nape of her neck. 'A baby Guinness and a gin and t, please.'

Scarlet lobsters on the white marble counter, flamboyant red and gold plush upholstery and vast gilt mirrors were a perfect foil for Mary in her muted colours.

'I can't stay long today, mama, I am meeting Alma for luncheon at Sweetings.'

'She is a nasty common woman with tits like an old sow and the belly of a poisoned pup.'

Mary could feel her temper rising. She was fond of Alma and it was difficult to make women friends with her irregular background and her relationship with William. She glanced away from her mother's mischievous face, and caught sight of the old lady's feet clad in a pair of second-hand riding boots bought for half a crown in Kensington Gardens Market from one of the totters. 'You like the boots? They are excellent quality; my feet are swollen now so I take a size one. It's the fault of the chilblains.' She took a malicious pleasure in taunting her daughter on every possible occasion.

'Mama, I can't stay here any longer to see you make an exhibition of yourself. I am leaving. I suppose you want another drink before I go?'

At that moment Louis walked into the bar to pour oil on troubled waters. 'What are you drinking, mother? Half a pint of Guinness and a gin and T for you, Mary?'

He joined their table, and was on great form.

'You can tell I'm feeling flush at the moment. I've found a marvellous way to make money. I travel round the country in our old jalopy, tap on doors, and ask if there's anything old-fashioned for sale. I'm on the knocker! You should try it some time, sister dear. You could be mistaken for the Lady Bountiful in that rig-out, and the cottagers would think you were doing them a favour. Thank you for calling, milady.' He gave her a mock bow and touched his forelock.

'Have another tipple? It's the Irish sickness you know.' As soon as he disappeared to the bar, Mary placed three pounds on the table. 'There is your money, mama.'

'That reminds me, Mary, can you lend me twenty pounds for a week or two? A distressed gentlewoman has some old porcelain for sale, and I think there may be a pair of Chelsea figurines.'

'Another of your pipe dreams? No way, mother, William would be furious. The last time I lent you money, I took my gold mesh bag to the pawnshop because I couldn't stretch the housekeeping allowance any farther. I have a thousand pounds a year to cover all the expenses apart from the rent, Marianne's governess and the bills for coal and champagne. This time I am afraid you will have to manage in your own sweet way.'

Anna prodded a stubby forefinger stained with button polish at the broad-tail coat. 'I like the new furs, Mary. Let me count the skins and I will tell you how much William paid for the coat.' (One of papa's second cousins had been a furrier in the Rue St Honore and she had learned a few tricks of the trade.). Mary ignored her.

Anna stood up and pirouetted like a plump little ballarina. 'I got my furs out of cold storage this week,' she chortled, 'I keep them in the cellar during the summer.'

The musquash coat had already seen better days when she picked it up in the market from one of the totters. Now in its fifth season with Anna herself, it was balding on the collar and cuffs and stretched at the seams. Some of the skins were split and Anna had joined them together with big, shiny safety pins – far quicker than a needle and thread. A silver nappy pin fastened the coat across her ample bosom.

Mary rose to leave as swiftly as possible, and Anna decided it was time to open her antique shop across the road and feed the moggy, Tinkerbell. Anna overheard two women at a nearby table discussing her appearance 'It's a disgrace, the daughter wears expensive clothes and gets herself up like a dog's dinner, while the mother dresses like a tramp.'

Anna paused for a moment on her way to the door. 'You, my good woman look like the whore of Babylon.'

Louis watched her exit, wrapping the fur coat about her person and leaving The Seven Stars like a galleon in full sail. The old girl might be eccentric but she was still damn good value.

*

The shop was divided from the back parlour by a portière curtain hiding the brown pottery sink in the scullery, and the copper pots and pans ranged above. The aroma of beef stew with herbs was enriched by the smell of medicinal rubs and potions emanating from amber, blue and green chemist's bottles on a wooden shelf near the window.

Louis was wont to hold his nose in mock disgust and chant, '"Bubble, bubble, toil and trouble". It is like a witch's coven. What evil brew are you concocting today, mother dearest? Perhaps you are casting a spell on the bricklayer.'

Looking through the lattice window, Anna could see her pots of bittersweet geraniums, nasturtiums and marigolds lining the crooked path to the earth closet, but now the autumn was here, and the view was bare save for a few evergreens.

The shop window faced south and caught the sun. Bead necklaces, amber, cornelian and ivory hung against the door, and tinkled like windbells whenever a stray customer entered. Collectors were few and far between.

Anna was hungry as a hunter after crossing swords with Mary and those dreadful women in The Seven Stars. She locked the door behind her, drew back the heavy curtain on its brass rail ladled some of the casserole into a brown pottery bowl, and tore off a hunk of crusty French bread.

The sleek black and white cat weaved its way between her legs as she squatted on a low oak stool to enjoy her meal in peace.

An old phrase of John's came to mind: Monarch of all she surveyed. She remembered so many of his sayings: 'never let the sun go down on your wrath', 'warm your hands at the fire of life' from Dr Johnson, and 'as good as bread'.

Anna ignored the rattle of the letter box, and only made her way towards the shop door after a ripe peach and drinking a strong cup of black coffee. The bills could wait, time enough.

One of the letters was addressed to Madame Anna Rose Donelly, the Madame was unusual these days, and it was not Uncle André's handwriting although it bore a Belgian stamp. She slit the envelope with a carved ivory paper knife her curiosity aroused and skimmed through the contents, headed by the name of a firm of solicitors well known to her in the past.

'If Madame will be kind enough to contact us immediately, something to her advantage... etcetera, etcetera.'

Anna read the letter again very slowly then began to wash up the dirty crocks from her meal, piling them in the old brown pottery sink while she boiled a kettle and set to work. Her mind was a whirlpool. 'Keep your hands moving and take one step at a time. There might be some mistake.'

Her heart was racing. This affaire was beyond her wildest dreams. She dried her hands, crammed the old felt hat on top of her head, put on the offending musquash coat, and set out in search of Louis with the letter tucked away in her handbag.

'Oh God, there's mater jigging up and down on the doorstep like a Zulu warrior with St Vitus' Dance. Can we stretch the remains of the high tea?'

'There are two or three eggs in the larder. I can always make an omelette.'

Anna's old felt hat was askew, and her hands trembled as she fumbled in her handbag. 'I have had the most fantastic news... a letter from Monsieur Garnier.'

'And who might he be, dear Mamma?'

'You remember the Van Maaskens solicitor in Brussels? He writes to say that Uncle André is dead. No crocodile tears, he was a fine age, ninety-four years, and I must contact the firm at once and learn something to my advantage. It may only be one or two oil paintings, but we must telephone now and I haven't any cash.' (She had forgotten the remittance money from Mary in The Seven Stars.)

'We are completely skint after doing the weekend shopping, mamma,' but there must be some way out of this ridiculous impasse. Of course the office might be shut, it is getting late.'

'I have Monsieur Garnier's private number. The letter is most insistent.'

Catherine was always the practical one in the family. 'There is plenty of small change in the children's piggy bank if you are really desperate.'

Louis smashed the blue china pig on a corner of the mantelpiece, and the small boys began to howl as a shower of pennies and threepenny bits fell across the carpet. They scrabbled on the floor retrieving odd coins and pieces of jagged china. 'Don't cut your fingers. Be quiet boys, we'll get you a bigger one tomorrow.' Louis spread the money across the old gateleg table and began to count their ill-gotten gains.

'Don't want another pig, want that blue one.'

'Stop caterwauling and granny will buy you a present, a football to kick around the Lanes.'

The noise ceased as if by magic, and David and Jonathan gazed silently from the hearth rug.

'You know my black cat Tinker? She was only a kitten when we rescued her from a dustbin in Middle Street, sleek and black as night. Your father wanted to christen her Scheherazade after the Princess in the *Arabian Nights*, but I call her Tinkerbell. I will give you sixpence a week each if you feed her every day while we are away. She loves cod's head and pussy's pieces, but they stink. She will eat scraps from the table when she's hungry. Is it a deal?'

'Yes, Gran.'

Louis put on his old tweed overcoat. 'Come on, mater, we can use the telephone in the Old Ship Hotel.'

'One moment, if you please, sir, I will see if Monsieur is available.' The maid fetched her master to the phone.

'Chère Madame, how kind of you to call.' Louis was almost crawling into the earpiece.

'As you know Monsieur André Van Maaskens died at the great age of ninety-four, and will be sadly missed by all. We have found an old will made in 1910 in which our client leaves his entire fortune to you, his niece. In any event, you appear to be his next of kin. It would assist us greatly if you were to leave for Brussels at your earliest convenience in order to comply with the necessary legal formalities. I am sure you are aware that your uncle has left a considerable estate, chère Madame.'

There was a quick intake of breath in the telephone booth. Anna's fingers clawed at Louis' sleeve. 'I shall travel with my son Louis, Monsieur Garnier. One has certain commitments, but we should be able to arrive in Brussels the day after tomorrow.'

'We shall always be eager to welcome you to our beautiful city, Madame. My clerk will reserve a suite at the Palace Hotel on your behalf.' The telephone clicked, the line was dead.

They hugged one another and performed a little war dance in the foyer of The Old Ship to the utter amazement of the residents. Louis paid for the call with his store of odd coins. 'Many thanks, you may keep the change,' and they swept out of the building, arm-in-arm, two shabby clowns. 'Panache, my dear little mother, panache. I am sure that poor girl is convinced we have robbed a gas meter.'

Catherine had put the boys to bed, and peace reigned. Louis unearthed the dregs of a bottle to toast the future. They drank, and the fiery liquid burnt her throat. 'My God, Louis, it's poteen. I shall be pissed as a newt in paradise.'

'Moonshine, only moonshine. Here's to the luck of the Irish!' He raised his glass, and they sat dreaming of a rosy future.

'I shall buy wonderful extravagant presents for my grandchildren and...'

'The money is burning a hole in your pocket already, mater. Don't count your chickens before they're hatched.'

'You are a fine one to talk, Louis, always searching for the crock of gold at the end of the rainbow. I know this is my last chance.' She took a deep breath, and braced herself for the next move. 'I need a clear head to cope with Mary. Call a cab, Louis, we must tell your sister the glad tidings. I can pay the fare out of my remittance money, I forgot it was lying at the bottom of my handbag all the time. I loathe asking her for money, but we need tickets for the journey and new clothes. We are not arriving to claim this inheritance looking like a couple of down and outs!'

They drove along the promenade to Mary's new flat on the drawing room floor of twenty-eight Brunswick Terrace. It was a godsend that Anna's son-in-law would be absent at this time of the week. Anna paid the driver, and mounted the stairs, butterflies fluttering in the pit of her stomach.

A maid answered the door, dressed in a frilly white cap and apron and black uniform for the evening.

'Your mistress is not expecting us – Mrs Donelly and Mr Louis Donelly.'

'If you will be kind enough to wait in the hall, I will tell Madam you are here.' She looked askance at Anna's fur coat and riding boots. Louis raised a finger to his lips, and they sat side by side on two hall chairs.

'The lady of the house is entertaining.'

They could hear a low buzz of voices behind the closed doors of the drawing room. 'May I take your coat, Madam. This way please.'

Anna stripped off her outer garments to reveal a paisley shawl in flame colours seamed to form a dress.

'Très avant garde, maman, Liberty's best.'

'Hand-me-downs from the market.'

Mary rose from a low settee to greet them. 'My dear mama and brother Louis. It is a most unexpected pleasure at this hour. You should be tucked up in your little cot, mother. May I introduce my friend, Tiny Smith? My mother Mrs Donelly and my brother Louis – Miss Tiny Smith. Take a pew. Two more glasses please, Alice.'

They were all players in a drawing room comedy. Mary gazed at her mother through clouded eyes. Thank God that ghastly frock was out of focus, a blur of cream, terracotta and black. Still Louis was clad in his very old heather tweeds, and he at least looked distinguished.

'Tiny' wore a short beaded dress, and a black velvet band round her forehead, with an aigrette in the middle fixed by a diamond pin, slightly askew.

Anna dismissed her as a plump silly little thing.

A Chinese shawl embroidered with blood-red paeonies, was thrown across the grand piano displaying photographs of William, Mary and Marianne in embossed silver frames. Blue Italian brocade covered the cane and walnut bergère suite. A shallow black Wedgwood bowl stood on a low table by the window, near a vase filled with artificial apple blossom.

There was a long empty silence.

'Tiny' took a Turkish cigarette from her shagreen case, Louis rose to light it for her, and the fluffy creature bridled.

A light tap on the door, and Marianne came into the room to say good night. She kissed her mother, shook hands with 'Tiny', then ran to hug Anna and Louis. 'You've come to see us at last, grandma. What a shame it's bedtime.'

'Dance with me, my little UD. Play something lively on the gramophone, Louis... rag-time... "It's a Bear" or "Teach me to Shimmy like my sister Kate". That's better, little brother. UD can do the Black Bottom, can't you, darling?'

Louis wound up His Master's Voice, and music blared out loud and fast through the horn. Mary grabbed her daughter by the hand and they danced, wiggling and twirling, till she twisted an ankle and almost fell on top of the child.

'I'm tipsy.' She dismissed Marianne with a vague wave of the hand. 'Go to bed, UD, we're all very tired. Nightie, Night.'

Marianne loathed Tiny Smith. She hated her fat little feet pushed into black patent leather winkle-pickers with gobs of beige flesh protruding over the sides, but most of all she detested the scent of violet cachous on her breath.

The child ran down the corridor to the nursery she shared with Nanny, brushed away her tears, sniffed hard and began to read Hans Christian Andersen's Fairy Tales.

Louis was trying to make conversation, and give his mother an opportunity to broach the reason for their visit. 'Why on earth do you call that poor child UD?'

Because she is my tame little Ugly Duckling who might change into a swan one of these days – *une belle laide*. She knows she is not pretty, even at ten years of age, which is rather sad. Ring for Alice, Louis, I want her to call a taxi and bring my wrap.'

'We are going to The Lotus Club tonight, Mrs Donelly. It's too divine, everything is oriental like Limehouse.' It was Tiny's first long utterance.

'I do not frequent night clubs at my time of life. Utter gutter!' Anna had picked up the expression from a 'bright young thing in The Stars'.

'I want to ask you a favour, Mary.'

'Let us drink a toast to the Roaring Twenties! More music, Louis, while we drown our sorrows. Have another glass of fizz.'

The record turned to the tune of 'I'll be loving you, always' and Mary began to gyrate.

'For Heaven's sake turn off that bloody noise.' Anna grasped the metal arm, and the needle scratched across the grooves. 'Uncle André is dead. Louis and I are travelling to Brussels the day after tomorrow.'

Mary ignored her, dancing across the room, her dress glowing like a stained glass window, a length of purple chiffon drifting across her face. Silence fell. At last she turned on her mother. 'The vultures gather to pick the bones white. I am sure you want money mother, take it.'

Picking up her gold evening bag, she pressed the jewelled clasp and flung a pile of small change and a wad of notes into Anna's lap. 'For God's sake go home before I lose my temper.'

'You do not understand why we are here, Mary.'

'To sponge on your daughter, dear mama, and squeeze her dry. You like my friend 'Tiny?' She lives with a lord so you see we are both kept women although she is higher in the social strata of mistresses!'

The deadly stillness was broken by a knock on the door. 'Your cab is waiting, Madam.' Alice brought a facecloth coat with a bearskin collar, and a bunch of Parma violets.

Mary thrust the flowers into her mother's hands. 'Happy memories, a last gift from your dear John. Goodbye mother. You killed my father as surely as God made little apples. I have always loathed you since the night he died in agony, and I never want to see you again as long as I live.'

Tiny stubbed out the butt of her Turkish cigarette in the ash tray. 'This is a howwible scene... Tiny is going to the Lotus Club for a drinky-poo.' The aging flapper teetered towards the door in her winkle-picker shoes and burst into tears. 'Tiny wants... Tiny wants a baby!' She followed Mary down the stairs weeping and wailing.

Anna picked up the money and thrust it into her handbag, shaking like a woman with the ague. 'I am going to see my grandchild before we leave.'

'I'll wait here and drink another glass of champers. Don't let my sister get you down, mater. It's not worth it.'

The maid was lurking in the corridor to see them off the premises, but Anna was on her mettle. 'Take me to Miss Marianne, Alice, before we leave.'

Marianne was busy drawing a picture of daddy in a bowler hat and a stiff collar with a carnation in his buttonhole, carrying a furled umbrella. She signed it 'The Kid', his special nickname for his youngest child. When Anna knocked on the nursery door the little girl sprang to her feet. 'I thought you'd gone home, Grandma. Come and sit in the big armchair. I want to talk to you.' She curled up on the floor at Anna's feet and sat looking down at her hands. 'Tiny says I'm a bastard, and I don't understand what it means. I was hiding under the grand piano to escape from that awful woman, and they were talking about me. I know daddy loves me but he says I'm the skeleton in the cupboard. You know I have never met any of the brothers and sisters. It's like being an only child.'

Anna put an arm around her shoulders. 'Poor baby. I expect mummy and daddy will marry one day.'

'Daddy's always saying, "Do it now!" But it's always one day... one day you can learn to sing and dance and go on the stage. Last Christmas daddy took us to the pantomime at The Grand Theatre and there was a funny fat old man dressed as a lady who sang: "Potatoes have eyes, Oooh what a surprise".' She giggled at the memory. 'I would love to do that.'

'Maybe one day Marianne' you might be on the pictures like Mary Pickford.'

There was a long comfortable silence broken by the child. 'Mummy went into a nursing home to lose a baby. Alice said she was going to die.'

'Well, Alice was wrong for once in her young life.'

Out of the mouths of babes and sucklings – Anna had never heard of the abortion. 'I am going to Brussels with uncle Louis and I will bring home a present. What shall it be? Would you like a puppy or a kitten?'

'You choose, grandma. Uncle Mike bought Mummy a goat, and they hauled it upstairs on a rope, but it ate all the cushions in the drawing room and smelled disgusting so it's gone to live in the country now. He wants to marry mummy, uncle Mike, not the goat. I like him but I'd hate living with him all the time instead of daddy.'

Mike Leverson had been around for years, and was unlikely to be a threat now.

'You have seen the little griffon bruxellois? They are small brown dogs with fierce black whiskers, very brave. I came to England when I was nine with a little black pug dog called Mopsy.'

'Would it be dreadfully greedy to ask for two presents, grandma.'

'Ça depend, ma petite.'

'I would love a white satin tutu with frills like the fairy godmother in the pantomime, my very own ballet dress.'

'The puppy and the dress, I promise. Isn't it time for bed?'

Marianne undid the pearl buttons on her dress and dragged it over her head to reveal a Liberty bodice, chilprufe vest and drawers.

'Come here, child, and let me help you. Where is Nanny tonight? She seems to have disappeared.'

'She has a follower, he's a policeman on the beat, and it's her half day off. Alice is supposed to look after me.'

'She's doing a grand job.' Anna loved this little girl very much indeed. 'Climb into bed and I will tuck you up. Don't forget to kneel and say your prayers first. Night, Night, mind the bugs don't bite.' She kissed Marianne on the tip of her nose. 'Au'voir. God bless.'

'Au 'voir, my dear little grandma. You *must* come to see us more often. *Je te donne un gros bec*, a big, big kiss. You see I have not forgotten our French lessons in the allotment. Bye-bye.'

'I will be your doting grandmaman always – *la mamie gâteau*.'

'You're the bee's knees, the cat's whiskers a l'Americaine!' She curled into a ball but there was a parting shot as Anna left the nursery.

'I will do a spectacle in my new tutu when you come back to England.'

The maid showed the eccentric old woman and her son out into the night. 'Take good care of the child while she is alone.' She slipped a ten shilling note into Alice's hand – it would have been one-sixth of her weekly remittance money.

Louis took her arm. 'Come on granny, we'll find a taxi somewhere along the seafront. There's a busy week ahead of us, stop snivelling.'

Chapter Thirty

That night Anna had a macabre nightmare: Uncle André was sitting alone in his garden watching himself die in the looking glass hanging on the old red brick wall. She woke up with a splitting headache, but choosing the least horrendous clothes from her wardrobe, set out on the first shopping expedition for years. Barrance & Ford on the promenade was her main port of call, and she emerged with a black costume and a small hat with ospreys, French knickers trimmed with lace, and a pair of pink stays to be packed into a green crocodile suitcase from Shorland Fooks, the leather merchants.

Mary had thrown the entire month's housekeeping allowance into her mother's lap by mistake.

Louis profited from his share of the spoils, buying a Donegal tweed suit and cap, and a new Gladstone bag.

Anna was on her way home, dying for a glass of wine, her mouth was as dry as the bottom of a parrot's cage, when a high clear voice called out to her from above.

'Anna, dahling, after all these years.! Come and have a cocktail with me on the terrace.' A creature in a flapper dress was leaning over the balustrade of the Metropole Hotel waving a long black cigarette holder.

'Mimi!'

Thank heavens she was wearing her new costume and the little black hat with a feather on one side. She would hate to meet Mimi clad in her mangy furs.

'I have been out shopping.' She was laden with carrier bags and a dress box – her purchases for the journey to Belgium the following day.

'Drink with me Anna, for old time's sake. Waiter, two White Ladies.'

They sat opposite each other at a small iron marble-topped table sipping their drinks.

'I heard that John died and you were short of money for a while, but you are looking very chic.'

'My Belgian uncle died. He was a very wealthy man.'

'I share a garret in Montparnasse with my lover, and we drink at The Dome and *Les Deux Magots*. Does that shock you? We are known as les inseparables – the love birds. Father left me all his money and I have learned that everything is for sale. Women, alcohol, cocaine.'

Mimi leaned towards her. 'Anna, have you ever kissed a woman?' She did not expect an answer.

'No, never.'

'I am spending a few days by the seaside with dear old Hannah. She will be here at any minute. I can assure you the relationship is quite Platonic, my dear.'

'Anna, how lovely to see you again... a school reunion!' She kissed her old friend on both cheeks.

'Where have you been, Anna? I know you were an heiress when your father died, and of course mother told me all about the handsome Irish husband, and the Laird of Cockpen.'

'I am going to Brussels tomorrow, and staying at The Palace for a few days.'

'We have a brace of fine healthy children, a boy and a girl, and four grandchildren. Do you remember planning the future when we were seventeen? Charlie has a roving eye, but what else can you expect?' The raw-boned girl had become a handsome woman, with broad hips and an ample bosom.

'I am on a diet. Charlie spends a naughty weekend in London: Daly's, Ciro's and The Kitkat, then comes home to me feeling very, very, guilty and bearing gifts.'

'John died.' The blank statement of fact was greeted by a dull silence.

'I am so sorry Anna, I never knew.'

'Dahling, let's have another. Life is hell. The younger generation is knock, knock, knocking at the door. Perhaps we are all a little passé?'

She applied a scarlet lipstick to her Cupid's bow and powdered her retroussé nose with a scrap of swansdown from a gilt compact.

'Poor Mimi. I think I will go home for luncheon, it is quite a long walk and I am a little tired.'

'Take your afternoon siesta, Anna. Bye-bye.'

Louis came in a taxi to collect his mother en route for Brighton Station. 'We could easily become accustomed to a life of luxury. I made all the arrangements through Thomas Cook: we travel Dover, Ostend, Brussels and should arrive mid-afternoon.'

'Bagages, Bagages,' the old cries of the foreign porters. The meadows edged with poplars took her back to Trouville more than fifty years ago when the world was young. Mantes-la-Jolie, *The Hirondelle*, Michel Besançon with his stories of adventure on the high seas.

She heard again the newsboy selling papers on Brighton seafront: 'French Empress dies... Buy a paper.'

Eugénie died in 1920 in her beloved Spain at the great age of ninety-three. She had sent Anna a coquette parasol as an engagement present. 'Marquise or coquette, for use in the carriage when you flirt with your fiancé. It was all so long ago.'

'Bruxelles Midi.'

'*André Van Maaskens, Scrap Metal Merchant*' was still emblazoned on the side of a building near the shunting yard, but the lettering had faded over the years.

A fiacre took them to the Palace Hotel near the Grand Place. 'If Monsieur Garnier fails to pay all the bills, we shall be forced to do a moonlight flit.' They wallowed in the luxury of hot baths after the journey and admired the black and white marble tiles, gilded furniture and a log-burning stove in the drawing room of their suite. It was a far cry from the Lanes.

Anna splashed eau-de-cologne on her wrists, and dabbed her nose and cheeks with poudre de riz to hide the flush of excitement. She rang the bell and ordered pâté de foie gras and a bottle of Veuve Cliquot from the room waiter.

A cab drove them across the Grand Place past the chocolate sellers and lace makers to their solicitor's office on the first floor of a fine old building.

Monsieur Garnier rose from his desk to kiss her hand. They met for the first time since her father's death. 'Madame Donelly, what a pleasure to meet you again after so many years. I remember a dinner at Claridges with your uncle.'

'Monsieur,' the matriarch inclined her head, 'may I introduce my son, Louis, Monsieur Garnier, the family solicitor of the Van Maaskens.'

'Pray be seated. It is a sad occasion and we ask you both to accept our condolences, but I am happy to inform you that our client, Monsieur André Van Maaskens, died a very wealthy man.'

Smelling salts! Dear God she must not faint until she knew the extent of her fortune.

'Although he retired from active participation, many years ago he was a prudent man who alway kept his finger on the pulse, as you might say. The business continued under excellent management, and all monies were well invested. Your uncle leaves a fine collection of antiques, paintings and objets d'art including many exquisite enamels by Monsieur Fabergé. He was a shrewd connoisseur not a dilettante, a respected member of society who will be sadly missed. As you know, he still owned a scrap metal yard on the outskirts of the city as well as the house on the Avenue Louise – our Belgian equivalent of your Park Lane. There are many investments and liquid assets.'

'Monsieur Garnier, we have travelled from England to ascertain details of my uncle's estate and his last testament. I am a little tired, pray come to the point as quickly as possible.'

'Madame Donelly,' he paused for dramatic effect like an actor. 'To the best of our knowledge and belief, Monsieur Van Maaskens made his last will in 1910. Perhaps he still refused to accept the idea of his own mortality. At least he did not wish to dwell on the thought and sign a recent document. At the time of his death, the entire estate passed to you, his closest relative.'

Everything went black before her eyes, but when Garnier swam into view he was still talking.

'Perhaps Madame would care to visit the house now to view a small part of her inheritance. I remember the occasion of your daughter's long holiday in 1908. We were made aware that our client intended to make a will leaving everything to the young lady, but he changed his mind when she returned to England. My clerk is at your disposal for the evening, Madame. Pray call on our services at any time. You will need to stay in Brussels for a few days to comply with certain formalities. The firm will attend to all expenses out of the estate, you understand.' He bowed low over her hand with the deference due to a lady of property.

They descended the staircase, Anna's hand resting on Louis' arm for support.

'Cabbie, number fourteen, the Avenue Louise.'

Louis' face was a study: impassive, unsmiling, blasé, until he turned towards Anna and winked. 'What is the quotation? "Today is the first day of the rest of your life".'

'Permit me, Madame.' The clerk helped her alight from the hansom cab, flourished a large decorative iron key, and admitted them to the mansion.

A long stained glass window at the head of the stairs cast red and purple shadows, fleur de lys against a blue ground, and the arms of Brabant shone in the pale autumn sunlight.

'Monsieur Van Maaskens' study is situated at the back of the house, overlooking the garden where he died. We have tried not to disturb anything pending your arrival.'

They mounted the stairs to the first floor, and entered the drawing room. 'Madame Donelly may decide to reside here and retain the furnishings, together with her own possessions.'

Anna had a sudden absurd vision of a chipped blue enamel bowl, pots and pans, a bidet and a rusty old iron bed in these surroundings.

The humble little man droned on. 'I understand that some of the pictures are of great value. You are connoisseurs of the arts? I will show you the gallery later. The housekeeper Mademoiselle Dupont has retired to live with her brother in Bruges – a man of substance, a merchant.'

Louis joined in the conversation. 'Uncle André had flair... some of these paintings are fabulous.'

Anna's heart was racing. She pressed the throbbing pulse in her throat with a gloved finger and tried to breathe slowly, but her chest ached.

She must lie down and rest for a while otherwise she might fall in a dead faint. 'I need to be alone. I suggest you look around without me.'

'Are you feeling ill, mater?'

She kissed her son on both cheeks.

'It will pass…Tout passe, tout lasse, tout casse. Uncle André's death has been a great shock to me.'

The clerk opened the door of the principal bedroom, the atmosphere was stale and oppressive. Anna opened a window and breathed deeply, took off her jacket, and loosened her stays. She wished Kate were alive to see her now. All the wasted years were dead and gone, this was the beginning of a new life for an old, old woman, an heiress once again at sixty-six years of age. She took a few drops of sal volatile to regulate the heartbeat. Dear God, she might die before receiving her inheritance, then Mary and Louis would share the spoils! Rising to her feet, she wandered around André's bedroom touching her possessions: an enamel box, the tortoiseshell hairbrushes on the dressing table.

André's old walnut bureau stood between the two windows. He liked to work and watch the street below in an idle moment. Anna pulled out the lopers and lowered the flap, but the desk was empty. Curiosity killed the cat. Ernestine Dupont or the solicitors would have removed all documents to the office for safe keeping.

A secret compartment might be hidden behind the columns at either side of the central door. Anna pressed a small brass catch hidden in a pigeonhole, and one of the wooden columns moved forward to reveal a piece of black tissue paper covering a diamond brooch, a rose tremblant on delicate springs, the petals quivering on stems of white gold. Beside it lay a card inscribed in faded sepia handwriting:

To Marguerite with all my love, André.

This was the secret he had hidden away for years. He loved maman, the lovely Marguerite de Savonnet he met years ago in the park when he was a penniless urchin in Brussels. This was the reason he wanted to adopt Mary as his own granddaughter. She wondered if her mother had loved André far more than his brother Jean Jacques.

Anna pressed a second catch. An envelope and a single sheet of parchment lay in the hiding place. Smoothing the crumpled page she began to read the last will and testament of André Van Maaskens dated 1920, witnessed by the gardener Johann Witte and his wife Marthe. (Now deceased.)

'I give and bequeath all my worldly goods to my loyal and devoted housekeeper Mademoiselle Ernestine Dupont with one exception. I leave the portrait of myself now hanging over the mantelpiece in my study to my dear niece Anna Marie Rose Donelly in remembrance of me.'

Anna's head was breaking into a thousand fragments. The house was silent as the grave. The envelope was addressed to her, marked 'Personal', and read as follows:

My dear Anna,

I never forgave your behaviour to Mary when she was a young girl in love. The whole wretched business could have been otherwise. You have ruined her life.

I shall always remember your John quoting from The Ballad of Reading Gaol, 'lying in the gutter but some of us are looking at the stars'.

We have only one thing in common, Anna – we are a dying breed.

May God bless you and keep you.
André

She flung herself on to the bed, drumming her fists against the wall. Ernestine Dupont was not even André's mistress. She was an elderly domestic servant. The idea of the old spinster living in this house was a nightmare.

She imagined Mademoiselle Dupont tending the Gloire de Dijon roses in the garden where André died, living off the fat of the land, while she scrabbled for pennies in the back streets of Brighton.

'Shall I die in a dark little room with bare boards, mice and cockroaches crawling over my body, or spend the rest of my life in this lovely house. I have the right to choose. Courage mon ami, le diable est mort.'

The sheet of parchment had fallen on to the Turkey carpet, and she snatched it from the floor, digging her nails into the signature. André Thierry Van Maaskens – she lacerated the italic handwriting, picking at the scarlet sealing-wax. Like a mad woman she tore the last will and testament to shreds, scattering it in the water closet like snowflakes and the sodden scraps of paper floated away into the sewers of Brussels.

Anna walked slowly to the head of the stairs and down the blood red carpet. The brass chandelier cast a rainbow of light across the embossed ceiling. Louis and the clerk were waiting in the hall, but Anna pulled the mourning veil over her eyes and walked alone into the twilight on the Avenue Louise.